Praise for

THE DRAGON WARRIOR

★ "Zhao's impressive and captivating debut adventure novel brings mythology and magic to life. . . . For fans of Rick Riordan's Percy Jackson series and Roshani Chokshi's *Aru Shah and the End of Time*." —*Booklist*, starred review

"Zhao seamlessly incorporates Chinese terms and themes into the fast-paced plot. . . . The story takes intriguing twists with its cultural background." —*Kirkus Reviews*

"Inspired by classic Chinese mythology, this #OwnVoices fantasy adventure delivers on action, humor, and heart." —*School Library Journal*

"Those looking for a story in line with the surge of modern mythological quests will find this take on Chinese mythology a worthy addition." —*BCCB*

"With engaging characters, a fast-paced plot, and a skillful blend of modern culture and ancient traditions, this series opener will appeal to fans of Percy Jackson and Aru Shah." —*Publishers Weekly*

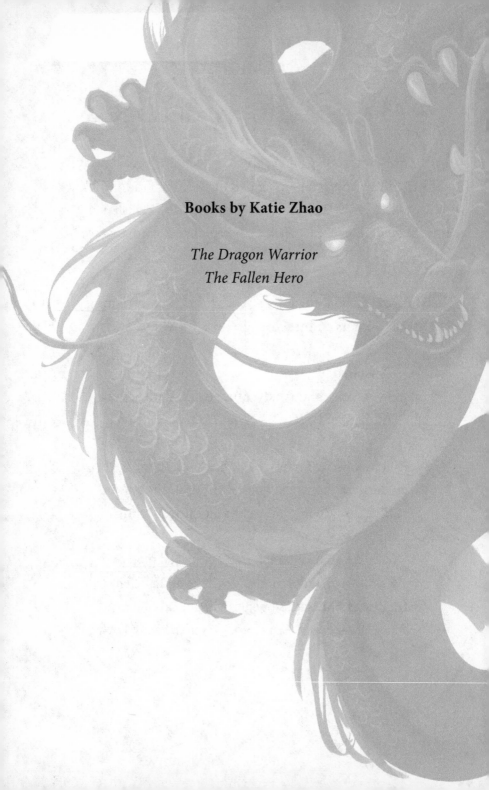

Books by Katie Zhao

The Dragon Warrior
The Fallen Hero

THE
DRAGON
WARRIOR

Katie Zhao

BLOOMSBURY
CHILDREN'S BOOKS

NEW YORK   LONDON   OXFORD   NEW DELHI   SYDNEY

BLOOMSBURY CHILDREN'S BOOKS
Bloomsbury Publishing Inc., part of Bloomsbury Publishing Plc
1385 Broadway, New York, NY 10018

BLOOMSBURY, BLOOMSBURY CHILDREN'S BOOKS, and the Diana logo
are trademarks of Bloomsbury Publishing Plc

First published in the United States of America in October 2019
by Bloomsbury Children's Books
Paperback edition published in October 2020

Bloomsbury books may be purchased for business or promotional use. For information on bulk
purchases please contact Macmillan Corporate and Premium Sales Department at
specialmarkets@macmillan.com

ISBN 978-1-5476-0479-1 (paperback)

The Library of Congress has cataloged the hardcover edition as follows:
Names: Zhao, Katie, author.
Title: The dragon warrior / by Katie Zhao.
Description: New York : Bloomsbury, 2019.
Summary: Twelve-year-old Jade Society member Faryn Liu may be destined to
command the Jade Emperor's army of demon-fighting dragons, but first she must
complete a daring quest across several Chinatowns before the Lunar New Year.
Identifiers: LCCN 2019004273
ISBN 978-1-5476-0200-1 (hardcover) • ISBN 978-1-5476-0201-8 (e-book)
Subjects: | CYAC: Adventure and adventurers—Fiction. | Demonology—Fiction. |
Dragons—Fiction. | Gods, Chinese—Fiction. | Racially mixed people—Fiction. |
Chinatown (San Francisco, Calif.)—Fiction. | San Francisco (Calif.)—Fiction.
Classification: LCC PZ7.1.Z513 Dr 2019 | DDC [Fic]—dc23
LC record available at https://lccn.loc.gov/2019004273

Book design by Danielle Ceccolini
Typeset by Westchester Publishing Services
Printed and bound in the U.S.A. by Berryville Graphics Inc., Berryville, Virginia
2 4 6 8 10 9 7 5 3 1

All papers used by Bloomsbury Publishing Plc are natural, recyclable products
made from wood grown in well-managed forests. The manufacturing processes
conform to the environmental regulations of the country of origin.

To find out more about our authors and books visit www.bloomsbury.com
and sign up for our newsletters.

For immigrants, children of immigrants,
and diaspora readers everywhere: never forget
that you are the dragon warriors and
heroes of your own stories

CHAPTER

1

On the eve of the Lunar New Year, the demons invaded.

I was pretty used to this happening. Demons swarmed the streets of San Francisco's Chinatown every Lunar New Year. Of course, these demons were just humans dressed as fearsome beasts, like golden lions and red dragons, who danced down the streets to the beat of drummers and exploding firecrackers.

Real demons would make the annual San Francisco Lunar New Year parade a whole lot more interesting. But nobody had seen one around here in decades.

I couldn't see much through the tiny window on the south side of our small one-room house. It was almost seven in the evening, and the sun had set over an hour ago. But I didn't need to see clearly to visualize what was happening out there. When I closed my eyes, my nose filled with the scent of fried dumplings and dough twists, my favorite desserts of the holiday.

A shiver of excitement ran through me as I held a glittery green-and-gold mask up to my face. Pretty soon—if I was successful—I'd be out there for real, at the parade.

I was glad to wear this mask tonight. I'd been born and raised in the Jade Society, a group of warriors who had emigrated from China to San Francisco, California, decades ago, to protect the people of Earth by fighting demons.

But I looked a little different from the other warriors. Dark-brown hair and eyes identified me as half-Chinese and half- . . . Other. A blend of Egyptian, Greek, and Turkish ancestry gave me brown eyes and tan skin that, for the most part, defied the black-eyed, pale-white-skinned standard of Chinese beauty.

But once I put this mask on, nobody could tell.

Footsteps creaked the floor behind me, and a familiar voice teased, "You're still here? Slowpoke."

I turned toward my brother, Alex. With his arms folded across his chest and a serious expression, he appeared like a grumpy old man, much older than his eleven years. "I was about to leave."

Alex pressed a finger to his lips. "Shhh. We don't want to wake Ye Ye from his nap. You know he's sick."

Our grandfather lay on his bed, only a few feet away from us. Thankfully, he probably couldn't hear us over the sound of his own chainsaw-like snores.

"You're sure you'll be fine on your own out there, right?" Alex whispered.

"Of course. It's not like I haven't been to Chinatown before."

"I know, but this time . . . it's different."

My brother was right. I rarely ever snuck out, but tonight, a new kind of energy sparkled in the air like static—as though hinting that real demons were preparing to crawl out of their hiding places, just like the legends said.

"You could sneak into Chinatown instead," I offered. "Or come along."

My brother's cheeks colored. "You know I can't. Someone has to stay with Ye Ye, and . . . well, you're . . . better at combat than I am." He said the last part all in a rush, like ripping off a Band-Aid.

Grinning, I cupped my ear in an exaggerated movement. "What was that?"

"Nothing," Alex mumbled. "Anyway, we'd better go over the plan." He swept his curly black bangs aside to wipe sweat off his forehead and leaned against our small TV. "What's step one?"

"Sneak into town and buy medicine from Zhao's Herbal Center," I rattled off dutifully.

"Good. Step two?"

My stomach growled, and I thought of my favorite meat-filled dumplings. "Eat ròu bāo zi."

"Faryn!" Alex glanced nervously at Ye Ye, whose long, gray

goatee fanned out with each gentle snore. He rolled over, his expression pinched.

"Fine," I huffed. "Run back home as quickly as possible, before Ye Ye notices I'm gone."

"Step three?"

"There's a step three?" I paused. "Eat ròu bāo zi?"

Alex rolled his eyes. "Faryn, you're always hungry. Step three is what happens in case you see a demon—you're supposed to run. You aren't going to try to be cool and play the hero, all right?" He gestured to the hand-me-down video games stacked by our secondhand gaming console. "This isn't *Warfate*. You won't be able to start over if you die."

I scowled, even though he had a point. "Thanks, Alex. I'll be careful—but I *can* handle myself. Ye Ye has been training us for years. You should know—I beat you in practice matches all the time!"

Mao hadn't invited Alex and me to train with the other kids, but our grandfather made sure we'd still learned martial arts and swordplay. Training with Ye Ye was better, anyway. Mao just wanted the warriors to look powerful, not to become good fighters. She'd taken a strong stance on not bothering the demons as long as they didn't bother us.

Ye Ye's training would make me into a true warrior. He once even told me that my best friend was a plank of wood. Then he whacked me in the shoulder with it, yelling, "Too slow. If I were a real demon, you'd have died five times by

4

now!" He repeated the process, and I got really good at ducking.

But I was also learning how to fight back.

"Fighting me is different from fighting a demon," Alex pointed out, pulling me away from my thoughts and back to the present.

"Yeah, the demons probably smell better," I said.

"I'm serious. Be careful out there in Chinatown, okay?"

Alex's gaze locked on the far back wall, which was decorated with huge maps of the entire world that tracked our father's journeys through Chinatowns, mostly in the United States. Shoved against that same wall sat a small wooden kitchen table, every inch covered by colorful stacks of more maps, all belonging to Ba. The paper's edges were yellowed with numerous tea stains from over the years. Its weathered state reminded me of how long it had been—four years—since our father's disappearance.

No wonder Alex was worried about me. After Ba had disappeared, we were all that we had left. And we needed each other. Ba's relentless warnings about the demons' growing strength had angered Mao and some of the other Jade Society adults. Now, without Ba around, they treated us as outcasts.

"Don't worry," I told Alex. "I'm not going to run into any demons. It's like what Mao loves to say, right? 'We've been demon-free—'"

"'—since 1983,'" Alex finished. He scratched his chin.

"I guess we should be safe. The eighties were pretty much, like, right around the time dinosaurs went extinct."

"Exactly." But even as I flashed Alex a reassuring grin, my stomach clenched up. And I was pretty sure it wasn't from the slightly moldy stinky tofu that Mao had given us to eat earlier for dinner.

Ye Ye had warned Alex and me not to go into town tonight. That he could feel the demons' evil stirring, which made it harder for him to breathe. At the time, I'd scoffed. My grandfather said that every year, and yet they still hadn't risen from Chinese hell, Diyu.

Ye Ye let out a loud snore that shook the empty teacups stacked on the kitchen table. When he quieted, Alex shoved a wad of dollar bills into my hand and whispered, "Go. And seriously, be careful. We don't know what's out there."

I nodded. Moving as quietly as I could, I slid out the door and shut it behind me. In the sky far above my head, another shower of fireworks exploded.

Beyond the walls and apartments of the quiet, tucked-away Jade Society lay the heart of San Francisco, and its famous Chinatown. Average residents knew better than to turn up uninvited at the doorstep of the wealthy, powerful families who ran the Society. If they tried, intimidating guards would stop them at the gates with their Ultra Doomsday Glares.

I dashed across the grassy lawn and through the black gates. A tall oak tree stood just outside the Jade Society's massive entryway, which was almost as tall as the trees themselves. I walked toward the oak tree, reached up, and spread some of the leaves apart until I spotted what I was looking for: a small black lever. The lever gave after I yanked it, and a gaping hole the size of a door appeared in the middle of the tree trunk.

To keep ourselves as separate as possible from the outside world, the Jade Society warriors traveled to San Francisco's Chinatown and other parts of the outside world using this underground tunnel. I was pretty sure that if I wanted to, I could take this route clear to China, or Narnia. I looked down at the smooth floor of the tunnel and found what I was searching for—one lone rusty black bicycle at the near-empty bike rack next to the entrance. The characters for "property of the Jade Society" were written on the bike's surface in red. Normally the rack was full, but tonight the rest of the bikes were gone, since almost everyone had taken them to the Lunar New Year parade. Only the oldest, rustiest one—which Alex and I were forced to share—was left.

After grabbing the bike, I steadied it and swung my leg over the seat. There wasn't a moment to waste. I had to get Ye Ye's medicine—and quickly. I pedaled so hard and fast down the dark tunnel, I could practically see the light. Then I really *did* see the light. The end of the tunnel drew into sight, which was good, since I was panting and wheezing like I'd just run a marathon while being chased by demons.

I braked to a stop and left my ride near the tunnel exit,

racking it haphazardly next to all the other bikes. I ran along the tunnel, which was dimly lit with torches, toward the growing light: San Francisco's Chinatown.

The tunnel exited into an abandoned alley on the outskirts. I emerged from it and breathed in the cool evening air, filled with too many yummy scents to identify. I'd seen the neighborhood at night many times by now, yet its beauty never failed to take my breath away.

Red lanterns lit up every corner. The sidewalks teemed with people purchasing dumplings from shouting vendors and exchanging red packets of money, hóng bāo, to ring in the Year of the Horse. I strolled through the streets, taking as much time as I dared, before I was forced to stop where the crowd had reached a standstill.

"Look, sūn zi," said an old woman next to me. She nudged the college-aged guy beside her. Based on the Mandarin Chinese term she'd used, he was her grandson. "It's time for the annual parade of the Jade Society warriors."

I couldn't resist pausing to watch the show. The Lunar New Year only comes around once a year, after all. A procession of teenage boys and their fathers marched to the beat of fast-paced traditional songs toward the brightly colored costumed dragons. Clad in bronze armor from head to foot, the procession followed four men on horseback. The horses had been brought in specially for the occasion.

Both lines stopped when they met under the towering

green Dragon's Gate at the intersection of Bush Street and Grant Avenue.

The crowd quieted in the presence of the most powerful men and boys in Chinatown. I mean, these guys literally sat on their high horses.

My fists clenched as I noticed Luhao, a lanky teenage boy with a long, narrow face that was permanently fixed in a sneer. The heir of the richest family in the Society, he'd taken to teasing both Alex and me over the years—but especially Alex, calling him names and stealing his books. To Luhao's right waited a brown mare with an empty saddle, probably meant for his father, Mr. Yang, to ride. He must've been off as usual attending to the shady business dealings that made his family so wealthy.

But everyone else's eyes focused on the boy in the very front. His tall, sturdy build and coal-black eyes commanded attention. And it was hard to ignore the costumed figure behind him, too—humans hidden within an elaborate outfit designed to resemble the half-lion, half-dragon demon called the nián.

"Every Lunar New Year, nián, you return to our village in the hopes of destroying the crops," boomed the fourteen-year-old heir to the Jade Society. He thrust a weapon at the nián's fabric mouth—the jagged blade of a custom-forged sword. "But this year, I, the great Wang, will banish you forever!"

The people in the crowd whooped, and their cheers grew louder as Wang and the costumed demon pretended to fight each other. Firecrackers exploded near their dancing feet, sending blasts of light shooting out into the night.

"I love you, Wang!" screamed a nearby girl. Probably Wang's girlfriend, Wendi Tian.

I rolled my eyes and muttered, "Crowd-pleasers."

"Our so-called protectors from evil," scoffed the old woman, startling me. Had she read my mind? "How far they have fallen."

Her grandson snorted. "When were those boys anything but a bunch of show ponies, nai nai?"

"Bèn sūn zi," the woman scolded, "don't speak about things you don't understand. The Jade Society warriors used to do great things."

"Shhh. Nai nai, they'll hear you."

"I hope they do. Maybe then these warriors will remember they were once the heroes of Chinatown. When I was a young girl, they worked tirelessly to capture rogue demons and protect the Earth. These boys don't look like they could capture anything. Zhēn méi yòng."

Useless, she called them. She wasn't wrong. Once the warriors had chased most of the demons out of San Francisco, the Society's goals had shifted from honoring the gods' wishes and going on hunts to making money and turning our headquarters into an impenetrable fortress.

I had pictures and memories of my own father to remind me what a true warrior looked like. With short black-and-gray streaked hair, a bulbous nose, and a stern poker face, my father looked—and had been—fearless. Even his name, Liu Bo, felt powerful. Though Alex and I went by our Americanized names, first name before last name, Ba, like Ye Ye, followed Chinese tradition, with our family name appearing first.

And he was the hero of countless stories. Even though San Francisco remained demon-free, Ba sought danger out across the world. On his travels, Ba had bested hundreds of demons and stopped floods. He'd even gone head-to-head with trickster gods who'd rebelled against the Jade Emperor, the ruler of the heavens and the most powerful deity we worshipped in the Jade Society. Ba could've become a general in service to the Jade Emperor—but he had me, and then Alex—before vanishing.

"Demons? Never even seen one," the boy said. "They've gotta be too scared to show their faces now since the warriors are protecting us."

The old woman's frown deepened. "Demons can disguise themselves as humans—they could be anywhere, even now! You should be careful what you say, silly boy. The demons are at their strongest during the fifteen days of the New Year celebrations, before the moon is full."

The old woman's words reminded me of the history behind

the festival. Thousands of years ago, the Lunar New Year celebrations had been designed to ward off evil spirits. But the world had a way of balancing everything out. As the demons grew more powerful, so did the gods—and warriors. Or so Ye Ye had told me.

Ye Ye. *Oh no.* I'd come here to get his medicine, not watch the warriors' show. I pushed past laughing elders and squealing children, plodding down the brightly lit Jackson Street until I reached a large herbal store with a sign hanging over it that read: ZHAO'S HERBAL CENTER.

I entered the store and walked past rows of jars, big and small, filled with unidentifiable substances, selecting a container of pí pá gāo, a nasty-smelling black liquid for curing coughs.

I took a deep breath, slowly moving toward the counter. *Please, don't let it be Moli, don't let it—*

But there stood Zhao Moli, the pale, willowy daughter of the local medicinal guru, Mr. Zhao. Moli fit the Jade Society's idea of beauty so perfectly, it was as though the gods had designed her themselves; every girl wanted to be like her. She donned her riding clothes constantly—brown riding boots pulled over white pants, paired with a fitted black, long-sleeved jacket and a black riding helmet—to remind everyone she was a two-time state junior equestrian champion.

Moli's black eyes met mine as I made my way to the counter. I resisted the urge to flinch. She couldn't recognize me under this mask.

Or maybe she could. After all, we'd once been best friends, until Ba disappeared. I fixed my gaze on my feet as I placed my grandfather's medicine on the counter.

"We closed two minutes ago," Moli said sourly. "We won't open until two weeks from today, when the Lunar New Year is over."

My heart sank. Two weeks from now, who knew how much my grandfather's sickness would progress?

"Now, turning customers away isn't in the spirit of the New Year." Mr. Zhao, a short, round man with almost no hair, came up behind Moli. He put his arm around his considerably taller daughter. She frowned and wriggled out of his grasp. Mr. Zhao smiled at me. "I'll ring you up. No one should start off the Lunar New Year sick."

"Thank you, shū shu," I said, keeping my voice low and distorted. Unlike some of the Jade Society adults, Mr. Zhao treated me with as much warmth as he did all the other kids. Still, if I'd greeted him the usual way, Moli would know who I was.

"How many times have I told you that you can't let the customers take advantage of you?" said Moli. "You're too kind, bà ba. But you can't save the whole world."

My hand jerked while reaching for the medicine Mr. Zhao had bagged, nearly knocking it to the ground. I caught it in midair, my heart hammering.

"Are you okay?" Moli asked.

"Y-yeah."

"Hey . . ." She squinted, leaning against her broom. "Don't I know you from some—"

Yes. I'm Faryn Liu. Your former best friend turned enemy—remember?

Without responding, I ducked my head down and bolted past the rows of herbs. I pushed open the door. The loud cheers and explosions of firecrackers thrummed in my ears.

My fingers curled around the jar of medicine, and I pictured my sickly grandfather at home without his medicine. There was no time to gawk.

My feet took me down a shortcut leading toward the underground tunnel's entrance. Passing teeming restaurants, bubble tea shops, and beauty salons, I rounded the corner and slammed straight into a convincing red-and-gold nián—not unlike the one Wang had fought during the parade. The demon had the body, nose, and muzzle of a lion, along with a full mane and long, razor-sharp teeth—but combined with the scaly skin and pronounced brow ridge of a dragon. Even though it was swathed in shadow, I could tell that the costume filled up half the alleyway. It loomed before a group of four children, two boys and two girls who couldn't be older than six or seven.

"We aren't scared," shouted a bald little boy. "You can stop pretending to be a demon. The real nián isn't such a stupid-looking creature."

"Don't be mean, Ah Wen. I bet they worked really hard on

their costume," scolded the girl next to him. "I really like the fangs, shū shu. They look super real. Can I touch them?"

A deep, rumbly snarl came in response. These parade participants were *really* committed to this demon act.

"Maybe we should leave whoever it is alone," the other boy suggested nervously.

But his friend ignored him. "Fetch, fido!" Ah Wen reached into his pocket and chucked something at the dragon: a dumpling. It bounced off the costume and landed with a *plop* on the pavement. "What's the matter? You don't like vegetable dumplings, either?"

"Ah Wen, you're being rude! *No one* likes veggie dumplings."

A low, feral growl rumbled through the alley, shaking the ground. I looked at the costume, really *looked* at it, and was doused with a sudden icy realization.

No human feet poked out from under the scaled underbelly of the beast.

CHAPTER

2

Fear seized me, keeping my body rooted to the hard ground beneath my feet. Every cell in my brain screamed for me to turn and—what had Alex said?—*run like the wind*. But my legs each seemed to weigh more than a block of solid gold. I could do nothing but stare at the beast before me.

I'd never seen a demon outside of my grandfather's handbook, *Demons and Deities through the Dynasties*. I'd lost count of the numerous types of Chinese demons that populated its pages, some as epic as winged horse creatures with the heads of dragons. The more powerful ones hid in disguise among the humans, though a good warrior like my father could detect the demons based on scent alone. Apparently, they smelled like stinky tofu and pickle juice.

This demon was definitely not in hiding, and its appearance was as horrid as its smell.

The demon's vicious-looking claws were each the size of small horns. They'd probably have no trouble ripping into human flesh. *Nián* literally meant "year" in Chinese, and according to Ye Ye, the name had originated because, back in his hometown of Beijing, he and his neighbors had had to defeat this same ferocious demon every Lunar New Year to protect their citizens.

Every fiber of my being yelled at me to run, but there was no way I could leave these kids to fend for themselves.

The nián reared its head back and roared. The beast's limbs were fuzzy, coming in and out of focus. A mouthful of yellow fangs more than capable of shredding me in two glittered in the mass of black chaos that was its face.

"Get out of here," I barked at the kids.

Ah Wen shrieked as he and his friends scattered down the alleyway. "Sorry! Next time I'll bring real dumplings!"

I tossed my grandfather's medicine to the ground and rolled up my sleeves, resisting the urge to flee with the kids. For years, I'd trained for a moment like this, to battle and defeat a real demon. Yet my arms and legs couldn't stop shaking.

The demon lunged. Dodging the creature's swiping claws, I jumped onto an empty wooden crate leaning against the wall. I spotted a still-smoking, charred incense stick on the ground and snatched it up before the nián could make another pass at me.

Seeing the burned stick reminded me of Ye Ye's favorite advice: to pray to the gods whenever I was in trouble.

Deities, help me bring down this demon. Right now.

The nián's fangs elongated. It charged at me with a growl and leapt through the air. I closed my eyes and screamed, certain that moments from now I'd find myself in the nián's stomach. And that was so *not* how I wanted to ring in the New Year.

But the fangs didn't tear into my throat. I peeled open one eye and—saw. Really *saw*.

All sound ceased. The fireworks had frozen in the sky, and so had the nián. I rolled out from under its path and examined the fine details of its scales, the tiniest cracks in its yellowed fangs, a milky whiteness in its eyes that told me it was at least partially blind.

Details about the alley I'd missed before popped into focus. Moss lined the cracks between the bricks in the walls. Ants scurried along the asphalt. The fireworks exploded in my ears, sounding louder and closer than ever.

As the demons grow more powerful, so do the gods—and warriors.

The thought dropped into my head just as something else dropped into my hand. My fingers closed around a cold, firm hilt.

My incense stick had been replaced by a gleaming, double-edged silver sword.

I gaped at the weapon. I'd practiced using swords with Ye Ye and Alex, and watched my father use them before he disappeared. But this wasn't practice. This sword felt much heavier, more real, than any weapon I'd used before.

Power coursed from the roots of my hair down to my toes. If the nián left this alley, it would prey on the innocent, unsuspecting people. Like children. Like my family. My palms turned so slick with sweat that I could barely hold my sword. But I couldn't let fear get the best of me. In the Jade Society warriors' place, with the gods' blessing, I had to protect them.

With a *snap* that shook me to my core, time began moving again. The *pop pop pop* of firework explosions mirrored the strength that crackled through my veins. As the night sky above lit up with colorful bursts, my short hair blew up with the force of an invisible wind.

When the nián lunged again, I stood my ground. I envisioned something less threatening but still punchable— Luhao's face, right after he'd tripped Alex in front of our house last week. That was all the incentive I needed.

My first swing went wide. Instead of chopping off the nián's front leg, my sword only sheared a tuft of its fur. The beast glowered at me. I swore it was laughing. Its claws swiped at me before I could dodge, and I muffled a scream as I dove out of the way. Sharp pain seared up my arm, and this time, I cried out. The beast had shredded part of my shirt and left a cut on my left arm that oozed blood.

I imagined Alex teasing me. *You punch like a toddler. Is that really the best you've got?*

Gritting my teeth against the throbbing pain, I pressed my

palms against the asphalt and jumped to my feet. My grand-father's advice sped into my head. *You're small, which means you're quick. Use that advantage against bigger opponents.*

The nián leapt through the air. I made myself as tiny as possible and slid under it onto the dirty, cold ground. I stabbed the sharp end of my sword upward into where the nián's heart should have been.

A satisfying *squelch* followed by a roar of pain told me I'd nailed my target. The demon collapsed and skidded away from me, taking my makeshift weapon with it.

"There," I panted. "Go back to King Yama!"

King Yama, the king of Diyu, was in charge of locking up all the demons. He'd know what to do with the foul creature.

My first kill. I collapsed onto the ground, my hands trembling and my palms coated with sweat. Though my stomach felt queasy when I saw the fearful beast I'd slain, the high of victory also roared through my veins.

I waited for the nián to disappear, for its soul to depart and return to Diyu like it was supposed to according to legends. But the creature stirred and climbed unsteadily back onto its legs, turning around to face me. Its eyes flashed a furious red.

A rush of fear replaced my short-lived joy.

"Um, good nián," I squeaked. "Roll . . . over?"

"Not so fast, you great ugly brute!"

A low, gruff voice, followed by thundering footsteps, echoed behind me in the narrow alley. A tall, skinny greyhound leapt over my head and barreled the nián to the ground.

"Good boy!" shouted the same voice. An old man wearing black robes and wielding two swords came at me.

I rolled out of his way automatically and screamed, "Shū shu, no! That's a demon!"

But the old man jumped toward the nián, swords twirling through the air.

The creature ducked the brunt of the blow and batted the man and his dog away with its paw. The stranger's swords only managed to shave off part of the nián's mane. The dog careened into the wall, then slumped onto the ground.

"Oh, you've done it now," the man roared, landing lightly on his feet in front of me. "I'm going to turn you into ròu bāo zi!"

The creature turned its ferocious yellow eyes on the man. Apparently, it didn't relish the thought of becoming a meat bun.

I opened my mouth to scream a warning—and the words were ripped from my throat when the man leapt high above the creature, much higher than humanly possible.

I saw every shiny scale on the demon's body, the rivulets of dark-red blood running down its arm and claws. The sliver of unprotected green skin wedged between its back and head.

The man must have seen it, too. He swung his sword down, aiming for the sweet spot at the base of the neck. It sliced off the demon's huge head in one clean stroke. The head rolled down the alleyway, where the four children had gathered when I wasn't looking.

Oh no. They hadn't fled to safety after all.

"A dragon head!" the girl hollered, and fled farther down the alley.

"Cool! We can use it to play soccer!" said Ah Wen. He and the other boys ran after their friend.

The demon's headless body collapsed in a movement that shook the ground. It shuddered. Then it dissolved, leaving behind a small white wisp that floated upward and disappeared.

The scrapes and bruises along my arms and legs throbbed, and the world swam around me, shouts and sounds of fireworks ringing distantly in my ears. The reality of the past fifteen minutes began to sink in.

I pictured my father's warm smile. *I did it, Ba. Demons are here in San Francisco, like you always said, and I helped kill one.*

I just wished he could've seen me do it.

The old man stood up and dusted himself off. He urged his hound to get to its feet, and then patted its head. "That's a good boy, Xiao Tian Quan. I'll feed you some demon souls when we get back home."

The dog barked and sat on his haunches, wagging his tail.

Xiao Tian Quan. The name sounded so familiar, but I

couldn't quite figure out why. I knew one thing for sure, though. This was no ordinary man. My mind whirred to Ye Ye's stories about the gods, how they'd sometimes take human form to blend in with society.

Or maybe this man was just a Chinatown chef. Those guys were seriously skilled.

"Who are you?" I asked.

The man pressed the blades of his swords together, and they molded into one long, black spear with a three-pointed, double-edged blade. I blinked and stumbled backward. "Whoa! H-how'd you *do* that?"

"I have been hunting that nián for weeks," the man said, ignoring my shock. "Though I hate to admit it, mortal, you deserve some credit for bringing it down. Who are you?"

My mouth went dry. This man—could he really be—a god?

The man cocked his head skyward, as though he was listening for something. Then he took a slow step forward. "Wait. I know who you are."

How could he? I was a nobody. Maybe what the man meant was that somehow he'd seen through the mask I wore. He knew I was the daughter of the Jade Society traitor Liu Bo.

Panicked, I lurched back and bumped into a small container on the ground: Ye Ye's jar of medicine. It reminded me that the longer I spent here, the longer my grandfather spent in pain back home.

I didn't wait to find out what the heck was going on. I grabbed the medicine and sprinted down the alley.

"Hey," the man yelled, but I kept running through the crowd.

I didn't stop until I'd entered the underground tunnel and biked all the way back home, then jumped over the fence before I tiptoed through the grass.

The rustle of grass and sound of soft laughter made me freeze in the middle of the courtyard, right under a tall tree. "Who's there?" I called softly, my heart pounding as I scanned the empty area. But everyone had left to watch the parade. Only the wind responded. I was alone with the silence and the stars.

Shaking off the feeling of being watched, I climbed up a set of stairs near the gates. When I reached our house, I cracked open the doors and snuck inside in the dark.

Alex slumped facedown and snored on the kitchen table, a black notebook flipped open under his right hand. His thick, curly black hair was glued to the side of his face with drool.

I sighed. "You were supposed to stay awake in case Ye Ye needed anything."

Alex must've been exhausted, like I was. Poor kid. I ruffled his hair fondly, the way I used to when we were younger. Before Ba disappeared when I was eight years old. Before Alex decided he was no longer a kid, that he needed to grow up fast, and that he didn't need anyone—not even his big sister—to look after him.

Swallowing hard, I placed the jar in Ye Ye's medicine drawer for him to use when he woke up. I'd risked life and limb to buy the thing before the stores closed, and I'd do it all over again.

I lay down. Now that Ye Ye's health wasn't an immediate concern, all I could do was think about the nián.

And who was that man—or was he a god?

I pulled the mask off my face, sucking in fresh air and wiping away the sweat that had condensed beneath the disguise. Through the only window in the room, directly opposite my pillow, I watched the fireworks explode high above me in the air. The snores of my grandfather and brother lulled me into an uneasy sleep.

CHAPTER

3

On the morning of the Lunar New Year Day, I didn't dare mention that I'd helped slay the nián. Ye Ye would be too busy scolding me for sneaking out to congratulate me on slaying a demon. That's Asian-style tough love for you.

Instead I went outside into the small clearing behind our home and threw myself into training, pretending the damp, bent tree branch I wielded was a sword. As Ye Ye looked on, Alex danced in front of me, blocking my jabs with his own makeshift weapon. He was a decent opponent, but I could usually take him. My brother's skin was slightly paler—more properly "Chinese," Mao would say—than mine, yet still not quite enough for some of the Society members.

Training always brought memories of Ba to my mind. He'd been the one to show us weapons for the first time, to demonstrate some basic combat moves while we watched from the sidelines. He'd be the one training us today—if he hadn't left on a quest to reach the gods' haven of Peng Lai Island four years ago so he could ask for their help in fighting the demons wreaking havoc across the country. Mao and the other Society members had protested, to no avail.

"It's my duty," Ba had told us with a sad look on his face on the day he left. He crouched down until he was eye level with us both. "Even if everyone else thinks we should ignore the demons as long as they ignore us, I still must work with the gods to find them and bring them down."

"How long will it take?" I asked.

Ba had given us a warm, confident smile. "I've traveled this path once, before you were born, remember?" He raised one of the maps of his past travels and winked. "I can do it again, and faster this time. I'll be back before you know it."

As Ba hugged Alex and me, we'd begged him not to leave. Many Jade Society members had scoffed that he was off on a fool's mission, chasing down creatures that were no longer around. They assumed that Ba would be back within the week.

And then one week went by. And then another week. And then another, until weeks became months became years.

Ba never returned.

Why had Ba left us, his only family? And, unless he was dead, why had he never come back from his quest?

The questions brought a lump to my throat. But there was

no way I'd cry during training, not in front of Alex and Ye Ye. To force the tears back, I put extra oomph behind my next attack.

Down Alex went with a muffled yell.

He wasn't bad. But I was better. I'd helped bring down a demon yesterday. I'd never say that out loud to Alex, though. He already felt bad enough that he wasn't a tough, skilled warrior, like all male Jade Society members were supposed to be.

Ye Ye sat down in the grass. Thanks to the medicine—which Alex and I had persuaded him had been in the cabinet all along—he wasn't coughing this morning. His eyes followed our every movement.

"You've improved, Falun," my grandfather said. Ye Ye referred to us by our Chinese names, even though nobody else bothered.

"What about me, Ye Ye?" Alex asked, leaping up from the mossy ground.

My grandfather gave him a stern look. "And you, Ah Li. You . . ."

Alex leaned forward eagerly.

"You're a scholar—that's where your strength lies."

My brother's face fell. I patted him on the shoulder and gave him an encouraging smile, at which he rolled his eyes.

Ye Ye's features softened. "Don't worry about the Society's expectations, Ah Li. There's nothing wrong with being a scholar rather than a warrior. Your mother loved books, too."

Tears stung my eyes, as they did every time my grandfather mentioned our deceased mom. A fierce woman who had been half-Greek, a quarter Egyptian, and a quarter Turkish, she'd swept our father off his feet when he met her on his travels.

But then she'd died giving birth to Alex. Ye Ye alone remained to look over his grandchildren.

"Sure," Alex mumbled. "Scholar. That's me." He reached into his back pocket and pulled out a small black notebook, pressing it so close to his face that it must've rubbed his nose. "Being book smart is *cool*," he said, as if to convince us as much as himself.

"Sure," I said, "but have you ever slain a demon?"

"Have *you*?" Alex countered.

Actually, yes. Also, I think I met a god last night. Also, I might have saved Chinatown. How's your Lunar New Year so far? As if I could say all that, confessing to Ye Ye that I'd snuck out last night. Diyu hath no fury like an angry Ye Ye.

When I stayed silent, Alex smiled smugly. "Didn't think so."

"There's no need to bicker. The gods have an honorable destiny in mind for you both," Ye Ye reassured us. "You just need to believe it right here." He pressed his hands over our hearts. "Your father had big dreams, and he came close to achieving them. He dreamed of being the first warrior to be named an immortal general since the great Guan Yu two thousand years ago. Guarding the Jade Emperor in Heaven is—"

"The highest honor possible for a mortal warrior," Alex and I finished together.

Ye Ye smiled, the wrinkles on his face turning upward with his mouth. "Good that you remember. A man with your father's ambition, strength, and sense of filial piety would never abandon his family. He will return." My grandfather took each of our hands into his. "We'd better get to the temple before the sun rises. You know how long the line for prayer gets during the Lunar New Year."

I stifled a groan. "But we go every day."

Ye Ye raised his eyebrow, as if surprised that his twelve-year-old granddaughter wasn't leaping for joy at the idea of spending hours kneeling on a cold stone floor. "It is good practice to pray to the gods. The day will come when you need their help."

I was pretty sure that day had come many times already. Like when Ba had left us. Or every time Mao opened her mouth. And even though that man last night seemed like a god, well, he could've just been a skilled fighter in an even better costume. But I didn't say anything.

Ye Ye set off at a surprising pace. Alex and I raced after him out of the woods to make sure he didn't tire himself out. As dawn stretched across the sky in pink-and-orange streaks, we reentered the Jade Society's rectangular arrangement of towering black apartment complexes. Though the Society headquarters had originally been built decades before, when the warriors had first emigrated here from China, Mao had commissioned these new buildings fifteen years ago, with funding from Mr. Yang. I guess they were accommodating enough on the inside—definitely better than our house, which had once been a shed—but they clashed with the more classically designed buildings that surrounded them.

Ye Ye headed straight for one of the surviving original structures, a three-story, square-shaped red pagoda: the temple.

Gray stone walls with images of dragons carved onto their surfaces lined both sides of the temple entrance. Evil spirits couldn't turn corners, so the shadow walls kept demons outside the temple. Though they didn't stop annoying little brothers from entering. A big oversight I planned to bring up with the architects.

Ye Ye heaved open the golden doors in one breathless motion and stumble backward.

"Ye Ye!" Alex and I rushed forward, each catching one of Ye Ye's elbows before he fell. Even though he grumbled, he allowed us to help him into the worship hall. He reached into a red basket and grabbed a fistful of incense sticks right before heading inside.

The large room was empty—at least, of mortals. Our footsteps echoed in the silence. The vast interior was dark, the sole source of light coming from the gilded statues of the gods.

Ye Ye headed straight for the central altar, which housed

the statues of golden warrior-type figures, the guardians of Heaven. Each had his or her own altar.

"You two know what to do," Ye Ye said. "Don't pray for silly things like video games today. The gods are watching with careful eyes. It's the Lunar New Year, after all."

Ye Ye handed out and lit our incense sticks. We prepared to place them in the sand-filled holders in front of each god.

First, we placed one for the Jade Emperor, the ruler of Heaven and all the gods. He wore a robe embroidered with dragons—his symbol—and a hat with tassels made out of pearls. The guy was seriously impressive. As Ye Ye liked to tell the story, the Jade Emperor had once been a regular immortal—well, as regular as an immortal could be—who cultivated his Tao, his powers, in the mountains. He passed more than three thousand trials, each one lasting three million years. They should've let him be ruler of Heaven for that feat alone. After he beat up a baddie that all of Heaven's other gods couldn't defeat, the gods named the Jade Emperor their supreme ruler. I bet they were scared that if they didn't, he'd beat them up, too.

Next, we placed a stick for the Jade Emperor's wife, Xi Wangmu, the Queen Mother of the West. The statue wore a floor-length dress with a phoenix, her symbol, sewn into the fabric. An icon proving that girls *could* be powerful, she ruled over the paradise Mount Kunlun.

And after that we placed sticks for Guanyin, the goddess of mercy. Her statue wore a white headdress and white robes, along with a serene smile. Guanyin carried a thin vase full of pure water, the divine nectar of life, compassion, and wisdom.

Next was Nezha, the Third Lotus Prince, third son to Li Jing, the Pagoda-Bearing Heavenly King and playful, protective deity, who served the Jade Emperor. He took on the appearance of a young boy with long hair who wore golden armor and blue pants.

After Nezha was Erlang Shen, a god of war and waterways. The fiercest-looking of the lot, Erlang Shen's statue wore battle armor, and he had a third eye in the middle of his forehead.

In the old days, the gods and warriors alike teamed up to fight demons. These days, we still prayed to the gods for protection, so they could work their magic over society and keep the demons away. So far, it had been working.

My brother and I knelt on either side of our grandfather. I coughed as the incense entered my nose, then knelt on the ground, pressing my palms together against my forehead. I didn't know what Ye Ye and Alex prayed for, but my wishes remained the same as always: for my grandfather to recover from his worsening sickness and my father to return home after years of silence.

Because it was the Lunar New Year, I added another wish.

Ye Ye's time is limited, and he's always wanted to see a deity. Please, this year, let the gods join our banquet once more.

Though no wind blew inside the temple walls, the incense

sticks flickered and threatened to go out. My heartbeat quickened. The gods couldn't have heard my thoughts—could they?

We finished by placing our palms and foreheads against the cold stone floor in a deep bowing motion, repeating it three times. Then Ye Ye reached into his pocket again and pulled out several wrapped slices of sticky rice cake, nián gāo—literally translated to "New Year's cake."

"May the deities prosper and bring us good fortune this year," my grandfather murmured.

After we'd lit incense for them all, Ye Ye placed a nián gāo in front of each statue.

The plates looked barren and sad with only one slice of cake sitting on them, but that wouldn't be the case for long. Soon, many of the aunties and uncles would flood the temple with offerings, putting on a big show of their loyalty to the gods for the Lunar New Year. Kind of like how I'd floss my teeth the morning of a visit to the dentist's office and act like I did it all the time.

After Ye Ye was satisfied that we'd honored every god, we left the hall. Before the golden doors shut behind us, a draft blew through the gap and extinguished one of Guanyin's sticks. I thought I heard soft laughter behind me.

I twisted around, and my heart jolted in my chest. My eyes zeroed in on the nián gāo we'd placed on Guanyin's altar. Maybe the shadows were playing a trick on me, but a huge chunk appeared to be missing.

"Falun, why are you lingering?"

"C-coming."

Maybe Ye Ye had gotten hungry earlier when he was preparing the offerings. Still, I couldn't shake off an inkling that maybe the gods had really been listening to me.

I quickly followed my grandfather and brother back into the crisp morning air.

CHAPTER

4

When we got home, Alex and I threw ourselves into working on our big, ongoing project: studying Ba's notebook for clues of where he might be. My brother eagerly spread his hands across the huge map of Ba's journey mounted on the wall, raising our father's black leather-bound notebook in one hand, and ran his finger along the bottom coastline of North America with the other. Muttering to himself, Alex pulled a thumbtack out of Australia and stuck it off the coast of Massachusetts.

Alex had always believed our father was still out there. His optimism made me dare to hope, too. I helped him by sorting some of Ba's maps into neat piles.

As he shined a pair of shoes in the corner, Ye Ye asked, "Have you two made progress?"

"We're getting there. Ba's writing makes chicken scratch look like calligraphy," my brother grumbled.

Colorful thumbtacks marked Ba's travels on his search for Peng Lai Island, the mythical realm of the eight immortals. Each tack, trailing from the West Coast to the East of the United States, represented a hotspot for the gods' and demons' magic alike; most of them were Chinatowns. These markers connected sacred temples, to demon-infested areas, to the Chinatown where Ba had met our mother: Washington, D.C. We'd used the one tiny picture we had of her to mark it. She had lush, light-brown hair and kind green eyes, and looking at her conjured a familiar loneliness inside me—the loneliness of never knowing a mother.

Alex flipped through the notebook feverishly, and I stepped up behind him to stare at the faded, illegible characters my father had scrawled over ten years ago. He turned the page. "Wait. Go back."

"How about you read faster?"

Alex flipped the page back anyway. I squinted. Studying the crossed-out, hastily scrawled Chinese characters gave me a throbbing headache. "On second thought, I'll let you handle this."

My brother rolled his eyes. "*I'm* the scholar, Faryn, remember? It's about the best I can do."

We both jolted at the sound of a bang on the door.

"Are you up? You'd better be!" I recognized the high-pitched, simpering voice—Mao, the mistress of the Jade Society. She hammered on the door again, and dust from the ceiling trickled over the maps and onto the ground. "It's the first day of the Lunar New Year, and you know what that means—I've got *gifts!*"

"Hóng bāo?" Alex called hopefully.

"Even better. Extra chores. I'll be at the main house in ten minutes. Don't keep me waiting."

With a final, unnecessary bang, Mao left. Miserable old hag.

Ye Ye placed the now-shiny black boots—Ba's old boots, I realized—beside his statue of Buddha. He pressed his long, frail fingers to the boots. "Your shoes are waiting whenever you're ready to come home, ér zi."

Alex looked away. My own throat suddenly felt a lot tighter.

After I helped my grandfather swaddle himself in layers of clothing, the three of us left the house. We crossed the courtyard to reach the main house, where Mao lived.

Dusty white steps led up to a huge brass door with a knocker shaped like a dragon. To our left and right stood two jade-colored stone lions with snarls sealed onto their expressions. There were four Chinese characters written above the door that outlined the mission of the demon-slaying Jade Society, reading: GIVE LIFE AND DESTROY EVIL.

Well, if we were talking about the mistress of the Jade Society, more like give life *to* evil.

Evil took the form of a small, rail-thin woman with an obnoxiously large nose that put Rudolph's to shame. Mao's hair was so long that it graced the ground with its soft black tips.

When her husband had passed away, not too long after Ba's disappearance, Mao's reign of terror had descended upon the Jade Society. She made it clear that, even though the warriors should train to keep up appearances for the gods and scare the demons away, we should all stop seeking out danger on purpose and mind our own business. She declared that anyone who did go hunting, like Ba, was a fool, and would be treated as an outcast. Ye Ye, Alex, and I, of course, became the prime victims of Mao's rule.

"Here." Mao greeted us by thrusting someone at me: a skinny girl around my age with a waist-length braid. "This is my niece." She paused and scratched her head. "My niece, er . . ."

"Ying Er," the girl provided.

"Right. Ying Er. She's staying for the Lunar New Year." The mistress placed a firm hand on Ying Er's shoulder. "Tell them why your mother sent you here."

"I'm visiting some medical schools," Ying Er said with a dutiful smile. She could model for a prep school brochure. "I'm going to make my parents proud by becoming the first doctor in the family."

"A doctor. Wonderful," Mao said.

I resisted the urge to roll my eyes. Under Mao's guidance, we girls of Jade Society had our life paths sketched out in precise detail: get the perfect grades and test scores, graduate from Harvard medical school, and make our parents proud by becoming doctors. We weren't supposed to be brave or strong or courageous like the boys. That seemed pretty unfair to me, especially since *I* was always the one who'd kill spiders when Alex was too scared.

"My annual Lunar New Year banquet is tonight. It's sure to be a smashing hit, as always," Mao said.

The mistress liked to hold lavish outdoor banquets several times a year to remind everyone how rich she was. The Lunar New Year feast was the biggest, and the only one she allowed my family to attend. Even evil had to rest at least one night of the year, I guessed.

"That's why I need you four to set up the decorations," she continued.

Or maybe not.

The mistress picked up a large black garbage bag from behind her and shoved it into my arms. "You girls can put up the paper lanterns and streamers."

She turned her cold gaze to Alex and Ye Ye. "And you two. The courtyard needs cleaning, and the tables need to be set up."

Why don't you decorate the courtyard yourself, then? I wanted to snap.

Alex groaned. Ye Ye closed his eyes and nodded, resigned.

"But the courtyard is huge," I protested. "They'll never finish in time. Besides, Ye Ye is ill."

"Falun," my grandfather said sharply, "hold your tongue."

Anger simmered beneath my skin, but I pushed it back.

Everyone in the Society was supposed to treat the elderly, retired warriors with utmost respect. But Mao always made a point to treat Ye Ye rudely, as if to make him atone for Ba spreading his "false, loathsome" ideas about the demons' existence.

Mao turned her sneer onto me. "Did I ask for your opinion? Don't forget—the Society's generosity is the reason you three still have a place to stay. Otherwise, we'd have sent you packing long ago."

I balled my hands into fists.

"I suppose it *is* the Lunar New Year, after all. Liu Jian," she addressed my grandfather, "you're off the hook—as long as you cook up something good for the banquet tonight."

Alex and I both sighed in relief as Ye Ye bowed his head. My brother placed a hand on the small of my grandfather's back, slowly helping him to the apartment.

I grabbed the bag and stormed down the steps, with Ying Er scurrying after me. I reached into its depths, pulled out a handful of red and gold streamers, and handed them to her. "Hang these up on the trees, as high as you can reach."

Ying Er obeyed, stringing the streamers over the lowest branches of the four oak trees in the yard. Mao must've told her not to talk to me too much. Like aunt, like niece.

After hanging one paper lantern from a branch, I could already feel my muscles growing sore. My earlier training session with Ye Ye had really done a number on me. This was going to be a long afternoon.

The courtyard of the Jade Society—the sì hé yuàn—was a grassy, rectangular space that contained worn stone benches and four towering oak trees. I could see Alex raking fallen leaves and branches out of the open area.

When we finished in the courtyard, we strung up decorations in the rarely used training hall. And finally, we approached the stable, where the horses whinnied in greeting. I held my nose to block out the stench of horse manure.

When Moli had been younger, we'd taken turns riding her white stallion, Longma. The ghost of Moli's once-kind laughter echoed in my mind.

While Ying Er watched, I made my way down the line, first grabbing a bag of sugar cubes from next to the stable door and then feeding one cube to each horse.

"You're looking plump there, aren't ya, Longma?" Moli's prized white stallion bit at my pinkie. I swept it out of the way just in time. "Yow! It was just a joke . . ."

The horses tugged on their ropes. Though we kept them for traditional reasons, they were always restless from lack of exercise. Demon hunts were in the past now, and at least half the families owned cars, which were faster and didn't require bathroom breaks.

Longma bared his teeth at me and snorted, tossing his hair back and forth. His eyes went wild as they fixed on Ying Er.

"Whoa." I pulled on his ropes and patted his mane, to no avail. "What's the matter with you, boy?"

Longma's black eyes filled with urgency—and fear. He lunged forward, forcing me to jump back and let go of the rope.

"It's the Year of the Horse," Ying Er said, her voice startling me with its hardness. "You should be honoring these magnificent creatures, not locking them up."

"Hey, it wasn't my idea."

"Besides, this horse is *extra* special." Ying Er stepped toward Longma and whispered something in his ear. Unless my eyes were deceiving me, the horse nodded, like he understood her words.

"Um . . . what're you doing?" I asked.

"Indeed, what a majestic beast you are," Ying Er breathed, her eyes blazing with a frightening intensity. Maybe she did have something in common with Mao.

"Okay, don't do anything crazy now," I said nervously. "Just back away from the horse. Nice and slow."

Ying Er pulled out of her pocket something that glinted in the sunlight—a pocketknife—and sliced through the horse's ropes.

"No!" I lunged for the torn rope, but Longma shook it off and raced out of the stable.

"There. Much better."

Longma kicked up his hooves, letting out a joyous neigh. He sprinted out of the stable toward the woods. I ran after him, but he was too fast. Within moments the trees absorbed Longma's white flank.

I whirled on Ying Er, who was still smiling and looking entirely too pleased with herself. "Why did you do that?"

"I did him a favor. Now Longma is free to find his true family."

"Not if animal control picks him up first," I groaned.

Forget decorating for the New Year. I needed to decorate for my funeral. Once she realized her prized horse had disappeared, Moli was going to kill me.

I should've known anyone related to Mao would only stir up more trouble for me.

It was dark when Ying Er and I finished, and even darker by the time Ye Ye, Alex, and I headed over to the banquet, the smell of my grandfather's nián gāo making my mouth water. Ye Ye made the same sticky rice cakes every year for Mao's banquet, and they were always a hit.

Doors slammed around us as neighbors poured into the courtyard, seating themselves at four long tables draped in tablecloths of deep crimson red.

Mao greeted guests in a red floral qí páo, a high-necked, formfitting traditional dress usually reserved for special events. The mistress's brain must have frozen from the cold, because she forgot to be horrible to us.

"Put the nián gāo there." She pointed at a spot on the table between a tray of dumplings and a plate of bok choy. "The banquet is about to start. Go sit down, won't you? Ying Er should be around." Mao barely glanced at me before plastering on a smile for the next family. "Mr. and Mrs. Xiong," she said warmly. The short man and his considerably taller wife nodded at Mao, and gave Alex and me a friendly smile, too, but Mao quickly showed them away from us. "Are those your spicy noodles? They're a favorite every year . . ."

A group of men emerged from the training hall, hoisting something big onto their shoulders. Grunting and heaving, they thrust the object into the grass in the middle of the four tables. A hush fell over the crowd as people turned to admire the object: a gleaming spear, black as night, with a thick, double-edged blade attached to one end. They kept the weapon encased in glass.

"Fenghuang," Ye Ye breathed. "Beautiful as always."

Legend told that the weapon, named after the phoenix, had been forged underwater by the Dragon King of the East Sea, one of the four dragon gods who looked over the seas for the Jade Emperor. Fenghuang had only one equal on Earth—Ruyi Jingu Bang, a weapon that had disappeared centuries ago. I would never get to wield such an incredible weapon.

Fenghuang had once belonged to Guan Yu, slayer of one thousand demons and the only mortal warrior in two thousand years to become a general for the gods. The spear was too heavy for any mortal to lift alone—except for Guan Yu's destined successor, who would be called the Heaven Breaker. This warrior would prove their worth to the gods, follow in Guan Yu's footsteps, and command the Jade Emperor's army of immortal soldiers—as well as all dragons.

Even Mao still touted the Society's long-held belief that becoming Heaven Breaker, receiving the deities' accolades, and serving the Jade Emperor would be the highest honor any of us could receive.

So that was why every year the young warriors lined up to try to claim Fenghuang as their own. And every year, we all watched them make fools out of themselves.

"I wonder if anyone will be able to lift Fenghuang this time," Ye Ye said.

"Doubt it," Alex scoffed. "But watching these idiots fail is good dinner entertainment. I wonder who'll end up in the hospital this year."

Laughter filled the air as aunties and uncles caught up with each other, gossiping about whose children had or hadn't made it into an Ivy League school. A group of small kids shrieked as they chased one another around the oak trees. I thought of Ah Wen the dumpling-thrower and the nián from the night before, and I had to shake my head. All thoughts of demons could get lost until I had my first plate of traditional Chinese food.

Everyone sat by unofficial rank. Important people, like Mao and the retired warriors and their wives, sat around the table closest to the food. These leaders were the figureheads of the Jade Society. The young warriors took their places at the two tables farthest back. Of course, none of these warriors had ever seen a real battle with a demon. But the Society still praised them for . . . well, basically doing nothing.

Ying Er was nowhere to be seen, and the only open spots were next to Moli and her posse of overachieving girlfriends. They'd donned their best dresses for the occasion, wearing billowy, glistening semiformal gowns under expensive fur coats, funded by their parents' high-paying jobs as doctors, engineers, and lawyers. Next to them, I felt way underdressed in my simple jeans and brown down jacket.

When we sat down beside them, the girls not-so-subtly gave us a wide berth, although some of them gave us pitying looks. I knew they were too scared of Mao to sit next to us, but the snub still stung.

Alex sat next to Moli and stuck his tongue out at her. She fumed and turned away.

Alex rolled his eyes and mouthed, "She's totally into me."

I groaned. The poor kid had had a crush on Moli since he was five years old. Talk about not being able to take a hint.

Before I could smack some sense into Alex, a hush fell over the families. In the center of the courtyard, one by one, the young warriors tried and failed to lift Fenghuang.

Luhao kicked at the weapon until one of the men had to stop him from breaking his toe. Wang had wised up from last year's failure; he hooked the spear to the back of his father's motorcycle and tried driving off with it. To his credit, I think Fenghuang shifted a centimeter, but at the cost of Wang nearly crashing into the nearest apartment building's lobby.

"It's just an old legend," Luhao said as he and his friends ducked their heads to the laughter of the aunties and uncles. "Bet it's all made up."

Ye Ye's eyes urged me to try to lift the spear, but I didn't have a social death wish. Not only was I part of a family of outcasts, but I was a girl, and no other girls ever tried to lift the spear, anyhow. Next to me, Alex's nose wrinkled. Ye Ye hadn't given my brother the same look he'd given me. I would've tried to comfort him—tell him being the Heaven Breaker was stupid, and a high-stress job with no health care at that—but I didn't want Moli or the other girls to overhear.

Moli, meanwhile, offered the perfect distraction.

"So I finally met Wang's girlfriend of two months, Wendi Tian," she said. Her friends leaned in as if this was the juiciest bit of gossip they'd heard all year.

"Are the rumors true?"

"Is Wendi as beautiful as that Chinese actress Fan Bingbing?"

"Did she really play piano at Carnegie Hall?"

Moli pointed toward the table with all the food. "Why don't you ask her yourself?"

I craned my neck and managed to pick out Wang's girlfriend.

Wendi's petite frame was dwarfed by Wang's form on one side, and Luhao's on the other. She had big, dark eyes and long, silky black hair. Her looks fit Mao's definition of the ideal Chinese wife.

Wendi's eyes narrowed when they met mine.

"Whatcha readin'?"

A too-innocent voice startled me, and my attention shifted. Luhao. He'd swaggered up behind Alex and leaned his head over my brother's shoulder. The jerk never got tired of reminding Alex that he wasn't as tough as the other boys in the Society. But at least Alex wasn't as knuckleheaded as them, either.

"None of your business," Alex snapped, his fingers clenching the edges of the notebook.

"*None of Your Business*? That's my favorite." Luhao tore the book out of Alex's hands and dove out of the way when my brother tried to snatch it back. "What are these funny maps?"

My fists bunched at my sides. "Hey!"

"You idiots aren't still chasing some stupid dream of finding Peng Lai Island, are you? Your father couldn't do it, and you've only got half the warrior blood in your veins. No way *you* can."

Alex's face reddened. "Give it back!"

"Luhao, don't you have to go steal lunch money from six-year-olds or something?" I asked.

Luhao's sneer widened as his eyes flickered from us toward Mr. Yang, who was staring at his son with cold approval.

Some of the other adults shifted uncomfortably in their seats but said nothing.

Mr. Zhao rose from his seat with a glower. "Hey, cut that out," he said. Around him, Mr. and Mrs. Xiong stood up, too, shouting their agreement.

If Luhao heard the adults' warning, he didn't heed it. "I'd much rather destroy your little fantasy book."

Rip. Rip. Rip. Luhao tore the thin, weathered binding in half, scattering pages all over the floor.

Each shredded page felt like a tear in my heart. My father's work, all his travels and research, lay in pieces.

"There. It's as good as new." Luhao laughed like he'd told the funniest joke on the planet.

"Dude." Wang came up behind his friend, a frown on his face. Wendi stood right next to him with a sinister expression. I blinked, and then it was gone, replaced by a piteous look. "That was too far, don't you think? You didn't have to do that."

Luhao glanced from Wang to his girlfriend, his eyebrows pulled together. But within seconds, he was smirking again. "You're right. I didn't mean to do that. My hand must have *slipped.*"

Blood thundered in my ears as my brother scrambled to gather up the pages. My arm whipped toward Luhao. "You—"

A hand reached out and blocked my attack. Ye Ye held me back, grasping my trembling fist firmly in his hand.

"Ye Ye, this piece of scum just destroyed Ba's work!"

"I don't condone his actions," Ye Ye said coldly, "but I don't condone violence, either." His pinched-up brows, thin lips, and unblinking eyes told me he was in Super Saiyan Grandpa Mode. "Yang Luhao, the gods are watching. Your unkind actions will be your undoing one day."

Ye Ye bent down to help Alex gather up the last of the pages. After a moment, so did Wang and Wendi.

"Too bad you won't live long enough to see my *undoing*, you old fart," Luhao retorted.

"Luhao!" Wang hissed.

My vision flooded with red. I stood up and prepared to deliver Luhao's first course to him: a knuckle sandwich.

An unseen force wrenched Luhao backward. The boy stumbled and butt-planted onto the ground. Some of the girls laughed. But the laughter faded into gasps as the torn pages from Ba's notebook zipped out of Alex's and Ye Ye's hands and hovered in the air above our heads. A burst of light claimed the pages, leaving a glowing, newly bound book hovering in the air. The black notebook floated into Alex's limp, outstretched hand.

Some of the teens started screaming, while the younger kids shouted with excitement.

An unfamiliar man stood behind us. At the sight of his glowing form, more people gasped and pressed their hands against their mouths. Mr. Xiong knocked over a whole table in his shock. Someone fainted. I rubbed my eyes to make sure I was seeing properly.

The man wore deep-plum-colored robes and clutched a familiar, wicked-looking black spear with a three-pointed, double-edged blade. He appeared to be a normal twenty-something-year-old Chinese guy, except he was big, buff, and brutish, with a weathered, scarred face.

And unlike the rest of us, he had a third eye in the middle of his forehead.

CHAPTER

5

The man surveyed the banquet with a dismissive look on his face. Then Mao did something I'd never seen her do before. She rushed over and knelt before him, her entire body shaking.

"W-welcome to our banquet, E-Erlang Shen, nephew to the J-Jade Emperor, and h-his most fearsome and f-f-frightening fighter."

Erlang Shen—the god of war Ye Ye, Alex, and I had prayed to just earlier today. Mao had always said the gods left us alone because they saw how powerful we were on our own. Yet here she was now, groveling on the floor in front of Erlang Shen. So much for being the respected leader of a warrior society.

Gasps echoed in the courtyard. Mr. Yang fell out of his seat, but no one dared to laugh at one of the Jade Society's wealthiest men as he scrambled back onto his stool.

All eyes were on Erlang Shen as Mao led the god to the table with all the food. Surrounded by pork buns, dumplings, noodles, and many more dishes, Erlang Shen sat at the head of the table like a king.

A god, right here in the Jade Society. This proved they hadn't abandoned us—Ba had been right all along.

"I knew this day would come," Ye Ye whispered. His hands trembled where they gripped the table's edge. "The gods haven't attended our banquet since before we immigrated to America, but I knew they'd never forsake their warriors."

As fathers and mothers, warriors and scholars put their heads together to whisper, Mao seemed to decide that she'd handle this highly unusual circumstance by trying to act like nothing out of the ordinary was happening. She poured Erlang Shen a cup of tea, but her hands shook so badly that she spilled all over her red tablecloth.

"Humans. Hundreds of years, and your kind hasn't wised up one bit," snorted Erlang Shen. He put up a dainty pinkie as he sipped on a cup of oolong that Mao had just poured him. Then he lifted his nose and took a whiff of the air, recoiling with a pinched-up expression. "Don't get any nicer-smelling, either. This is why we deities never want to leave Heaven."

Mao turned her nose down to her shoulder and sniffed it.

Although the god clearly thought none of us could hear his mutterings, his voice was so sonorous that it was impossible not to. "But at least you warriors still get to fight your own fights. I'm always getting bossed around like some personal servant, forced to take care of the most mundane tasks on Earth. I'm sick of it. I'm the god of war! I should be rallying warriors to fight demons, not attending silly banquets!"

As Erlang Shen continued his not-so-subtle rant, a commotion parted the crowd. The Five Elders, the oldest and baldest men living in the Jade Society, paraded past us, on their way to take their usual seats at the front table. Then they stopped, stunned, at the sight of the three-eyed god.

Erlang Shen patted the stools next to him. "Come. I don't bite."

The Elders looked at one another and shrugged. I guessed when you were that old, stuff like random visits from deities didn't bother you anymore. Stuff like beard hygiene didn't bother these old men, either. They spent more time napping and growing their beards than actually attending to their elders' tasks, like meditating and communicating with the gods.

"Here, Xiao Tian Quan." Erlang Shen whistled. A dog barked in response. I watched, wide-eyed, as a familiar greyhound swooped down on a cloud and landed on the table in front of Erlang Shen, upending the spicy noodles.

It took me a moment to process where I'd seen the dog. I gasped.

Erlang Shen's hound had helped his owner and me take down the nián in the alleyway. If Xiao Tian Quan was here, his owner couldn't be far. Not even a foot away from him, probably.

When my gaze met Erlang Shen's, I stared into a pair of black eyes. The black eyes of the warrior god. And also the black eyes of the old man with two swords.

"It can't be," I breathed.

"I know, I'm in shock," Alex said, fanning himself with Ba's notebook. "Erlang Shen and Xiao Tian Quan. They're legends. Do you think Erlang Shen will sign my forehead?"

"I doubt Erlang Shen, nephew to the Jade Emperor, will want to go near *you*," Moli said loftily. Alex's face fell.

My hands curled into fists at my side. Punching Moli in a god's presence probably wouldn't be the brightest idea, but I made a mental note for later. *That's punch number three hundred ninety-two that I owe her.* If Moli thought I wasn't keeping track, she was sorely mistaken. Emphasis on *sorely*.

Erlang Shen examined the tables of people. A tense silence filled the courtyard, broken only by Ye Ye's coughs and my growling stomach. At the next table over, the boys eyed the food like predators zeroing in on their prey.

But the god took no notice of our hunger. "I've come on behalf of the Jade Emperor, bearing a proclamation."

Erlang Shen pulled something out of his ear—a tiny golden object. He blew on it, and it grew into a scroll. The warrior god unfurled it and cleared his throat.

"Last night, the gods sensed a presence we have been

seeking for two thousand years. The Heaven Breaker stirs among you."

Alex's book thudded onto the table. Everyone turned their gazes toward the black spear in the middle of the courtyard.

"Who is it?" cried Mao. "Who's the Heaven Breaker?"

She wrapped her arm around Wang as though prepared to shower him in hugs and kisses the moment the god announced the Heaven Breaker was her son.

Erlang Shen continued reading from his scroll. "In light of this momentous occasion, my uncle, the Jade Emperor, would like to invite the Heaven Breaker on a quest. As the worthiest warrior of them all, the Heaven Breaker will aid the Jade Emperor as his new general."

Gasps rose from the crowd.

Ye Ye shook Alex and me by our arms. His eyes lit up with excitement, brighter than I'd seen them since my father left. "This is the chance your father and our ancestors have waited for. At last, the warriors—*you*—will see true glory."

I shook my head. "Didn't you hear him? Only the Heaven Breaker is worthy."

"You are worthy, sūn nǚ er."

Erlang Shen rolled up his scroll, and his eyes zeroed in on me. My pulse raced, but he looked away in an instant. "The Heaven Breaker must pass the Jade Emperor's tests of valor. For that, my uncle has asked me, the most courageous and brilliant god of all, to compose a shī."

A classical poem. The idea of the fearsome god composing poetry made me want to laugh, but I figured that would be a bad idea.

Erlang Shen made a show out of clearing his throat and held the scroll up.

First, seek the city named after the Empress to save the animal named after the Emperor.

Second, travel east to the city of a goddess who brings sleep, to free the fallen beasts.

Third, find the city in quiet ruins and reclaim a lost treasure.

And finally, prove the tests have been fulfilled to gain entry to Peng Lai Island.

When he finished, Erlang Shen paused and gave us an expectant look. Everyone stared at him in silence. Then it became obvious what he was waiting for. We all brought our hands together in a smattering of uncertain applause.

"That was so bad. That wasn't even a poem, much less a classical one," Alex muttered under his breath. "I guess there's a reason Erlang Shen is the god of war, and not poetry."

I jabbed Alex in the elbow. "Shhh. He'll hear you."

Erlang Shen said, "On the fifteenth and last day of the Lantern Festival, the Jade Emperor and the eight immortals will hold their annual banquet atop the mountain on Peng Lai

Island. If the Heaven Breaker can make it to the banquet, the Jade Emperor will welcome the brave warrior as his general, in preparation for a new era."

"The mountain on Peng Lai?" Alex gave me a wide-eyed look. Hadn't Peng Lai Island been Ba's final destination on his demon hunt?

Erlang Shen continued, "During the next two weeks, the demons will be more powerful than ever, emerging from hiding places even in havens like San Francisco. Already we gods have felt the presence of beasts that haven't roamed Earth for thousands of years. The Jade Emperor is testing the Heaven Breaker's physical strength, mental fortitude, and loyalty to the gods."

More murmurs swept through the crowd.

"But who *is* the Heaven Breaker?" Mao asked, gripping Wang's arm so tightly he winced.

Erlang Shen fixed her with his cold eyes. "I sense you will soon know. It is only a matter of time before such power reveals itself."

"This is impossible." One of the Five Elders stood up—the Eldest. He looked like a wizard because of the long white beard hanging past his stomach. Also, he liked to wear funny hats sometimes. "We've never heard about mortals setting foot on Peng Lai Island before. Even if the Heaven Breaker is among us, he will not be able to find this banquet."

Alex's hands clenched against Ba's book.

Erlang Shen raised an eyebrow. "To the best warriors, the impossible is merely another challenge. When a nián attacked last night, only the Heaven Breaker was courageous enough to take it down with me."

I pressed my hands into my sides to keep them from shaking. Unless I'd heard wrong, Erlang Shen had just called me the . . . Heaven Breaker.

Nobody, not even my own family, would believe that I'd brought down the fearsome demon. That someone like me was the Heaven Breaker.

Erlang Shen's lost it, I thought. *Maybe he hit his head really hard last night.*

Ye Ye turned and narrowed his eyes at me. As if he knew.

"But demons like the nián have been dormant for decades," said the Eldest, looking pale and shaky. "We would have sensed if it had been anywhere near us."

Erlang Shen snorted. "Your senses have dulled, old man."

The Eldest sat down and mumbled an apology.

Erlang Shen summoned a cloud beneath his feet, and he crossed his arms over his chest as he floated above us. "If I were my uncle, I wouldn't choose any of you to be my general. Not until you've proven your loyalty and vigor. You've been slacking off. Growing soft and weak. Failing to pay your respects to the gods."

Erlang Shen thrust his spear in the direction of the temple, and a bolt of purple fire shot out of the end. The powerful blast crumpled one of the shadow walls. Several people screamed.

I groaned. Guess who'd get to clean up that mess later tonight?

"*And* I hear you've turned your backs on demon-hunting in order to pursue other, less honorable activities." Erlang Shen's three eyes fell upon the guilt-stricken faces of some of the men: Mr. Yang in particular.

Erlang Shen rose higher in the sky, and Xiao Tian Quan followed him on a gray cloud. "Two weeks, Heaven Breaker. The Jade Emperor awaits."

"Wait! You haven't even tried the wine yet," Mao called after the god.

"Or told us the name of the Heaven Breaker!" shouted Mr. Yang.

Yet the god said nothing. We watched with bated breath as he disappeared high into the sky. For a moment, Erlang Shen's departure was met by only stunned silence. Everyone turned to look at Wang.

He gulped. "Wh-what?"

CHAPTER

6

As predicted, Mao forced Alex and me to clean up the destroyed shadow wall. She tried to rope Ye Ye into doing her dirty work, too, but relented after seeing that his cough had worsened, and my grandfather returned to the house. Shocked by Erlang Shen's appearance, everyone else had gone home early, too.

Alex and I swept up the rubble quickly. There was no salvaging the wall—the warrior god had blasted it to smithereens. Until we got an architect in here, I guessed the statues of the deities would have to fend off the evil spirits themselves.

"Of course Wang is the Heaven Breaker," Alex muttered sourly. "He's the future master of the Jade Society. It makes perfect, disgusting sense."

He threw down his broom, making a *whoomp* that echoed across the empty courtyard.

As if on cue, Wang climbed up the steps toward Alex and me, taking them two at a time.

"Have you guys seen Wendi?" he asked.

"No," I said. Wang's forehead glistened with sweat, and there was a large brown stain on his shirt. I'd be lying if I said part of me—okay, a *lot* of me—wasn't glad to see Mao's perfect son all frazzled.

Alex didn't bother hiding his glee. He leapt up onto the remaining shadow wall and kicked his feet in the air. "Lost your shadow—I mean, girlfriend—have you?"

Wang sighed. "She probably thinks we're nuts. Especially after Erlang Shen visited." He buried his face in his hands. "That wasn't what I meant when I told her we'd be 'eating food fit for the gods.'"

"If I were Wendi, I wouldn't want to see you again," Alex threw in. I cut him a look, letting him know enough was enough.

Wang brushed the back of his head, biting his lip. "Look, I know you guys don't like me. My mother can be a bit . . . much."

I raised my eyebrows. "A bit much" was the most generous description of Mao I'd ever heard.

"Yeah, so why bother talking to us? Mao would be upset if she found her precious Heaven Breaker with *us*." Alex spat out the last word.

"What did you come here for?" I asked.

A pained look crossed Wang's face. "I just wanted to—"

"Waaaaaaaaaang! Where are you, silly boy?"

Wang winced as Mao's croon echoed in the quiet court-yard. He glanced toward his house, then back at us. "I wanted to say—"

"Your precious mā ma is waiting," Alex said softly. "A good, filial ér zi wouldn't make his mother worry. 'Specially not the Heaven Breaker."

Scowling, Wang shoved his hands into his pockets. "Every-one keeps calling me that, but I don't know anything about being the Heaven Breaker, all right? Just let me know if you see Wendi."

He thudded down the steps, his shoulders hunched over.

I raised my eyebrow at Alex, who leapt down from the remaining shadow wall and shrugged at me. I bit back a lecture. It *had* felt nice to see Wang out of sorts.

Alex was so hyper from all the leftover nián gāo that he couldn't stand still or stop babbling. "Ba searched for the island before we were even born, and now the gods have granted the Heaven Breaker a quest to find it. This is fate. I bet—" My brother whirled around and nearly slammed into me. His brown eyes burned bright in the light of the red lanterns. "I bet this means our father really *is* alive. He must have hunted all the demons along that path and is waiting for us at the island!"

"Maybe," I said. But even as hope rose within me, doubt slithered into my mind to crush it. I mean, if Ba had been alive this whole time, why hadn't he bothered to send a post-card or something? Did he even want to see us again?

"Or—or maybe Ba got lost along the way," said Alex. "Maybe he's in trouble and needs our help. Faryn, we have to go with the Heaven Breaker. This is our chance to find Ba."

He had a point, but I didn't return my brother's enthusiasm. "Yeah, right. You think Wang would appreciate us, of all people, tagging along on his quest—especially after you talked to him like that?"

"Bet he would if we gave him this," my brother countered, waving Ba's black notebook. "The Eldest might not know anything about the island, but *we* do."

"Don't be stupid. You know we can't go."

"Why not?" Alex demanded. "You don't seriously believe Mao's nonsense, do you?"

I stared at him, aghast. "Of course not! I just meant—if we leave, who'd look after Ye Ye?"

Alex softened. "We could . . . bring him with us?"

"You really think Ye Ye is well enough to make that trip?"

The hopeful light dimmed in my brother's eyes, and guilt tore through me. It wasn't like I didn't want to find Ba—I just knew we couldn't leave our grandfather here, alone and helpless. Especially not during the Lunar New Year.

"Alex . . ."

My brother forced a smile. "You're right. Plus, I'd never make it to Peng Lai Island, anyway. I'm not a great warrior like Ba. Or even as good as you."

"That's not what I meant . . . Even though you're totally right—I am more awesome than you."

Alex smacked me on the shoulder. "Race you back to the apartment!"

"Alex!" I started after my brother but froze at the sound of a loud creaking noise behind me. The golden temple doors slowly opened—on their own.

My heart dropped into my stomach. "Wh-who's there?"

Evil spirits.

Erlang Shen had destroyed one of the shadow walls when the demons were at their most powerful. My eyes darted to the surrounding trees, searching for—I don't know—a Chinese boogeyman.

A chilly breeze swept through the air. The lanterns and tree branches danced with the wind. Nothing was there.

Then candlelight flickered alive inside the worship hall, lighting up the space in a golden glow. I had to enter the temple to get a better look.

I walked inside to see the calm, stony faces of Buddha, goddess of mercy Guanyin, Third Lotus Prince Nezha, the now all-too-familiar god of war Erlang Shen, and other warrior protectors stared back at me. Their altars overflowed with food from the offerings of New Year's Day: fruits, rice, meat—even Pocky. The familiar sight of the gods did nothing to reassure me.

Visits from warrior deities and now possibly Chinese ghosts—I had to be dreaming. I slapped myself and yelped. Not dreaming.

My eyes fell upon something that hadn't been there this morning: a black spear with a wicked blade, encased in glass.

Fenghuang. The spear of the Heaven Breaker, the most powerful one of all.

My breath stilled. All thoughts of evil spirits lifted from my mind. Without thinking, I reached my hands out toward the spear. I didn't care that there was no chance I could lift it. Fenghuang drew me in, its presence calling to me like an old friend—or maybe a friend from a past life.

I knelt before the glass, pressing my fingers into the cool surface. I lifted the thin cover up easily and moved it aside. Trembling, I reached inside and grasped the cool shaft of the spear and pulled with all my might.

I felt like a toddler trying to lift a barbell weighed down by elephants instead of plates. My muscles strained, and then gave up. I winced and shook out my aching hand.

Guess that meant I wasn't the Heaven Breaker after all, even if Erlang Shen seemed to think so. Knowing the tales of great warriors' deaths—heads lopped off in battle, poisoned by enemies—I could live with that.

I started to stand up, and then hesitated. Someone, or more likely several someones, had deliberately moved Fenghuang to the worship hall. And what else was there to do in a worship hall except worship?

The incense grew brighter in front of the statue of the Jade Emperor's wife, Xi Wangmu, as if welcoming my prayer.

I turned away from Buddha and the other deities and folded my hands in front of the Queen Mother of the West. I pressed them to my forehead.

Queen Mother of the West, if I am the Heaven Breaker, please grant me the power to wield Fenghuang.

After I'd bowed my head three times, the incense stick glowed even brighter. Energy pulsing through me, I reached inside the glass case again, firmly grasping Fenghuang in my hand. I inhaled and pulled.

This time, the spear came up with my fist, lighter than any of the spears in our training hall. I gasped. I would've dropped it in shock if it weren't stuck fast to my hand.

"Gods, this isn't happening."

The black spear shook and glowed, burning white-hot in my palm. I muffled a scream and looked away from the blinding light.

When the glow faded, I held a brilliant golden spear. Its shaft molded perfectly to fit into my hands. Chinese characters were crafted along the base of the spear, and a red-and-gold bird was carved around the width of the shaft. The bladed tip held a small, glittering white crystal.

I whipped my head around. The place was empty, as were the faces of the deities that glowed in the dim light. "I just . . . King Arthur'd."

"That's a pretty weapon you've got there."

Cloaked in shadow, Wendi Tian stepped through the open

door, her eyes glued to the spear in my hand. I swear they flashed red.

"You shouldn't be here." Casually, I hid Fenghuang behind my back. Maybe Wendi would think it was an elaborate back-scratcher. "Wang's looking for you."

"You," Wendi croaked in a distorted, accusing voice.

I blinked. "You okay? You sound . . . sick. And old."

"You helped Erlang Shen bring down the nián. You are the Heaven Breaker."

I backed away until my legs hit Xi Wangmu's altar. My palms grew sweaty around the shaft of my spear. "Wh-wh-what? No. C-can't be."

Wendi tossed her head back and growled. "I can't allow you to make it to the Lantern Festival banquet, mortal. No hard feelings, all right?" A sinister change swept over the girl, elongating her nose, coloring her hair and eyes from black to a fierce red.

"Wh-whatever it is you're doing, stop it now," I said. "I do not like that. Nope. Do you hear me? That is not good future-Chinese-wife behavior."

A snarl contorted her face. Her now cracked, dry lips pulled back to reveal a set of gleaming fangs. A reddish orange layer of fur sprouted over her body. With one last convulsion, a set of not one, not two, but nine tails burst out of her backside. Wendi landed onto the ground, paws first, now a fully fledged fox demon. A hú lì jīng.

"I knew you were too good to be true!" I cried. With a silent apology to the statue of the Third Lotus Prince, Nezha, I flung the nián gāo from his altar at Wang's girlfriend.

The creature, now only a half-dozen paces away, dodged the rice cake like a school-food-fight champ. It shrieked in anger, a horrible screeching noise that left my ears ringing. I racked my brain for what I knew of the hú lì jīng. It hoodwinked men by transforming into beautiful women—and it could only be killed by slicing off all nine of its tails.

If I held Fenghuang now, that must mean I was the Heaven Breaker. It was impossible, but the thought strengthened me.

I swung the magical spear from behind my back, raising it above my head as the creature closed the distance. With a growl, I arced the spear downward. Though my aim was true, my trembling hands stole my strength. The fox dodged to the side, the sharp blade of Fenghuang only managing to sever two of its nine tails. I cursed. At the moment it mattered most, Ye Ye's training had flown out of my head.

The fox lashed out with its remaining tails, which I managed to avoid by leaping onto the Jade Emperor's altar and knocking his bowl of grapes to the ground.

"Sorry, dude." I forced a brave appearance even though all I wanted to do was crawl under the table and wait for the demon to go away. "They don't call me Heaven Breaker for nothing."

The hú lì jīng jumped to the other side of the altar, lashing out with its tails. I swung Fenghuang through the air and lopped off three with ease. A tail sliced across my cheek before I could back away, leaving a sharp sting.

The creature bared its fangs, eyes red as fresh blood, hissing and gloating at me. A pink tongue darted out as the hú lì jīng licked its lips.

In my desperation, I could only think to do one thing: pray. *Please, deities, give me a miracle. Give me the power to slay this demon.*

Warmth shot from the top of my head down to my toes. Fenghuang glowed and heated up in my hands. As I grew accustomed to its light weight, the spear felt incredibly easy to maneuver in my grasp, like an extension of my arm.

"Eat this!" I leapt forward, toppling the Jade Emperor's bowl of rice onto the ground and slashing my spear at the demonic creature before me. Two more tails flew through the air, landing on the ground and dissolving with a hiss. Two to go.

The fox was cornered, and we both knew it. But that seemed to only fuel its anger. It whipped its remaining tails at me. I contorted my body into a painful position to avoid being sliced.

Two darts sailed above me, each slicing off a tail. With a wail, the hú lì jīng writhed on the floor. Then it shriveled into nothingness. Its soul was whisked away into the air, melting through the roof.

I spun around to see that my savior stood just inside the entrance—an older woman with long, black hair piled onto her head in a high bun, held back by a white headdress. She wore a long-sleeved white shirt and a floor-length, shimmering pale-blue skirt. White ribbon floated around her, held up by nothing that I could see. And her outline radiated light.

A deity.

I sunk to my knees, spluttering, "I—we—you—"

"Please, rise, child." The goddess waved her hand through the air and opened a bag strapped to her side. I gawked as the darts zipped inside. She flicked off some dust that had settled on the hem of her glittering blue dress. "You'll need to be more careful from now on. The power of Fenghuang will attract many enemies—demons and deities alike."

"Wh-who are you?"

"You know me as Ying Er," the woman said in an ethereal-sounding voice, "but in my true form, I am Guanyin, the goddess of mercy."

"Right," I said, somehow sounding calm even though every inch of my brain was screaming. Warrior gods. Nine-tailed foxes pretending to be Wang's girlfriend. Just another day in the Jade Society. "You're . . . a goddess. Whew. Right. Um. Okay."

After I knelt down to the goddess and paid my respects properly, Guanyin helped me to my feet. "I came here to fulfill your prayer and attend the banquet only. But there are some problems I must fix." The goddess cast a suspicious look around at the ruined altar. "We need to talk."

No kidding. "Why are you helping me? Did Erlang Shen send you?"

"But not now." Guanyin pointed out of the golden doors. "None of the gods know I'm here, but we'll discuss that later. Now, we have bigger problems."

My eyes followed her gesture. The shouting reached my ears before my eyes processed what was going on. A huge gang of men holding weapons surrounded a house.

My house.

My family.

Despite my aching, tired limbs, I could've sprinted across the courtyard to kick some major butt. But Guanyin's plan was a little better. She summoned a cloud under our feet.

"Whoa!"

My stomach lurched as we shot out of the temple and into the cool night air, leaving the mess of upended food and broken plates inside the worship hall.

Within seconds, I tumbled onto the grass in front of the men. Even in the darkness, I could see the dragon tattoos that stretched across their bulging biceps—marking them as members of Mr. Yang's shady business group. They pointed their shovels and rakes at the house.

But it wasn't just Luhao's father and his men who surrounded my home. The men flanked Mao, who crossed her arms over her shoulders.

"There's no use resisting," said Mao. "We've surrounded

your home, and my son is already inside. You're going to give up the maps to the *true* Heaven Breaker."

"Nobody's giving up anything, ā yí and shū shu."

The men whirled around at the sound of my voice. Their jaws dropped as their eyes zeroed in on my spear.

"Wait," Mr. Yang said, elbowing Mao. "Isn't that . . . Fenghuang?"

"Nonsense." Mao's stunned expression reverted back to disgust. "Fenghuang is black, not gold. Besides, my son, Wang, is the Heaven Breaker—not Faryn."

Most of the men murmured and nodded, keeping their shovels and rakes trained on me, although some frowned and lowered their weapons. Forget a spear. I needed a Captain America shield to take on these guys.

Or maybe a goddess of mercy.

"Put down those unsightly weapons," Guanyin snapped, drawing herself up to her full height. And then some. I gawked as she grew almost as tall as the houses in the Society.

The men threw themselves at the goddess's feet. "G-guanyin," they stammered in voices muffled by the grass. I guess even Chinatown gangsters knew where to draw the line.

Looking quite merciless, the goddess of mercy glowered down at the men, then lifted her head to address them. "So this is how greed has corrupted the once-noble Jade Society."

Mao's face turned as white as the lily she'd tucked into her hair.

"Not only have you treated my human form, Ying Er, with

75

ultimate disrespect," Guanyin reprimanded, "but you failed to recognize a hú lì jīng, Wendi, in your midst."

Mao's head flew up. "Wendi? It can't be. She had perfect test scores."

"Furthermore, you have shown shocking prejudice toward your own members. And over what? A silly grudge against their parents?"

A couple of the men murmured to each other and threw Mao mistrustful looks.

"Those two brats are not warriors," Mao snapped. "Their father decided their fate when he chose to wed that horrible woman over his betrothed."

Guanyin smiled coldly. "You mean, over *you*."

My jaw dropped. I'd never heard that Mao had been betrothed to my father. No wonder he'd hightailed it out of here as fast as he could.

Mao's pale face flushed with anger. "How dare you—"

Guanyin's eyes flashed. "How dare *you* talk back to me, mortal. Have you lost your mind?" Mao cowered before her. Guanyin winked at me and jerked her head toward the house. "A warrior is raised, not born. What you hooligans need is a refresher on the concept of loyalty . . ."

The realization sunk in. Guanyin was buying me time to get into the house and rescue my brother and grandfather. Keeping an eye on the kneeling men, I ducked around the side—only to see someone streak past me, sprinting away from my home. Wang.

I was about to take off after him, but my brother's scream from inside stopped me in my tracks.

"Ye Ye! Wake up. *Please* wake up."

I raced into the apartment. Ye Ye was lying down in his bed, where Alex was fussing over him.

My brother looked up, tears streaming down his face. "Whoa . . . what's that?"

The golden spear. I'd almost forgotten I had it.

"Wait. That isn't . . . ," Alex whispered.

"Fenghuang, in its proper form." My brother fell back in his seat, silent and disbelieving. I couldn't blame him. "I-I think I m-might be . . . the Heaven Breaker."

"The *what?*" Alex froze with tears still streaming down his cheeks. "That's gotta be a mistake. How—?"

Gee, thanks for the vote of confidence, little bro. "I'll explain later."

Letting Fenghuang clatter to the ground, I rushed over to my grandfather's side and felt his wrist for a pulse. It was there, but faint. His face had turned ashy.

My heart squeezed in fear when I looked up at Alex. "What was Wang doing in here? Did he hurt Ye Ye?"

Swiping at his red-rimmed eyes, my brother raised a piece of fabric that looked like it had been ripped off someone's shirt. "Th-they surrounded the house. O-ordered us to give up wh-what Wang needs. I couldn't do anything, and then Wang came in here and s-stole Ba's notebook."

"What?" They'd gone too far. "Then why's Ye Ye like this?"

"Ever since the b-banquet, Ye Ye has been—I think he . . . he's—"

"He isn't dying," I snapped.

My grandfather's eyes flickered open. He groaned and reached for something under his cot. His hand emerged clutching a sword, its sharp point digging into the ground. Ye Ye's eyes widened at the sight of Alex and me.

"You're not well," I said. "I'll get the medicine—"

"No medicine."

"You're right. You need proper medical attention. I'll call a doc—"

My grandfather held up a hand. "No doctors, either."

"What?" Alex spluttered.

"It is . . . my time." Tears shone in my grandfather's eyes. He lifted the blade. His hands caressed the gleaming silver surface. "And, Falun and Ah Li . . . Erlang Shen's visit has proven . . . it is *your* time . . . to . . . honor the gods. And in turn . . . restore our family honor."

The tears fell, though I fought to hold them back. "Please, we can't do that without you—"

Ye Ye stopped me by holding up his hand. He turned to Alex, pushing the sword into my brother's chest. "I gave your father . . . this sword . . . forged of the finest iron. Decades ago . . . when he set out . . . on his first demon hunt. I now hand it to you, sūn zi."

"Me?" Alex shook his head frantically. "But I . . . I'm no good with combat, Ye Ye. You should give it to Faryn."

"Nonsense. You have . . . unlimited potential. You need to get your head . . . out of those video games." Ye Ye coughed again, covering his mouth with his hand. When he pulled it away, it was shiny with blood.

Alex fell onto his knees, looking crushed. "But—but I love video games, Ye Ye."

"Take Ba's sword," I urged Alex. He hesitated for a moment before obeying, grasping the hilt with trembling hands.

"Oh no. Am I too late?"

The three of us turned at the sound of the sad voice. Guanyin wiped godly sweat off her brow. She filled up the whole doorway with her glow.

Ye Ye inclined his head with a great effort. "Guanyin."

"Liu Jian." The goddess appeared at my side. "It is time."

"It is."

"No, it isn't," I protested.

Guanyin gave me a patient look, which only fueled my anger. "We gods have taken note of Liu Jian's loyalty over the years. When his soul departs this world, there's a chance he'll join the ranks of the deities in Heaven. If that's the case, you can see him as much as you'd like through your prayers."

Alex gripped Ye Ye's hand, the silent tears streaming down his face faster than before.

"Your grandfather has been in pain for a long time," the goddess said. "In Heaven, he'll be treated with the greatest honor."

"What if he doesn't go to Heaven?" Alex whispered.

I bit my lip. Only the most virtuous souls would undergo deification and rise to Heaven. The majority had to pass through the ten courts of Diyu and atone for their misdeeds in life. That was a miserably long time to spend in court. Even worse, in Diyu demons and human souls alike were trapped together.

"Even if he doesn't go to Heaven, at least he'll no longer be in pain."

Our grandfather took one of my hands and one of Alex's into each of his. "You . . . must be brave. As brave as you were when . . . you slayed the nián, Falun."

Alex's eyes snapped to mine. "You did what?"

I gaped at my grandfather's proud expression. "How did you know?"

His weathered fingers traced a tear that fell onto my cheek, and he smiled. "You are your . . . father's daughter. Liu Bo's bravery . . . runs through . . . your veins. As soon as I heard . . . Erlang Shen's proclamation . . . I knew."

The sound of cheers ripped through the quiet of the apartment. I turned toward the window and peered into the darkness. A noisy crowd of people gathered outside the temple. The courtyard lit up with firecrackers, which illuminated a large brown chariot sitting in front of the temple stairs. Wang and Luhao were squeezed inside it.

When the next round of firecrackers went off, the chariot no longer sat on the ground. I rubbed my eyes to make sure I wasn't hallucinating. The chariot rose up into the air, pulled by two horses.

Alex gaped. "Are those horses *flying*?"

I fought the urge to let out a manic laugh. Sure, if ancient demons were running around Chinatown now, why shouldn't horses fly?

"The other gods are answering the warriors' prayers," Guanyin said in a frosty voice. "They've given those boys a magical chariot. They are . . . challenging you."

"Challenging me? T-to do what? Go where?" I stammered.

Alex smacked his forehead. "The island. They're leaving for the island! We have to go after them—now."

"What? *Now*?"

"Now," echoed Guanyin.

"Don't you see? If we don't leave, the gods are gonna turn Wang into the Heaven Breaker." Alex shuddered. "We can't let that happen. That guy can't even beat me at *Mario Kart*!"

Though my brother grabbed my arm and pulled me toward the door, I remained rooted to the spot. I cast a look at our grandfather, who lay there with a serene smile on his face. The rise and fall of his chest slowed.

"But Ye Ye," I choked.

"I care about Ye Ye, too." Tears streamed down Alex's cheeks, but his eyes reflected determination. "But *you're* the Heaven Breaker, right?"

"I . . . y-yes," I said uncertainly.

"So stop them before Wang steals Ba's work and goes to Peng Lai Island!"

Still, I couldn't move. Muffled applause traveled through the glass window. Elders, aunties and uncles, and little kids watched as the chariot rose high into the sky, accompanied by a shower of red-and-yellow light. The chariot soon disappeared among the stars.

"This isn't fair!" Alex yelled.

I couldn't believe that Wang was setting off in a blaze of glory that should have been mine and my brother's.

I couldn't believe that, while my grandfather was dying, the New Year's celebrations continued. The world should have been in mourning. The Jade Emperor should be putting off the Lantern Festival.

I'd prayed to the gods every day for as long as I could remember. How could they still be so cruel?

"Those warriors will get their comeuppance." Guanyin's voice had lost its warmth. "It's time you both left as well."

"How?" Alex demanded. "We don't have a flying chariot. We don't even have our father's notebook anymore."

I couldn't care less about islands or banquets. I ran back to Ye Ye's side and clutched his hand in mine. Alex took the other.

"Never forget," Ye Ye rasped. "The most . . . important thing . . . a warrior can do . . . is to put others . . . before himself . . . or herself."

"We'll remember," Alex said.

"Stay with us," I pleaded.

My grandfather's eyes were fixed on the window. The colorful fireworks were reflected in his black pupils, as though he was seeing something far beyond Alex and me. "Your children are . . . finally walking in your footsteps . . . ér zi. They are . . . warriors."

Ye Ye's hand stilled in mine. His eyes stared blankly, reflecting the fireworks far above.

CHAPTER

8

I waited for the shock of Ye Ye's death to set in, but it never did. Not when Guanyin pressed a white cloth over my grandfather's face. Not when she reached into her sleeve, pulled out an object that looked like the bottom half of a mop, and swept it over Ye Ye's body. When she backed away, his body vanished.

"What did you do?" Pain ripped through me as I sank to my knees. Seeing the empty space where my grandfather had lain only seconds ago felt like losing him all over again.

The Lunar New Year was supposed to be a celebration of family. Yet fate had wrenched my grandfather from me. The hollow numbness in my chest convinced me I'd never feel again.

Besides Alex and me, my wise, wonderful Ye Ye had no one to mourn his death or honor his memory. Our grandmother, Nai Nai, had died before he immigrated with his son to America. The Chinese side of my family all lived an ocean away. I'd never spoken to nor seen them, and neither had my grandfather since he'd left.

"Your grandfather's soul has passed on into the Underworld," Guanyin said. "It's cycling through Diyu, under King Yama's judgement. If Heaven's will is true, you will see him again as a deity, warriors. Now, dry your eyes. You have a quest to fulfill."

I gazed at the spot my grandfather had vanished from. I would never move again.

Alex, shivering, recovered before I could. He slowly pushed himself to his feet and turned to face the world map. He pressed his trembling palm against the small picture of our smiling mother. Then he banged his fist against the map, causing the wall to shake.

"Forget this," Alex bellowed. He whirled around with angry tears still in his eyes. "We have to leave."

I blinked, stunned. "Our grandfather just *died*, and you still want to go off to the island?"

"Somehow, the gods think you're the Heaven Breaker. And for whatever reason, they've decided to help you. You *have* to stop Wang and go to the island. Besides, didn't you hear Ye Ye's last wish? He wants us to go."

"But . . . but I can't." My head clouded with panic. "There's no way I'm the Heaven Breaker." I swallowed. "Help me, Alex. I can't do it. I'm not even a warrior."

Alex paced across the floor. I felt sicker by the moment.

"Here's what we'll do," he said at last. "We'll get that

notebook back, and then we'll use it to fulfill this quest. We'll find Ba. He's the greatest warrior in ages. He'll know what to do, and how to train you."

"But what if Ba isn't—?"

"He's alive, Faryn," Alex snapped. Then his eyes softened. "He has to be."

Alex was right. Yet I was frozen. Numb. Disbelieving.

We were interrupted by frantic pounding and shouting at the door.

"You'll want to answer that," said Guanyin.

Cautiously, I picked Fenghuang off the ground and inched open the door. A girl stormed into the house, her long, high ponytail whipping me in the face as she burst past. Moli.

"I'm sorry, this is an annoying-person-free zone—" I said.

"Where's Longma?" Moli interrupted. She barely registered the ten-foot golden spear in my hand, which told me the girl was definitely out of her right mind. "You took my horse somewhere."

Longma's escape had almost slipped my mind. I stammered, "Um, I—"

"I was going to feed him," she ranted, shaking a bag of sugar cubes in my face, "but he's *gone*. I know it's your fault. You're the only one who goes near the horses."

"Actually, that was my doing," interrupted Guanyin. "I thought your horse was due for a bit of a walk. And to tie him up so cruelly during the Year of the Horse? Shameful."

The sugar cubes fell out of Moli's slack grip and spilled onto the ground. She reeled until she backed into the doorway. "You're—you're a-a-a-a god-goddess—"

Guanyin swept past Moli. "You want to find your horse, right?"

"Why—I mean, yes, I—"

"Follow me."

Guanyin headed toward the horse stables.

"Okay, horses are flying, the gods and goddesses are real, and I've been forced to breathe the same air as you two for an extended period of time," said Moli. "This is the weirdest nightmare I've ever had."

I glared. "Come closer and I'll make it worse—"

"Come on," Alex urged, interrupting me very rudely. "Staying here isn't going to bring Ye Ye back."

Though I hated to admit it, Alex was right. My whole life, I'd stayed in one place, waiting for something to change. Waiting for Ba to come back. Waiting for Ye Ye's health to recover. Waiting for Mao and the others to finally welcome us into the Jade Society.

I was sick and tired of waiting.

Following the goddess, the three of us headed for the stables. Firecrackers exploded noisily in the courtyard. Everyone was too busy celebrating the others' departure to pay us any attention.

Moli ran down the line of horses. "Six . . . seven."

The last spot held only an empty rope. Her shoulders drooped. Moli buried her face in her hands.

"My father scrimped and saved to buy me that horse," she sobbed.

Her words stirred a memory: the moment jovial Mr. Zhao, cheeks red with pleasure, had presented seven-year-old, pigtailed Moli with the beautiful white horse. Moli had thrown her arms around her father and me—her best friend in the world back then. Mr. Zhao had been the only adult who had unconditionally accepted Alex and me. Once upon a time, Moli had been the only child to accept us, too.

"I set your horse free knowing you would be reunited one day soon," said Guanyin. "He's a very special horse."

"Of course he is," Moli sniffed. "*I* raised him."

But the mysterious look in the goddess's expression told me Moli hadn't understood the true meaning behind Guanyin's words.

Alex walked over to Moli. "Hey, you know, it *is* the Lunar New Year. And it's the Year of the Horse. Maybe Longma wanted to find his, I dunno, horse family, somewhere out there—"

Moli turned on him with tears glistening in her eyes. Her hair had fallen out of its smooth, high ponytail into a disheveled, tangled mess over one shoulder. "I *am* Longma's family. His only family. And *I* wanted to celebrate the Lunar New Year with him." She swiped at a tear. "I don't get it. I've been such a good owner."

"So have I," I said through gritted teeth. No way would I let her take all the credit for looking after the horses. "But think about it. If Longma returns, Mao will confine him to the stables again. Is that what you want for him?"

"He'll be happiest celebrating Year of the Horse in the wild," the goddess added. "If you truly do want to be united with him again, though, there is a way."

Moli went quiet, eyes blazing. "How? I'll do anything."

Guanyin whispered something into each horse's ears. They bucked their heads, as though they'd actually understood her. When she was done, the goddess stepped back. "Yes. I do believe it's time to put this old thing to use again."

She pulled something out of her pocket, a tiny gold disk, and threw it at the horses. With a burst of light, a large, luxurious chariot appeared out of thin air. There were two benches that could seat four people total, and a spot directly behind the horses for a charioteer. The horses were harnessed to the front of the gleaming chariot. They pawed at the grass, whinnying and neighing.

Alex fell to his knees. "The chariot of Zhao Fu," he said, his voice hushed. "The best vehicle in *Warfate*. Pulled by horses that can travel one thousand lǐ per day."

Moli rolled her eyes. "This isn't a dumb video game. Zhao Fu's chariot is just a made-up—"

Guanyin pointed at Moli. "Actually, this *is* Zhao Fu's chariot. And you're going to drive it."

"What?" asked Moli.

"You are descended from a legendary charioteer, Zhao Fu, whose lightning speed brought King Mu to Xi Wangmu's palace in this very chariot. You will make a fine charioteer."

Moli's jaw dropped. "I . . . what?"

This had to be a joke. There was no way Moli was tagging along with Alex and me on a quest to hunt down the mythical island. I'd rather take the nián. I'd rather walk.

Moli let out a sharp, derisive laugh. "Oh, right. The only place I'm taking these two is to a dumpster, where they belong."

I tightened my fingers around my spear.

"You will obey my commands," Guanyin said, her voice turning threatening, "and seek out Peng Lai Island, if you ever want to see your beloved horse again. It is the Year of the Horse, and any horse worth his carrots will be doing his best to get to the Jade Emperor's banquet. If Longma is a strong horse—"

"Oh, he is. The strongest," Moli said.

"—then he'll be waiting for you on this journey."

Moli patted down the horse's black mane. Finally, she stood and dusted herself off, her jaw set. "All right. I'm in."

"You're coming?" asked Alex. "Really?"

"The faster you losers shut up and get in the chariot, the faster I'll be reunited with Longma."

Alex rolled his eyes. "Girls and their horses."

We boarded the chariot, Alex and I each taking one of the golden benches.

Moli held the horses' reins in her hands. She shouted, "Jià!" and the horses trotted forward. "Wait. Do the horses even know where they're going?"

"You should know! You're the one driving," Alex cried out. He pulled out that small piece of shirt fabric from his pocket. "I got this off Wang earlier. Maybe it'll help?"

I grabbed it and waved it into each of the horses' noses. "Smell that stench? Kinda like old gym socks mixed with betrayal? Yeah, that's our friend Wang. Can you take us to him?"

The horses sniffed the air and kicked up their hooves. Their heads turned in unison in the direction where the other chariot had disappeared. I took that to mean yes.

Plodding forward, the horses slowly gathered traction on the unpaved path. I felt like I was on a parade float. At this rate, we'd reach Peng Lai Island when we were all ninety years old. We'd barely moved ten feet when the woods rustled, and something shadowy crashed out of the trees.

"Demon!" Alex screamed.

It wasn't a demon, but my brother had gotten it pretty close. Mr. Yang and his goonies tumbled out of the bushes, beat-up and covered in leaves and dirt.

"Oh, for crying out loud!" I shouted. "Can you guys go bully someone your own age for once?"

Alex drew out Ba's sword. I gripped my spear more tightly. Moli ducked under the seat and screamed, "I'm not here!"

A group of adults, led by Moli's father and Mr. and Mrs. Xiong, charged across the grass and slammed into Mr. Yang's group.

Moli raised her head to peek over the top of the chariot and gasped. "Bà ba! What're you doing?"

Mr. Zhao had pinned Mr. Yang to the ground and ignored the fists and curses the mobster was throwing at him. "Go, nǔ ér! Help your friends. I'm"—he ducked a punch—"doing what I"—he ducked another punch—"should have done"—this time Mr. Yang's punch landed square on Mr. Zhao's face, but to his credit, Moli's father didn't get off the other man— "long ago!" Now it was Mr. Zhao's turn to deliver a blow to Mr. Yang's nose. "Take that, you villain!"

"Bà ba!" Moli shouted, near tears.

Just as Moli looked ready to leap out of the chariot, Guanyin pulled a long, thin, green vase out of her sleeve and scattered droplets of a clear liquid over the horses.

The chariot jerked backward with sudden speed. Moli screamed. I thought we were going to crash.

Instead, golden dust enveloped the horses. They thrashed and writhed against some invisible force, causing the chariot to shake harder than ever. Then the horses . . . grew. Their manes lengthened. Their coats shone with fresh sleekness. They kicked their shiny hooves up into the air, and the chariot lurched upward.

We were flying.

CHAPTER

9

I broke the first rule in the flying handbook. I looked down.

The stunned faces of the aunties and uncles, along with the excited grins of the younger kids, glowed in the shower of fireworks. I would've given my golden spear to know what they were all thinking at that moment, especially Mao and Mr. Yang, watching the Liu siblings fly away in a horse-drawn chariot.

If we ever returned to the Jade Society, I'd thank Mr. Zhao and the adults who'd helped us escape.

We rose so far up into the air that the black rooftops looked like toy buildings, the people resembling tiny figurines. The city of San Francisco glittered below us, a mass of lights and dark buildings. We rose so high that, for a moment, I was terrified that an airplane would spot us.

"The blessings of the gods shield ordinary mortals from

seeing anything strange or magical, like demons and flying chariots," Guanyin said as if reading my thoughts. "Well, usually."

"Usually?"

"The blessing is strongest in the sky. In areas on Earth where there are curses or demons deeply rooted into the city, it's ineffective."

Great. Even the gods weren't strong enough to shield us from the demons. "A-and how are the horses doing this?" I stammered. "Flying?"

"All horses are born with the ability to fly, you know. They forget as they grow older and aren't given the chance. But since magic is strongest during the Lunar New Year—and especially in the Year of the Horse—they can remember."

Though we left some danger behind, the skies were even more treacherous—especially tonight. The horses neighed and jerked the chariot back and forth in earnest to avoid the explosions of fireworks. They climbed higher in a zigzagged, panicked motion, ignoring Moli's attempts to restrain them. My stomach swerved.

"Oh, this is *so* not what I signed up for!" Moli shrieked. "What am I supposed to do?"

"You can start by not screaming in my ear!" Alex yelled. "Just go with the flow. The horses know what they're doing."

As Moli and Alex bickered, Guanyin examined my spear. "This is a very powerful weapon. The Dragon King of the

East, Ao Guang, forged Fenghuang to be a weapon worthy of the gods, which means you, Heaven Breaker, can channel our powers when you use it."

This had to be a dream. All of it. I shook my head in disbelief. "What do you mean?"

"As long as you continue praying to the deities, we'll answer any call. If you're truly meant to be the Heaven Breaker and the leader of the Jade Emperor's army, you will wield our power well."

"Okay," I said, deciding not to let on that I could barely wield a hairbrush on most days. "Sure. Me, lead the Jade Emperor's army. Why not?"

And maybe while I was at it, I could find the cure for cancer, too.

The goddess frowned at the weapon. "This is going to be a headache to carry around." She flipped the spear over, as though searching for something. "There should be a way . . . ah. Yes."

I flinched when Guanyin shoved the spear under my nose. A few golden characters had been carved along the staff.

"Recite the incantation written here," she ordered.

"Um . . . yeah, no problem." I racked my brain for something, anything, that sounded like an incantation. "Bibbidi . . . bobbidi . . . boo."

The goddess raised her eyebrows at me. "Can you not read Chinese characters?"

"Not—not very many," I admitted, embarrassment heating my cheeks. "My brother can read, though. You should ask him."

Guanyin sighed. "No matter. You won't be doing much reading. Listen carefully, Heaven Breaker. I will only repeat this incantation once."

I listened as the goddess murmured, "Ǎn ma ne bā mī hōng," something that sounded like a Buddhist mantra. The spear shuddered and shrunk down to a fraction of its former size, turning into a golden hairpin.

The goddess brushed away some of my flyaway bangs and placed it into my hair. She smiled. "There. Lovely."

I blinked, my throat closing up. *Lovely.* I'd never been called *lovely.* Only *strange. Exotic. Not enough of a warrior.*

Guanyin's warm touch and smile made me wonder if my mother would have been this gentle and kind.

The moment was shattered by a loud, blaring tune from a song I recognized as a Top 40 hit.

"Oh, who changed my ringtone again?" Guanyin pulled a pink iPhone out of her apparently bottomless sleeve. "I've got to go. Urgent matters."

"Now?" The goddess couldn't leave. I had no clue what in Diyu I was doing. "But I—"

Guanyin pressed a finger to her lips and smiled. "Remember, the deities—and soon, your grandfather—are only a prayer and offering away. We'll meet again, warriors." She stepped out of the chariot onto a cloud, answering her phone. "Oh, Nezha.

I've sent the warriors on their way safely. Now, tell me more about this plan of yours . . ."

The goddess's voice faded as she floated away, turning into a star in the distance.

Nezha? Plan? Guanyin's words struck me as strange, but as we flew onward into the night, I couldn't make sense of them.

Besides, try as I might, the distractions around me made it impossible to even hear my own thoughts. The fireworks might have stopped, but the explosions between Moli and Alex only grew louder.

"Guanyin put me in charge, not you," Moli snapped.

"I'm trying to help," my brother retorted. "Your driving is awful."

"I've never driven anything before. And are you really making sexist jokes?"

The chariot rocked back and forth. The horses shot up in the air, as if chasing after something. My ears popped, and I clenched my hands around the edge of my seat. The chariot jerked as it leveled. The back of my head slammed into the chariot, and stars erupted before my eyes.

"Found the idiots!" Alex shouted, pointing ahead at a dark shape that loomed out of the clouds—a brown chariot.

Wang and Luhao hovered above us in their ride, apparently arguing. Both boys were standing. I wouldn't call myself an expert on charioteering, but I figured that wasn't good protocol, especially not thousands of feet in the air.

They fought over the reins, while Wang waved something

through the air with his free hand—Ba's notebook. As if he heard our approach, he whipped around. Wang's eyes widened. He yelled something I couldn't hear.

"Horses, get them," I shouted. Blood pounded in my ears. Even if this was all some weird dream, which I was convinced it was, no way would I let Wang and Luhao show me up. "Fifty sugar cubes per warrior!"

Moli screamed as the horses charged with a burst of speed. When it came to sugar cubes, these guys didn't mess around.

But the horses pulling the other chariot were fast, too. They spurted forward, yanking the boys ahead.

"They're getting away," Alex shouted at Moli. He stood, his hair whipping in the wind.

Our ride jerked back and forth as Moli yanked on different reins like a puppeteer. "I can see that, you stupid—Whoa!"

Wang's chariot plunged downward, blown off course by a sudden gust of wind that caused our chariot to careen slightly to the left. Moli pulled us upward to stabilize the vehicle.

"Go after them," Alex yelled at her. "If we don't get our father's notebook, we won't know how to reach the island!"

Another burst of wind blew the other chariot in a zigzag motion. Both boys were screaming.

I saw the source of the strange wind: a skinny man in a yellow cape, flying toward us. No. A closer look showed me a long nose, whiskers, and yellow teeth. The figure was a rat the size of a man.

"Yāo guài," Alex cried.

I gulped. A yāo guài was no ordinary demon, but an animal spirit that had grown powerful—and evil—by practicing Taoism. The demon's beady black eyes zeroed in on Wang's chariot, and then on ours. On me.

Guanyin's words rang in my head. *The power of Fenghuang will attract many enemies—demons and deities alike.*

Alex drew his sword, which shook as he held it in front of him. The horses bucked against their reins as Moli attempted to restrain them, threatening to shake us out of the chariot. The yāo guài hovered so close to us that I could see individual whiskers on its face.

"The sky is not your territory, warriors. Taste the wrath of the samadhi wind!" The yāo guài sucked in a deep breath. Before it could blast us into the next dimension, I reached for the pin in my hair.

But Alex placed his hand on my shoulder. "Wait. I've got this." He swung his sword wildly at the yāo guài, which flew higher to avoid the blade. Alex nearly tumbled over the edge of the chariot.

"Wow, way to show it," Moli screamed.

The yāo guài dove at the other chariot. Wang scrambled to one end, nearly tipping the vehicle and sending both boys to their deaths. Luhao pulled at the horses' reins. After rebalancing himself, Wang sliced at the yāo guài with his sword, but the demon was too quick. Another blast of wind from the creature sent their chariot careening past us.

Luhao's hands fumbled for the reins. "Help!"

I reached for Fenghuang again, but the yāo guài turned its attention back to us. It released another gust of wind from its mouth. The chariot rocked sideways and would've tossed me overboard if my fingers hadn't gripped the side at the last moment.

"Moli, charge!" I screamed.

"Don't tell me what to do!" Even as she said this, Moli yanked on the reins and urged the horses forward. They took off in a burst of speed. My head careened back into the chariot in a collision of pain.

"Good news," Moli bellowed. "This yāo guài is giving me a crash course in charioteering. Bad news—we might literally get a crash course in charioteering!"

The yāo guài flew above us with a cackle. The demon was toying with us. "I spent decades mastering Taoism to become this powerful, mortals. You won't kill me that easily!"

Alex thrust out with his weapon as Moli pulled the chariot upward, but the yāo guài dodged us with ease. I took advantage of our momentary stability to pull Fenghuang out of my hair.

I knew what to do. I repeated the incantation Guanyin had taught me: "Ǎn ma ne bā mī hōng!" Fenghuang shifted into its full golden glory in my palm. "I'll take this one, Alex."

My brother fell back wordlessly.

The yāo guài's white fangs glinted against the night sky as it paused at the sight of Fenghuang. The boys pulled up behind us, Luhao in full control of the horses, but the demon only had eyes for us now. The hungry look on its face sent a shiver up my spine.

"Fenghuang," it sneered. "I see you've brought me a present."

"Yeah," I said. "Xīn nián kuài lè! Happy New Year!"

Gripping the spear above my head, I thrust it toward the yāo guài. The demon dodged the point of my weapon, sailing through the air. The chariot rocked more violently, and my hip smashed against the side. Pain shot up my body.

"Kill it, Faryn! What're you waiting for?" Alex bellowed.

Answers. An instruction manual. I had no clue how to use Fenghuang. Cold sweat gathered in my palms. The fight with the hú lì jīng must've been a fluke. The power and warmth I'd felt before had abandoned me, and I had no clue how to activate it. I jabbed desperately at the yāo guài, gripping the side of the chariot for balance.

"Pathetic. You don't deserve to wield that magnificent weapon." The yāo guài swooped down. It spread its arms, yellow cape billowing in the wind, and sucked in another breath. This time the wind was so strong it sent searing pain through my body. Our chariot bashed into the three boys'. The horses whinnied in panic.

I pressed a hand to my stinging cheek. Blood came away on my fingertips, along with grains of sand.

"S-sandstorm!" Wang cried.

The yāo guài had paused its attack and was shaping

something with its hands. As it grew, I realized what it was—a tornado.

Wang lunged at the demon with his sword as Luhao pulled them within combat range, but his swings were useless. The wind billowed around us and threatened to yank my hair out of my head. As the horses fought to keep us in the air, their whinnies reached a crescendo. I lifted my spear and flung it in front of my face, keeping the other in a death grip on the side of the chariot. It was all I could do to hold on to Fenghuang.

"Useless!" Luhao screamed above the howl of the storm.

The wind bit at my exposed skin. He was right. I was useless. I was only half a warrior, unfit to hunt demons, much less become the Heaven Breaker. I held one of the most powerful weapons in the world—and had no idea what to do with it.

Despair twisted my gut. Why had the gods chosen *me* to be the Heaven Breaker?

"Faryn!"

Alex's scream jolted me out of my thoughts. The yāo guài's tornado had grown to easily twenty feet tall. The demon wound its arm back, as though preparing to unleash the storm. My brother clutched the side of the chariot with his fingers, his body blown so far backward that one good blast would send him over the edge.

I cried out. The wind was too strong. I couldn't move to help Alex.

Think. What had I done differently to kill the hú lì jīng in the temple?

The temple. The place of the gods.

Guanyin had said Fenghuang could grant me the power of the gods. Back at the temple—I'd prayed.

Even though the idea of owing more favors to the gods didn't sit well with me, I didn't see another choice. The split second before the yāo guài unleashed its tornado, I sent a silent prayer to the goddess who'd first given me the power to wield Fenghuang—the Queen Mother of the West, Xi Wangmu, wife to the Jade Emperor.

Xi Wangmu, please help me send this yāo guài to Diyu.

My limbs surged with power—the same feeling of invincibility that had helped me defeat the nián and the hú lì jīng.

As though they'd read my mind, the horses fought against the howling wind and charged toward the yāo guài. I squinted as much as I dared against the violent storm, and slashed Fenghuang at the demon. The crystallized point drove through the tunnel of wind and met its target with a burst of light.

With a shriek, the yāo guài dissolved under the force of the strike. The tornado vanished. The wind settled. Breathing heavily, I watched as its form crumpled into a wisp of smoke that floated away.

Alex slumped onto the bottom of the chariot. He was quaking from head to foot. For a long moment, there were only the sounds of the horses whinnying in protest.

"What"—my brother turned to me, openmouthed—"did you just do?"

Good question. "That's not important," I shouted, pointing

in front of us, where the wind had blown Wang and the others away. My eyes zeroed in on the black book Wang clutched in his hand. "Get the notebook!"

Moli obeyed. The horses kicked up bursts of cloud behind us, and we surged toward the brown chariot, gaining on the boys with each second.

But something was wrong. The other chariot had slowed. The wooden chariot first stuttered, then stopped, and then began to fall, dropping like a ton of bricks.

Wang and Luhao screamed. Moli urged our horses after the falling chariot.

Alex's fingers reached for Wang's outstretched hand, as though he were trying to catch him. Instead, my brother snatched the black notebook out of Wang's flailing arm, ignoring the fact that the boy was literally plunging to his doom. "Gotcha!"

"No!" I screamed. I lunged past my brother, shoving him aside to grab Wang's fingers. I hoisted with all my strength.

But Wang's fingers were too sweaty. I clung to his hand, desperate to get a solid hold. His eyes widened as they met mine; his mouth parted. For the first time, an anguished expression crossed his face. The face of a boy truly fearful. A boy looking upon death.

Wang's fingers slipped out of mine. His body plunged downward into free fall.

CHAPTER

10

As the boys plunged toward Earth, I knew I had to save them. Even if the gods seemed to have left Wang and Luhao for dead after we'd overtaken them in the "challenge," this wasn't right.

For one thing, the poor dead folks in Diyu shouldn't have to put up with these morons for eternity just yet.

"Moli, save them!" I shouted.

"Jià!" Moli drove the chariot downward, chasing the falling bodies. The chariot jerked until it was horizontal and caught the screaming boys.

Wang landed with a thud at my feet, and Luhao landed on top of Wang.

"Get off me!" Wang shouted.

"I can't!" roared Luhao. "There's nowhere to go!"

The decently roomy four-person chariot had now become

a very cramped space full of flailing arms and legs. I hissed at Wang when his arm whacked my foot.

The boys' chariot had plunged to Earth, but their horses twirled in joyous circles before soaring off into the distance.

"Deities, what kind of trash chariot was that?" Wang demanded, sitting up and rubbing his hair, elbowing Luhao in the process. "It almost killed us!"

"Miserable gods," Luhao grunted. "I can't believe Xi Wangmu gave us a faulty ride after we prayed to her."

Wang smacked his head. "And after I offered her my last pack of strawberry Pocky."

Somehow the image of the heir to the Jade Society offering strawberry Pocky to the goddess didn't quite process in my mind. But then again, how well did I know Wang, anyway?

And why had Xi Wangmu helped me—but not them?

"Faryn, you're too nice," said Alex. "Should've just let these guys fall to their deaths."

"Say that again," spat Luhao, but Wang held him back.

I blinked. The intense anger on my brother's face frightened me. "What? You can't be serious."

"It's the least they deserve."

Luhao raised a fist, with great difficulty, considering his foot was now in Wang's face. "Say that again, you filthy little—"

"That's enough," Wang interrupted, shoving the other boy's foot away. "They saved us."

Luhao looked stunned by the rebuke. He cast his eyes downward. "Whatever."

The heir to the Jade Society stood up, wincing and rubbing his neck. "We, um . . . we owe you guys."

"No kidding," I said.

Alex glowered. "You can repay us by taking a hike to Diyu. Three thousand feet, straight down. Can't miss it."

"Bye-bye, boys," Moli added in a sweet voice.

Wang bit his lip. "And we're sorry we took the notebook."

"I'm not," scoffed Luhao.

If Ye Ye were here, he'd want me to forgive them. But Ye Ye was gone. I swallowed and blinked back tears. And I wasn't prepared to let these guys off the hook.

"So why'd you steal the notebook, then?" I demanded.

"My mother—well, you know how she is," said Wang. "She insisted I was the Heaven Breaker. She told me I'd bring her honor—and riches—if I became a general for the Jade Emperor. She knew about your father's research and notebook, so I—I . . ." Wang closed his eyes. "But I'm not the Heaven Breaker. And I don't want to be a general." The tips of Wang's ears flushed bright red. "I—I want to be an actor, okay?"

Luhao nearly fell out of the chariot. "What?"

"Every Lunar New Year parade, I get to play the hero who slays the nián," Wang mumbled, "and it's the highlight of my whole year."

Luhao stared at Wang as though he were already looking at a dead man. "Dude, your mama's gonna kill you."

"You don't have to do everything Mao says, you know," Alex said sourly.

Wang shook his head. "That's just it. I do. Our families immigrated to America to follow the demons, so we could slay them with ease and protect the people of Earth. My mom's family sacrificed everything to come here. Going against her dream, it's . . ."

Luhao blinked. Then he put a hand on Wang's shoulder, sighing. "I get you, dude. When I was a kid—"

"Aren't you still a kid?" Alex muttered.

"—I wanted to be an engineer, but my old man said demon slaying is cooler. Well, before we stopped slaying demons."

"Being an engineer would be cool," Wang said. "Anyway, I . . . think I'm going back. It is the Lunar New Year, after all. We should be with our families."

Wang looked at Luhao for support. The other boy crossed his arms over his chest but finally nodded.

"How're you guys getting back to the Jade Society? You don't even have a chariot anymore," I pointed out.

"Uh . . . a taxi?" Wang suggested.

Luhao looked ready to smack him. "You sure you aren't more suited to being a comedian instead?" Then his eyes darted in Moli's direction.

Moli folded her arms. "Oh no. Nuh-uh. If you boys think

we're dropping you off to your mommies, you've got another thing coming. I'm not a chauffeur."

"But we own two of those horses," Wang pointed out. "Zongma. Feikuai." Each name he called was followed by the horse's whinny of response. "We'll take them and get out of your hair."

With those two horses gone, we'd lose almost half our speed—but our pace had been too fast anyway. If we kept it up all the way to Peng Lai Island, my skin would peel right off my body.

"All right," Alex said grudgingly. "Take your horses and scram."

Moli's scowl deepened as the two boys each released their horses from the reins. I didn't want to give up the horses either, but if we didn't, we'd have to take these losers with us. And none of us wanted that.

With difficulty, the boys mounted the flying horses. Luhao trembled from head to foot and squeezed Feikuai's neck so tightly that the horse bucked in protest.

Wang bowed his head. "Good luck."

He'd need luck more than we did, as soon as Mao found out he'd given up on being a Heavenly General to pursue acting.

The two boys kicked their horses and took off into a blaze of pink-and-orange sunrise, until they became specks in the distance.

Alex turned to me. "Okay, now it's time for you to explain how you're such a good fighter. You killed a demon just now, but that wasn't your first, was it? Ye Ye said you slayed the nián."

"What?" The chariot lurched as Moli yanked too hard on the horses' reins. "She slayed *what*?"

"Helped," I clarified. "Erlang Shen killed the demon. I just, um, beat it up."

"Beat it up." An incredulous expression stretched over Alex's face. "My dorky older sister. Beating up ancient demons. When did you turn into a kung fu movie protagonist?"

"Uh . . . about twenty-four hours ago."

My heart sank when Alex looked—as though I'd become a stranger. He buried his face back into Ba's book. "Look at you, defeating demons left and right. You're turning into the warrior Ye Ye and Ba always wanted. You might not even need Ba's help."

I swallowed. "Of course I do. I have no idea what I'm doing."

"Could've fooled me," Alex muttered. "Why do *you* get to do all the cool things?"

I didn't know what to say. I hadn't asked to face the nián or be the Heaven Breaker. What right did I have to wield the powerful weapon—a girl who had only one foot in the warrior world?

My eyes burned with tears. I pictured Ye Ye's smile. Grief

clawed at my heart, but I didn't let the tears fall. If I could exchange my grandfather's life for the spear, I would in a heartbeat. Guanyin had been convinced that Ye Ye would be deified. I had no idea how long that would take—if it was half as complicated as the United States citizenship process, I'd be dead before my grandfather made it to Heaven—but there was hope.

"As much as I hate to interrupt a fight between you siblings," Moli called from the front, "I think it *might* be a better use of our time to figure out where the heck we're going."

I hated to admit it, but she was right. Swallowing back my frustration, I recalled the riddle embedded in the warrior god's proclamation. "Erlang Shen said I—*we*—have to, uh . . . get some animal that's named after . . . somebody—"

Alex heaved a great sigh. "No, he said: 'First, seek the city named after the Empress to save the animal named after the Emperor.'"

My jaw dropped. "How did you remember that?"

"I use my brain?"

I scowled and rapped a knuckle against Alex's head. "So do I."

He swatted my hand away. "Ow! Quit it."

"If you're so smart, then why don't you figure out what the riddle means, too?"

"I already have," Alex said with the exaggerated impatience of an adult speaking to a toddler. "'The city named after the Empress' can only refer to the phoenix, a bird typically associated with the Empress. There's one on Xi Wangmu's statue, remember?"

I jogged my memory for the statues back in the Jade Society temple and gasped. Alex was right.

"As for the animal named after the Emperor, that can only be the dragon. As in, the dragon on the Jade Emperor's statue." Alex clapped his hands together. "So, first we have to seek 'the city named after the Empress.' That means we have to find a dragon in Phoenix, Arizona. Leave it to me."

Alex raised Ba's notebook, showing a hand-drawn map, and stuck his nose back into its pages.

"Finding a dragon shouldn't be too hard," Moli said sarcastically. "Maybe we can check the local zoo."

At least the gods wanted us to find a dragon, and not an ant or something. I figured there was a pretty small chance of us missing a huge mythological creature like that in the middle of the city.

Alex shouted out directions to Moli, and as much as she complained, she followed them exactly. This went on for long enough that I was feeling pretty useless looking down at the house-dotted landscape below.

"Most of Phoenix's Chinatown isn't publicly known the way San Francisco's is," said Alex. "They've kept the majority of the temples and other buildings in a secret neighborhood on the outskirts of town to avoid tourists and other unwanted visitors."

"Then how do you even know where we're going?" shouted Moli.

Alex held up Ba's notebook. "Well, I have insider info."

We were low enough to the ground that I could see the red lanterns dotting the city. "Wait—is that a Chinatown?"

Alex stood up, rocking slightly in the face of a gust of wind. He leaned his head over the edge and gasped. "Moli, we made it. Go down!"

"Whoa—aren't we trying to get to Phoenix?" I protested.

"That *is* Phoenix down there," Alex said, throwing me an exasperated look. "Phoenix's Chinatown. That's where we have to go. I'm sure of it." My brother opened the black notebook and squinted at the page. "Even though they don't have a society of warriors there like San Francisco does, Ba praised the wise monks who guard the temple. He said they knew the answers to all his questions." He snapped the book closed and flashed me a triumphant grin. "I bet they'd know where to find our dragon."

"You think a couple of bald men will solve our problems?" Moli spluttered.

"Do *you* have a better idea?"

Moli grumbled but commanded the horses into a rapid descent toward Earth. I clung onto the side of the chariot. Once we reached the island, I was never going to step foot on a chariot ever again. Or anything that moved faster than two miles per hour.

"Whoa, steady, horses!" Moli yanked on the reins, but it

seemed she'd lost control of the chariot. "Don't land there, idiots!"

But the horses wouldn't listen. We jerked toward the ground, and my stomach churned. As the horses panicked, I was reminded of Guanyin's earlier words about the gods' blessing weakening—near demons. I gulped.

A huge jolt nearly tossed me out of the chariot when we'd landed. I immediately spotted a skyscraper-tall black pagoda in the center of a small Chinatown. A long line snaked out the temple door and down the street.

Despite the fact that it was winter, the air in Phoenix was warm and dry.

The area where we'd landed was a metropolitan sprawl for the most part, with tall, glassy buildings, but in the distance I could see cacti and a desert landscape surrounding us. The streets of Chinatown were lined with run-down grocery stores and restaurants that had colorful green-and-red pagoda tops and curved eaves. The horses seemed to be back in familiar territory. They neighed and plodded forward.

Now that we were on the ground, the gods' blessings no longer shielded us, judging by the fact that people were screaming and scattering to get out of our way, dropping armfuls of food and incense sticks onto the ground.

"Clear out! Important people coming through," Moli shouted, tossing her hair over her shoulder as she urged the horses onward.

"The gods have answered our prayers!" gasped an elderly Asian woman. She pointed her walker at us. "I *just* wished for horses, and here they are. It's a miracle."

Gasps echoed throughout the streets.

"The gods?" a younger man behind her demanded. "Are those the gods?"

Everyone from the children to elderly fell to their knees before us.

A flash went off in my face. I blinked. A girl wearing a huge infinity scarf and too much eye makeup had taken a selfie with the chariot. "I'm filming *live* outside the temple in Chinatown, where the gods just dropped out of the sky."

"Hold on," I protested, "we aren't the—"

"'Scuse us. Gods coming through," Alex interrupted in his Darth Vader impression. "Important business at the temple, you know. Thanks for this, ā yí."

My brother swiped an apple out of a middle-aged woman's hand and bit into it.

"That wasn't for you," she protested. "That was for the god of fortune!"

I avoided looking at the people in line, aware that they were staring at us and murmuring. Moli ordered the horses to stop when we reached the front of the temple, a few strides away from the golden statues and food-filled altars on the inside. Two bald men wearing roomy orange robes stood before us, eyes narrowed. Monks.

Alex leapt out of the chariot. "Shī fù." He inclined his head to the monks in respect. "Years ago, a warrior named Liu Bo defended your temple from demons."

I jumped out of the chariot and joined my brother. "We're his children, and we'd like to ask for your help. We have to find a, uh . . ." There was no way to say *dragon* and get them to take us seriously, so I'd just have to do it with as straight of an expression as possible. "A—"

"Sorry. We've never heard of this Liu Bo," interrupted the monk on the left.

The other nodded and added gently, "Please go to the back of the line."

"What?" Alex flipped through the notebook. "No. This is Phoenix's Chinatown. Ba clearly wrote about saving the monks from demons here. He says, 'There was a yāo guài rampaging around the temple, breaking altars and terrorizing the monks. I eventually destroyed it, though it was one of the hardest battles I ever fought. The monks rewarded me with food, as well as the promise to honor my relatives forever.'" Alex pointed at the passage and held the book out toward the monks, who sniffed and turned it away. "With all due respect, shī fù, maybe you guys were taking the day off, or—"

"Children, we're quite busy today, as you can see," the monk said with a touch of impatience. "Please don't waste our time. I've never seen a demon here in Phoenix."

Alex kept arguing with the men, but a flurry of movement

diverted my attention. A boy snuck out of line, wearing a black T-shirt that contrasted with his strikingly white hair.

The boy sprinted up the steps. He almost made it past the black doors and into the temple. But then a monk turned and flung his arm to stop him.

"Cursed One," the man said, his voice trembling. I couldn't believe it. This monk was scared of a kid? "When will you learn that you can't enter a sacred temple?"

The boy, the Cursed One, gave the monk a pleading look. One of his irises was black, but the other was a brilliant emerald green. "Shū shu, please."

"Every day for ten years you've been trying to get in," said the monk. "Aren't you tired of it?"

"But it's the second day of the New Year. The gods are most generous now. Please, I have to talk to the god—"

"The gods don't even talk to *me*. Come back when you've rid your hair of your curse, and that awful white dye."

"This is my natural color!" the boy protested.

"More proof that you're cursed." The monk grabbed the boy by his arm and marched him down the steps. The white-haired Cursed One stumbled back into an old man who stood in line. The man shuffled away from him. So did everyone else.

My heart beat quicker. This wasn't right.

"The temples are supposed to be open to everyone who needs help," I said. "Aren't they?"

The monks folded their arms, returned to their posts, and didn't respond. I turned to the Cursed One—only to discover he'd vanished into the crowd.

"Let's get out of here." Moli sniffed, yanking the reins. The horses snorted and made a U-turn, causing more gasps from the crowd.

"Wait," I protested as Alex and I scrambled to climb onto the chariot. "We're leaving, just like that? We haven't even figured out where the dragon is!"

"For once, I agree with you," Alex said "Those monks have to be the ones who helped Ba. We've gotta talk to them. This is the only temple for miles, Moli—"

"So we'll keep moving forward and find another temple with monks." She yelled over her shoulder, "I'm totally giving you guys a one-star review on Yelp!"

I swallowed my anger. There would be more temples on our way. We'd find others to help us. But not here.

An ugly, tense silence fell over our chariot. Moli turned us down a street to get away from the crowd. The horses pulled us past a closed Korean beauty-supply store and a couple of restaurants with names like Golden Dragon and Emerald Restaurant. This Chinatown was much smaller than the huge, bustling one in San Francisco I was used to seeing. They probably didn't even have a Lunar New Year parade. It was a sad thought.

"What now?" Moli asked. The chariot halted in front of an Asian supermarket. The flashing neon sign hanging above the store read FRESH MART. Except some of the lights were out, so from a distance it read FEAR instead. Awesome.

A low growl split the silence.

"Demon!" Alex yelled, upending his notebook and yanking his sword off the floor.

"No, that was my stomach," I admitted. "Do we have any food?"

Alex reached into his pocket and produced a half-eaten granola bar. I gave him a withering look.

"Suit yourself," he said, tearing off the wrapper and then shoving the rest of the bar into his mouth.

"Ew!"

"There's bound to be some food in there." My brother nodded at Fresh Mart. He crammed the notebook into his back pocket and swung his legs over the chariot.

"I'm not going in there," Moli huffed.

"Why not?" I was already poised to leap out of the vehicle.

"Asian markets always smell like dead fish. You two stink enough. I'm gonna head up to the roof and get some air, thanks." Moli paused. "While you're at it, get some carrots for the horses. And fruit for me. I'm starving."

"We don't have money," Alex pointed out.

I bit my lip, inwardly cursing myself. We should've asked Guanyin for money before she left. That was, like, rule number one of cross-country quests: take the grown-ups for all they're worth.

"What kind of city dweller doesn't carry money with them?" Moli scoffed.

As though it were our fault that Mao had only ever given us enough money to cover groceries and bills. As though Alex and I had ever even been allowed to dwell outside in the city as freely as everyone else. I wanted to point out that not all of us had been as *spoiled* as Moli was.

But the hunger gnawed at my insides and fogged up my brain. I didn't have the energy to fight.

"Don't spend everything at once." With that, Moli directed the horses skyward.

The bustling market welcomed us with the pungent odor of fish and durian, not to mention the chaos of families yelling at each other across the store. I plugged my ears. Seriously, couldn't these people just text one another?

We pushed past swarms of people, moving through aisle after aisle of Asian junk food—everything from Pocky and shrimp chips to dried mushrooms that smelled more like dried feet. I had to drag Alex away from the candy aisle.

The fruit was located in the back of the store, next to giant transparent tanks where live fish swam. Their eyes gazed straight into my soul, begging me to save them. A couple of kids giggled and poked at the glass.

"What kind of fruit do you think Moli would like?" Alex asked, eyeing the colorful variety of apples, bananas, peaches, and more.

"Durian," I blurted out. "Yep. Durian. I'm positive."

"Really? How're you so sure?"

"She, uh, mentioned it to me back when we were still friends. Said it's good for the skin or something."

Alex hurried to select one of the stinky yellow fruits. I snickered.

I grabbed a bag of carrots and some dried meat and other snacks for us, joining Alex as we headed back to the front. There was a lovesick, puppylike expression on his face that made me want to punch him.

Instead I did something worse.

"Soooooooo, Alex. It's up to me to talk to you about girls, huh?"

"What?" Alex spluttered. "Why?"

Though I'd been trying to make a joke out of it, my grin faded. "Since . . . you know . . . our parents aren't around."

My brother looked at me as though I'd suggested we poke our eyeballs out and offer them to the gods. "You've got to be kidding me."

"You're reaching that age where you're interested in girls. It's only natural."

Alex's cheeks flamed. "Wh-what are you talking about?"

"I'm not blind. You totally have a thing for—"

"I don't have a thing for anyone!" my brother shouted. In a normal store he probably would've attracted stares from everyone in a fifty-foot radius, but since we were in the loudest place on Earth, I barely even heard him.

Grinning, I put my hands up. "Okay, whatever you say."

"You're so embarrassing."

"Just looking out for you."

"Well, don't."

Before I could respond, someone bumped into me, causing the counter to dig into my rib cage. "Oof!" I gasped. The person stumbled but recovered quickly and squeezed past customers in a mad dash for the exit.

"Thief!" a deep voice bellowed. "Someone stop him!"

CHAPTER

11

Like Chinese Wonder Woman, I saved the day. I reached into my grocery basket, grabbed the thorny durian, and chucked it at the white-haired figure while trying not to shriek in pain.

Note to self: never, ever touch durian skin with bare hands.

The spiky, smelly yellow fruit sailed through the air and thwacked against the thief's back. He went down in a flash of white, his body half-inside the store and half-outside, scattering the people nearby.

"She shoots—she scores!" I said.

"Seriously, is there an agency I can use to disown an older sister?" Alex muttered.

A Fresh Mart worker pulled the thief to his feet, and his face came into view. White hair and mismatched eyes. The Cursed One. This kid was a magnet for trouble.

A large man with a black beard shoved past me. He

mumbled something to the worker, who released the white-haired boy with a reluctant look on his face. The man yanked the thief by his ear. "Ren! You shameless boy. I take you to a store, and you decide to *rob* it? And during New Year?"

"Technically I haven't left the store yet," mumbled Ren.

"Uh-oh. Looks like that kid's in some big trouble," Alex whispered.

Something about this scene was definitely wrong. The man was tall and intimidating, with black hair piled on top of his head in a man bun. He wore a long, white shirt decorated with a column of gold buttons. His massive belly protruded over his tan, belted pants. He didn't look like the white-haired boy's father, but stranger things had happened.

The man let go of Ren's ear and snatched something out of the boy's hands—three white incense sticks and a golden statue of what looked like our familiar ally Guanyin, the goddess of mercy. "What's this nonsense?"

"You wouldn't let me buy the incense sticks or the statue," Ren protested, rubbing his ear.

"So what? You think that's permission to *steal* them?"

"I have to speak with the gods, Mr. Fan. It's urgent."

"What for? The gods won't help you get rid of your wretched curse, boy. C'mon. Back to training." Mr. Fan threw an arm around Ren and called over his shoulder, "Move along. Nothing to see here."

Ren wriggled out of the man's big, beefy arm, knocking over a shelf of wasabi peas. "I'm not going back with you!"

Mr. Fan's face reddened, and his beady eyes flitted around the crowd "Ren, don't make a scene. Think of how ashamed Jianfei would be."

"If my father were still alive, he'd be more ashamed that you—his *friend*—won't even let me pray to the gods!"

I probably should've let the Fresh Mart workers handle the situation. But if there was one thing Ye Ye had taught me, it was the importance of prayer. Showing loyalty to the gods was a privilege everyone was supposed to have.

I pulled my pin out of my hair and muttered the incantation. Fenghuang lengthened in my hands.

"Get away from him," I ordered the large man, whipping the crystallized tip under his nose.

I expected the screams. I expected the shocked look on Mr. Fan's face. I expected Ren to stumble backward.

I didn't expect Mr. Fan to keel over in a dead faint—or for the air around Ren to burst into smoke.

The families began bolting out the front door in a panic. Mothers grabbed their crying children in one hand and hauled a week's worth of groceries in the other.

As I looked on with a mixture of fascination and horror, Ren's skin began turning blue. Its texture bubbled, the surface turning from smooth to scaly. He screamed, the high-pitched sound deepening into a roar.

"He truly is the Cursed One!" someone screamed as the last of the customers and workers stampeded out of the door.

I backed away, feet crunching over spilled wasabi peas.

A gray smoke screen enveloped the white-haired boy, and as he writhed, his roars turned lower and more animal-like. Then he began growing at a rapid speed. He grew and grew until his body burst through the roof with a thundering *crash* that shook the building from ceiling to floor. Chunks of brick rained down on us.

Alex tugged at my sleeve. "Get out!"

"But—Mr. Fan," I said, staring at the man lying on the ground.

My brother hauled me along with strength I hadn't thought he had in him. "Forget him, Faryn. He's a complete jerk anyway."

I frowned. First Wang, now Mr. Fan. I wasn't the biggest fan of those guys, either, but wasn't my brother being a little extreme? "Just because people are jerks doesn't mean they deserve to—"

"More importantly," Alex interrupted as though I hadn't spoken, "Moli's out there!" He pointed through the rubble toward the outside. The panic in his voice bordered on hysteria. "We've gotta save her."

I felt guilty until I noticed Mr. Fan had managed to dig himself out of the rubble—and instead of checking on Ren or any of us, he was running away screaming and waving his arms. I shook my head. The real hero of Chinatown.

Together, the two of us dodged falling mortar and sprinted for the exit. We ran out into the parking lot, where the families were piling into their cars and driving off. In moments, the parking lot was empty.

I looked up. Moli's golden chariot soared high above us, safe from danger. I let out a breath of relief. If she was smart, she'd stay up there.

When the smoke cleared and dust settled, we found ourselves facing a full-grown dragon. The snakelike creature had emerald-green scales and two small horns that emerged from the top of its head. He hissed and emitted smoke out of his nostrils. He stood at least fifteen feet tall and measured easily twice that in length, with the body of a serpent and small arms and feet. The dragon hovered over the crumbling building.

"The riddle!" my brother shouted. "This is—"

"—the dragon we've been looking for," I finished. I squinted up at the majestic creature and gulped. "D-dragons are supposed to be good . . . right?"

Ye Ye had told me that dragons were honored beasts in Chinese tradition. Sure, there were a couple of dangerous ones, but almost all—especially the direct descendants of the Dragon King of the West Sea, Ao Ji—were intelligent, even if they were incapable of human speech. The creatures commanded great respect and power among humans and deities.

"Normally, yeah. Dragons bring prosperity and the rain," Alex said, his trembling fist clenched around his sword. "But it doesn't look like this one is, uh, that interested in prosperity."

The dragon opened his mouth to reveal fangs as tall and thick as poles and pointed enough to bite anything in two. He let out a roar that shook the trees. Birds scattered. Up above, the horses kicked up their hooves and whinnied in terror, drawing the dragon's sharp glare.

Moli screamed. She had no weapon to protect herself.

"Over here, Fish Breath!" Alex bellowed at the dragon.

"Alex, get back!" I said. "I'll fight the dragon with Fenghuang."

"*I* have to save Moli!" he shouted. "I don't care if you're the Heaven Breaker, the Chosen One, Girl Who Lived, or whatever. I can do this."

Shoulders steeled, my brother sprinted toward the dragon, slashing his sword through the air. The creature opened his mouth, shooting out a column of water at us.

I dove out of the way, my arm ramming into a shopping cart and sending it skidding into a curb. Pain shot up my side, nearly causing me to drop the spear.

Alex didn't scatter quickly enough and received the brunt of the blast. The pressure of the watery column threw him into a brick pillar in front of Golden Dragon restaurant. He fell into a wet, crumpled heap on the ground and stayed still, one of his legs bent at an odd angle.

"Alex!" Moli and I both screamed.

Moli drove the horses toward my brother. She grabbed his hand and yanked him over the side of the chariot. The two of them took off, spiraling into the sky and out of harm's way.

Moli urged the horses in my direction but swerved upward when the dragon shot a blast of water at her.

I threw myself behind a nearby rack of shopping carts. The water pummeled the RETURN SHOPPING CART, OR ELSE sign.

My brain went into overdrive. If this dragon was the one from the riddle, then I had to let him know I was the Heaven Breaker.

"All right, Faryn," I muttered. "Time to show this dragon who's boss."

I waited for the water to stop pummeling the sign before I jumped out. I craned my neck to look the dragon straight in the eye, aware that if I hesitated for even a second, I might find myself staring King Yama in the eye instead. This wasn't one of Alex's video games. There would be no do-over.

"I am the Heaven Breaker." My voice shook, just like the spear I held in front of me. If the Heaven Breaker was really meant to be master of the dragons, as the legend went, then this had to work.

Fenghuang's glow brightened, heating my hands and sending a surge of power through me. It was working. I cleared my throat and raised my voice. "You will obey me."

A deep, low voice boomed in my head, startling me out of my thoughts.

I transformed because I sensed the presence of your mighty spear, Heaven Breaker, so you must not be lying.

"Did you hear that?" I shouted to Moli and Alex.

Confusedly, they shook their heads. Did that mean I was imagining things? Or maybe . . . maybe as the Heaven Breaker, I could *communicate* with this dragon. The idea was crazy, but so was everything that had happened to me since the appearance of the nián.

"Are you *talking* to that thing? This is not some ridiculous Disney movie!" Alex shouted.

After thirteen long years of waiting for your arrival, said the dragon, *I must say, you aren't quite who I expected to see.*

I gritted my teeth. What did the dragon mean, I wasn't what he had expected? Why was that such a big deal, anyway?

"We're getting out of here," said Moli. "I'm coming!"

She squealed again when the dragon whipped his tail at her, yanking the horses upward, his mouth pulled back in a snarl.

Must protect master from the small villains.

"Whoa, buddy! You don't need to protect me from the small villains—I mean, those guys," I shouted. "They might look like villains, but they're my friends."

The dragon's great yellow eyes swiveled up toward the golden chariot. He bared his fangs and emitted a low, threatening rumble as I approached him. Steam spouted out of his nostrils. He opened his mouth, eyes glued to my spear. I figured we all had two seconds to scram before the dragon blasted us into smithereens.

Then the dragon lowered his horned head to me in a bow.

Forgive me, Heaven Breaker. I have learned not to trust humans, for many no longer respect and pray to the dragons.

"Humans kind of suck," I agreed. "I try to be one of the less suck-y ones."

Please accept me, Heaven Breaker, master of all dragons.

All dragons? If everyone around me started transforming into dragons, that was the last straw. I was going to hide in the mountains for all eternity.

I tried to keep my voice steady as I said, "I—I accept."

At my words, a gust of wind blew my hair back. The spear shuddered in my hand, shooting out a golden thread of light that formed between the dragon and me. It wrapped around my spear and the dragon's body. The string hung suspended in the air, glowing so strongly that I had to shield my face with my arm.

"Snake!" Alex yelled. "Oh gods, Faryn's a goner. Look away, Moli."

I peeked beneath my arm to see that the binding had dissolved. "But . . . why am I the master of dragons?"

Fenghuang was forged for the Dragon King of the East Sea, Ao Guang, the dragon explained. *Every time you use the spear, you send signals of power to every dragon in the vicinity. But be warned that you should not call upon us too often, Heaven Breaker, for power always has a price. Every time Ren allows me to take over, part of his own soul—that which makes him human—is lost in the exchange.*

Before I could ask the dragon what he meant, our chariot rushed past me in a blur of gold, the whistle of the wind accompanied by Alex's yell. A blade sliced through the air, its *whoosh* followed by a roar of agony. The dragon thrashed against the cement. The chariot climbed back up into the sky, avoiding the retaliating swings of his tail.

Alex whooped in victory, raising Ba's red-crusted sword high above his head. I looked down in horror. He'd shredded off part of the dragon's claws.

"No! Why'd you do that?" I snapped.

Alex's shoulders fell. "To—to help you. I know you think I'm the scholar but I can be useful in battle, too."

"Yes, your face could scare away an army of demons." Even as I teased Alex, I felt bad for raising my voice. I didn't exactly approve of Alex's violence, but I could see why he'd done it. "*I was trying to protect you.* I'm the Heaven Breaker—it's my job to fight, not yours."

The dragon groaned and then dissolved into a cloud of gray smoke that left only the boy with wild white hair in its wake.

Ren's shirt was slightly torn, exposing part of his chest. He clutched at his arm and cursed in pain. "Ow. What . . . happened?"

I shifted Fenghuang back into a pin and tucked it into my hair. My momentary elation turned to horror when my eyes landed on Ren's arm. Blood dribbled in thin red rivulets between his fingers.

Moli and Alex hung back, but I rushed toward Ren.

"We need to get that patched up," I told him, wincing as I absorbed the deep red gash.

The boy brushed me off. "It's fine."

"Seriously, you don't want to let that fester and—"

"Cursed One, right?" Alex called from behind me. Moli had brought the horses down to the ground, but my brother sat in the chariot, clutching his injured leg. "Next time you turn into a dragon, you might wanna give a heads-up. Some people like to be warned about that sort of thing."

"I . . . what?" Ren's face drained of color. "Dragon?"

"Did you forget already? You broke an entire *store*."

Ren wheeled around. "I did that? No. Not again. I-it wasn't me . . ." Ren slunk away with shame on his face, stumbling over a chunk of the roof.

Before I could coax him back, Alex snapped, "Don't bother."

I turned around, stunned. My brother massaged the injury on his leg, glaring in Ren's direction.

"What's your problem?" I asked.

"What's *your* problem? That thing tried to kill us! It almost killed *me*."

My mouth dried. Ren hadn't meant to, but he'd hurt Alex. Still . . . "First you wanted me to leave that shopkeeper to die, and now you've injured the dragon the gods wanted us to find. You've got to get a hold on your temper, Alex."

"Just trying to help," Alex mumbled.

I felt bad immediately and softened my voice. "I get it, but you're acting kind of—"

"Hold on." Alex turned away to sniff the air. "Are you smelling that?"

The scent of smoke wafted toward me. Ren had emerged from the rubble with his incense sticks and the golden statue of Guanyin. He placed them on the ground, his head bowed deep in prayer.

Moli yelled, "Goddess incoming!"

I thought Moli was boasting about herself again, until I spotted a glowing, human-looking figure off in the distant sky, rapidly coming closer to us.

A familiar woman in a white robe holding a thin green vase floated toward Ren on a cloud. That same long, white headdress held back her black hair.

"Guanyin," Ren said. He tumbled over onto his rear in shock. "You heard my prayer."

"Good to see you've made it here safely, Heaven Breaker," said the goddess of mercy. At the sight of her warm smile, relief washed over me.

Moli and I joined Ren, kneeling on the ground and bowing to pay our respects. Alex gave an awkward half bow, still unable to get down from the chariot on his injured leg.

"Can you remove my curse?" Ren asked the goddess, his voice still shaking.

Guanyin gave him a sad look. "I didn't come to remove your curse, child. That power lies with the caster, the Dragon King of the East Sea, Ao Guang."

Ren's face fell. "Ao Guang? How do I find him?"

"As one of the Jade Emperor's most trusted fighters, he has been busy attending to the Jade Emperor's tasks," said Guanyin. "I do not know of his whereabouts, other than that he, along with the Dragon Kings of the North, South, and West Seas, will be attending the eight immortals' banquet during the Lantern Festival. But first I have just the cure for all your injuries."

She tipped over the small vase in her hand, allowing just one droplet to trickle onto Ren's body first, and then Alex's.

I didn't know what was in that vase. Something stronger than Tiger Balm. A godly glow formed over the boys' outlines. They seemed to grow slightly bigger and stronger. Ren's shirt even mended itself.

As the light around his figure ebbed away, Alex stood up and slowly climbed down from the chariot, shaking out his leg to make sure his injuries had healed. Then he joined us in a bow.

"Thank you, Guanyin," he whispered.

Guanyin swept her robes up, as though preparing to leave. Panic jolted through me. Even though Ye Ye probably would've smacked me for being so rude and shameless, I flung myself forward in a deep bow, my forehead banging against the ground. I hardly felt the pain. "Guanyin, please help us like you did before. We don't have any food or money."

Guanyin said, "Since it *is* the Lunar New Year, and we deities are nothing if not generous—"

And confusing, and demanding, and very prone to threatening humans with sharp, pointy objects, I thought, remembering Erlang Shen.

"—it's only right to present the three of you with gifts. These come from my colleague Wenshu's new disciple, who's been watching over you carefully."

I blinked at the goddess. Why would the god of wisdom's disciple care about us? Did he have a special interest in the Heaven Breaker?

Guanyin pulled a wand with a thick brush at the end of it out of her long sleeve and waved it in the air. Four small red-and-gold-flowered packets—hóng bāo—materialized on the ground in front of us, with each of our Chinese names labeled on the fronts.

Out of her packet, Moli yanked not money, but something so large there was no way it should have fit inside: a gleaming bronze, double-edged straight sword with a golden hilt that had a dragon carved onto it. Then she swung it in an arc, forcing Alex to dive out of the way.

"Well, I would've rather gotten a pair of eyebrow tweezers," said Moli. "But this thing is all right, I guess. Even if swordplay is the violent, tasteless man's sport."

I rolled my eyes. If the gods really cared about Moli, they would've given her a personality makeover.

Ren pulled out a sleek black crossbow, along with a full sling of black arrows. Then he pulled out another, much smaller object—a music player. "Wenshu's disciple really wants me to have these?"

"The gods reward all who show us loyalty," the goddess of mercy explained with a smile. "Your efforts to enter the temple for years did not go unnoticed."

"Please be *Warfate II*, please be *Warfate II*," said Alex. His mouth froze in an O of shock when he pulled a brown, weathered book out of the packet, followed by a piece of cake in plastic wrap.

"*Demons and Deities through the Dynasties*," he said, marveling at our grandfather's old handbook. My brother's gaze dropped to the dessert, which he held with shaky hands. "And . . ."

"Nián gāo," I finished, my mouth watering just at the thought of the sticky rice cakes. "Just like the ones made by . . ."

Wenshu's new disciple—it couldn't be—

Heart hammering in my throat, I pried open my hóng bāo. I pulled out a small pocketknife, as well as a sheet of folded white paper with a phoenix printed on one side. I unfolded the note, and another small slip of paper fell out of it.

This is a prayer note, designed to replace incense sticks and offerings. When you're in danger, blow on this note and pray to Wenshu. I will hear and come to your aid—but only once, so use this note wisely. Wenshu's rules are strict.

And don't forget: you are both worthy, sūn nǚ er, sūn zi.

Wordlessly, I handed Alex the note. He read through it, and then his tear-filled eyes met mine.

"Ye Ye." My brother choked.

I nodded. "He made it to Heaven."

I wasn't sure if I wanted to cry or shout with joy. I squeezed the piece of paper between my fingers. The first real smile in ages stretched over my cheeks.

I turned around to face Guanyin, my heart filled with elation, and my head with questions. But the goddess of mercy vanished with a soft "Until we meet again."

CHAPTER

12

Guanyin must have taken the sunlight with her. Above us, gray clouds rolled over the city. As though sensing a storm, the four horses pawed at the ground.

Her new sword hooked to her jeans, Moli petted the horses and fed them carrots. Her eyes glinted with surprise when she looked up to find me patting down the mane of the brown stallion next to her. The horse snorted and turned its muzzle away from me, back toward Moli.

"Hey, it's me, boy," I said, confused. I must've fed this guy mountains of carrots, enough for the American Health Association to give me a medal. Yet he snorted and knocked my hand away.

"Looks like these horses are only loyal to me now," Moli gloated.

"Right," I muttered under my breath so she couldn't hear

me. "So loyal that one of them raced off to some mystical island to get away from you."

Moli gave Ren an uncertain look. "Are you coming with us?"

"Of course he is," I said. Ren looked at me, surprise widening his green and black eyes—but I needed to convince him to come along to prove I'd solved the first riddle. "You need the Dragon King Ao Guang to break your curse, right? Guanyin said he'll be at the Lantern Festival banquet. We're headed there, too." I paused. "Unless you'd rather stay here and celebrate the New Year with your family?"

"I don't have family," Ren said.

He swung his legs over the chariot and sat on my bench, turning away from us.

"Yay. Another freeloader." Moli groaned. "You people weigh too much. I'm not sure I want to take you to another banquet."

"Shut up and drive," Alex told her, sticking his sword into his hóng bāo.

I searched Ren's battered face for shock, panic, and denial: the Three Stages of Realizing Chinese Gods and Demons Are Real and Full of Teenage Angst. I found nothing. "You're taking this awfully well."

Ren shrugged.

"I think you owe us an explanation," I prompted.

Alex popped up over my shoulder. "Yeah, like who was that jerk with you at Fresh Mart? Your handler?"

"Mr. Fan?" said Ren. "He runs an antique weapons store. He's a friend of my father's who's, um—looking after me."

"Why? Where's your father?"

"Dead," he said shortly.

Alex's ashen face told me he already knew he'd gone too far. "Oh. S-sorry. But . . . are you sure?"

Ren gave an exaggerated movement of stroking his chin. "Hmm, wait, let me think just a—No. Of *course* I'm sure. I think I'd have noticed if I grew up with my father."

"That's not what I meant," Alex corrected himself. "It's just, they told us Ba was dead, too, only there's no proof and—"

"I know because I killed him. I killed my father."

Alex fell back in his seat. "I . . ."

"Not on purpose." A shadow passed over Ren's face at the same time the graying clouds grew even darker. "But I might as well have. I told you—I'm cursed. Or at least, that's what everyone else has always told me. I . . . I want to find my mother somewhere on this journey, if possible. My mom left me right after I was born, after I k-killed—"

He turned away without finishing.

I had no clue what to say. Maybe there was nothing *to* say.

Ren pulled something out of his pocket—the small electronic device he'd been given, with earphones attached. He jammed the headphones into his ears and closed his eyes, his head bobbing to the beat.

Alex rolled his eyes and opened Ba's book. "Erlang Shen

said our second task is to travel east to the city of a goddess who brings sleep and free the fallen beasts."

He bit his lip and stayed silent for almost three solid minutes. For once in his life, my brother appeared to be stumped.

"Can I see that?" Alex reluctantly placed the notebook in my palm. I flipped through the worn, yellowed pages, careful not to tear anything.

There wasn't that much I could read—the words on the page were almost exclusively in Chinese characters and barely legible anyway—but I paused on a map of the United States.

Ba had drawn a star next to Phoenix, Arizona, with an arrow that connected it to another starred destination somewhere in the Midwest, but the words he'd labeled it with had been smudged so I couldn't read them. No wonder Alex was stuck, too.

"Do any of Ba's anecdotes say anything about what this second destination could be?" I demanded. "Like . . . I dunno, another Chinatown, maybe?"

My brother blinked, his eyes focusing on me as though he'd been pulled out of a reverie. "Chinatown . . . huh. Can't believe I didn't think of that! Hold on. I think you're actually onto something."

"What do you mean, *actually* onto something?"

Alex snatched the book out of my hands and flipped rapidly through the pages. "Here. It's the passage that comes after Ba's accounts of Phoenix. Says . . . in Chicago's Chinatown, he held off demons with the help of Chuangmu, the goddess of love, and—" Alex gasped and snatched the book out of my hands.

"Goddess of what?"

"The next word is smudged but . . . I think it says she's also the goddess of sleep," he finished, showing me a page full of more characters I couldn't read. "See? It's the right number of characters long."

"Yeah, of course," I said, nodding like I had any clue what they said.

Alex snapped the book shut. "Chuangmu must be the one we're looking for. Moli! We're headed to Chicago's Chinatown! I'll help you navigate."

"If we die there like we almost did in Phoenix, I'll kill you both," Moli snarled.

"That isn't even possible," Ren pointed out, removing his earphones.

"You're on my list too, buddy." Moli swung her leg over the side of the chariot, landed in her seat, and yanked on the horses' reins. "Jià!"

When we lifted off, I only slightly felt like puking my insides out, a major improvement from the last time we'd ascended. I looked over at Ren to see how he'd take his first chariot-flying experience, but he seemed too distracted by his music and hóng bāo to care. He kept pulling the huge crossbow out of the tiny paper package and then shoving it back in.

"Magic," he murmured each time the bow shrunk to fit.

I fiddled with my pin and tried to forget Ren's words about his family, his haunted look.

After a short while, Alex surprised me by reaching over and tapping Ren on the shoulder. "Hey, you want a turn at this while I help Moli?"

He held up something—his handheld video-game device, which was emitting the pleasant sounds of automated demon shrieks and the squelches of decapitation.

"You brought a video game along on the biggest quest of the century?" I spluttered.

Alex flexed his thumbs and grinned. "I can't let these joints get out of practice."

Unbelievable.

Ren looked down at the screen and then gave Alex a strange look. "How'd you know I play *Warfate*?"

"Come on. Every kid plays *Warfate*."

"I don't play," I pointed out.

"Every cool, non-loser-older-sister kid," he amended.

"Hey!"

They both ignored me. Next thing I knew, Ren was sitting next to Alex, taking a turn with his video game.

Boys. But at least they were getting along now.

We flew on through the darkening skies, on the lookout for storms or demons. The minutes turned into hours, and the hours turned into days. The four of us took shifts sleeping and directing the horses, although every time something went wrong, we'd have to wake Moli and get her to help. By the second day since we'd left Phoenix, we were definitely in a state of disarray. The chariot floor was littered with empty beef jerky and Choco Pie wrappers, and Moli and her bloodshot eyes looked ready to kill one—or all—of us.

We were running out of food and energy, and we'd need to stop—and soon.

"I'm so hungry, I could eat a *horse*," Moli cried. The horses before her whinnied in protest, and the chariot tilted from side to side. "Sorry. It's just an expression."

Suddenly, a bolt of lightning crashed down from the sky. It whizzed so close to our chariot that the heat scorched the air and my hair stood on end.

The horses bucked against Moli's control, jolting the chariot. "I'll give you carrots!" she yelled. "Sugar cubes!" More rocking. "Dumplings! Oh, c'mon. Everyone loves dumplings."

The chariot dipped, and my stomach swooped.

Thunder boomed again, so loud and close that it shook me to my core. The chariot veered farther off course.

Lightning flashed again. The panicked horses bolted. We raced through a misty, muggy patch of gray clouds, emerging drenched and cold at the other end—only to run into a blur of orange and white. A hú lì jīng riding on a cloud.

The horses neighed and snorted in protest, jerking the chariot so hard I almost fell over the side. Moli screamed. It was all I could do to hang on. Alex let out a yell and slashed his blade through the demon. It disappeared in a wisp of smoke.

"Did you see that?" Alex shouted, giving me a look full of excitement and pride. "Who's the freaking man?"

"Look out, freaking man!" I shouted.

Alex turned around, just in time for a thundering cloud—an army of hú lì jīng—to shoot toward us.

"Ǎn ma ne bā mī hōng," I said, shifting Fenghuang into a spear. But the demons dove downward, the wind from their sudden descent blowing my hair back.

"You're not going to escape me!" cried an unfamiliar child's voice.

Moli yanked the horses' reins to the left hard, narrowly avoiding a head-on collision. "Oh great. Don't these demons ever take a day off?" she shouted.

But the glowing figure riding toward us wasn't a demon . . . and something about her was familiar, but I couldn't place why. She had two buns tying up half of her long black hair. She wore a red dress with intricate gold designs on it, and a sash of red fabric floated around her arms and waist. Two red hoops circled her ankles, and two fiery golden wheels lay beneath her feet. In one hand, the girl gripped a red javelin with a flaming red tip—an actual flaming tip—and in the other, she held a large hoop.

The creature she rode looked like something out of a

nightmare—or Ye Ye's book. Had I seen a drawing of it there before? It had the body of a lion, the wingspan of a majestic bird, and the head of a lion crossed with the fangs of a dragon. Instead of ears, one lone antler rested on its head.

"That creature is a pí xiū," gasped Alex. "Does that mean this is—?"

The girl jerked to a stop before slamming into our golden chariot and threw us an annoyed look. "Didn't expect to find warriors all the way up here. Earth is that way." She pointed downward. The flames grew higher as the volume of her voice increased. "Now, if you'll excuse me, I have to chase some—"

"Wait," Alex interjected, staring wide-eyed at the fiery girl. "You're—!"

"I am Nezha," she declared. "Third Lotus Prince. Protective deity. He who shields humans from danger with a pí xiū by his side."

Of course! An image of the altar and statue back at the Jade Society temple swam before my mind. But that Nezha, with purple skin, looked different from the real one.

"Oh!" I said. "You're, uh, wearing a different outfit than your temple statue does."

The flames in Nezha's eyes flared. Thunder boomed again overhead, causing the pí xiū to roar and buck its short, stubby legs impatiently.

"I like this outfit better," I added hastily. "It really brings out the . . . um . . . fire . . . in your eyes."

Nezha's face softened, but the flames danced even brighter in his pupils. "Why, thank you! Always nice to meet a fan who can appreciate my destructive sense of fashion. I'd love to talk more, but I'm on an urgent mission to hunt those demons and protect humans like you. Jià!"

Nezha kicked his boots against the pí xiū and made to swoop past us. He turned the creature back away from the demon.

"Oh, deities," Ren breathed.

Behind us stood a male deity with curly black hair, wielding a flaming sword in his right hand. He sat on a huge, ferocious-looking blue lion with sharp claws and teeth, its mouth curled into a snarl.

Nezha bowed his head toward the other deity, though he didn't look happy about it. "Nezha, are you causing a ruckus in Heaven again?" boomed the slow and sonorous voice of the deity.

The boy god straightened. "Wenshu, I'm protecting humans from the hú lì jīng."

Wenshu. God of wisdom and enlightenment. And, according to Guanyin, Ye Ye's new shī fù.

Alex's face reflected my own confusion and uncertainty. Should we ask about our grandfather? And Guanyin had mentioned Nezha when she'd visited us in the Jade Society. Did that have something to do with this tension between Nezha and Wenshu?

"The Golden War is coming," the god of wisdom declared, thrusting his sword at Nezha. "You need to heed the Jade Emperor and recognize your role on the battlefield. That means stopping all this childish silliness."

"Protecting humans from the threat of demons isn't childish nonsense," Nezha fired back.

"Insolence." Wenshu's lion pawed at the air and growled. "Most of those miscreants aren't worth saving."

Okay, that seemed a little harsh. Was Ye Ye really fine serving as this Lord Rude's disciple?

Nezha's face reddened. "You're lucky Guanyin isn't here. The goddess of mercy wouldn't be so merciful to you if she heard those words."

"Guanyin is a fool," Wenshu said calmly, "and so are you."

"Who's a fool?" With a gust of wind, another deity arrived on the scene next to Nezha: Guanyin herself. She stood on a large lotus, a flower formed by white petals and a green stem.

Guanyin and Nezha. Nezha and Guanyin. My head spun as I looked from deity to deity, trying to make the connection. How were these two linked?

Could we still trust them?

"Guanyin," Wenshu sneered. "How unusual for you to be up here instead of fraternizing with those sniveling humans. Do you really think preening in front of them will earn their prayers?"

Guanyin's eyes narrowed. "Nezha and I have important business to attend to."

"Let me guess. Protecting humans?" growled the god of wisdom. When neither deity responded, he let out a mirthless laugh. "I knew it. Defying the Jade Emperor's orders. Now, that I can't allow."

"Huh?" I blurted out. My heart hammered when the three gods turned their eyes to me. Wenshu's flaming sword and lion looked more threatening than ever. "Th-that can't be right. The Jade Emperor w-would *want* the gods to protect h-humans."

Wenshu's eyes flashed. "You dare question a god? Go back where you came from, little girl."

"Go!" shouted Nezha. "This isn't your fight."

"But—" I protested.

"But we're leaving," Moli announced, her voice an octave higher than usual. "Jià!" The horses jerked us down in their haste to get away. Roars and metal clashing on metal told me they'd begun fighting.

A sudden blast of wind knocked us off course, and the chariot careened out of control. I screamed as we plummeted toward the ground. We couldn't die here—our journey had only just begun. And plus, I wanted to die somewhere cool, like Timbuktu or Narnia. Who the heck dies in Nowheres-ville, USA?

I didn't have incense, food, or even a statue of a god. The

thought of using Ye Ye's prayer note crossed my mind, before I remembered I still had something at my disposal— Fenghuang.

I squeezed my eyes shut, tightened my hold on my spear, and prayed. *Whoever hears this prayer, please take us to safety. To Chicago's Chinatown.*

A low feminine voice, smooth and deep, entered my head.

As you wish, Heaven Breaker.

My spear burned white-hot in my palm, and the world around me was consumed by a flash of light.

13

The light faded, and the chariot landed on solid ground.

"I am awesome," Moli said, breaking the shocked silence. "Did you see that? I teleported us to safety. Amazing."

For the moment, I didn't care if Moli took the credit. I was just glad we were all in one piece. My fingers curled around the hóng bāo I had tucked into my jeans, containing Ye Ye's prayer note. I could've used it and saved us a lot of panic, but selfishly, I wanted to save it for later.

The next time I saw my grandfather might be the last.

Alex had recovered from the shock of our landing already, though I couldn't say the same for his hair, which now stood on end like a brown broom. "That—that was—that was so—"

"Terrifying?" I supplied.

"No, that was *cool*," Alex breathed. "Wenshu versus Guanyin and Nezha."

"That's a dream *Warfate* matchup," Moli said. Then she slapped a hand over her mouth.

"You play *Warfate*?" Alex asked.

"No!" Moli said too quickly.

My brother's smile faded slightly. "Man, I'd give my right arm to go back and watch that outcome in real life."

"If we'd stayed, it would've cost you more than that," I said darkly. Something serious was happening, driving a wedge between the gods. Did it have to do with the demons? Did it have to do with *us*?

Ren's face was almost as white as his hair, and he gasped for breath like he'd just run a marathon. "I should've . . . stayed home . . ."

The rain kept pouring down. I shivered, drenched to the bone. The horses trotted down the street, past a red welcome gate and a shadow wall carved with huge dragons.

We passed by a sign that told us we'd landed in Chicago's Chinatown. Ren sniffed the evening air. I sniffed, too, and caught whiffs of fried food.

"Smell any bad guys?" Alex asked anxiously.

"Yeah. Smells like gym shorts and stinky tofu."

"Really?"

"No." Ren rolled his eyes. "I'm not a dog. I can't just *smell* a bad guy."

"I knew that."

"Plus, demons smell like stinky tofu and pickle juice,"

I pointed out. "If you need a refresher, just get under Alex's armpit sometime and—" Alex elbowed me in the ribs. "Oof!"

Ren scanned the Chinatown area as though he expected a demon stampede at any moment. I thought of Nezha's and Guanyin's words, how they'd been determined to get down to the Earth to protect the humans from demons. Had they been headed here?

"Chicago's Chinatown is supposed to be one of the biggest in the country," Alex said, flipping through his notebook again and using one arm to shield the pages from rain. "Theoretically, I think that means it would attract tons of demons, too."

I swallowed. "Awesome."

"Ba spent weeks defending the people from demons here. He recommended pages of restaurants. And Chuangmu, the goddess who owes him a favor, supposedly lives here. The goddess who brings sleep, from the riddle."

"So where is . . . everyone?" Moli asked.

Forget goddesses. There weren't even any people in this Chinatown. A large parking lot sprawled under suspended train tracks, empty except for a few cars. The bright-red, scattered remains of firecrackers littered the streets, along with paper lanterns that had fallen from roofs. I saw a green tiled wall at the entrance with dragons carved onto it, and a huge mural with portraits of people—Chinese immigrants, maybe. I gawked at the mural as we passed by. There was so much history in this

Chinatown, and it was too bad I didn't have enough time to actually learn about it.

If we didn't get a move on, there wouldn't *be* a China-town—or any history—left to admire, I reminded myself. Shaking my head, I turned away.

Restaurants, grocery stores, and Asian barber shops lined the streets, but with hardly any customers inside them. The few adults out practically jogged down the sidewalk as though running away from an invisible pursuant. Maybe the wind. Maybe something more sinister.

I wasn't sure if I was just being paranoid or not, but I couldn't shake the sense that someone—or something—was following us. Only the near-empty street lay behind me.

"There's got to be demons here," said Alex. "Ren. Smell anything?"

"Like I said, I can't just—" Ren's nose wrinkled. He lifted it up into the air, frowning. "Huh. I smell stinky tofu and . . . pickle juice."

"Ha! What did I tell you? Demons," Alex said.

"Or someone's lunch," I pointed out.

Alex shook his head. "Can't be. Nobody actually eats stinky tofu."

"Hey, I do," I said indignantly. "And I like it!"

I wanted to urge the people on the streets to go home. But I couldn't exactly tell them there were demons running around. We could only wait out the demons and finish them off ourselves.

My heart raced as I imagined another battle between us and some ugly, fierce demons. But I couldn't back down. Ye Ye or Ba wouldn't have, either.

The chariot came to a stop in front of a store named Meng's Market.

Moli wiped long strands of wet hair out of her face. "The horses are exhausted. I'm starving, wet, and miserable, and you three look like drowned rats and smell even worse. We're going inside this store to get away from the rain, stock up on food, and figure out where to find this goddess."

"Did Zhao Fu rest his chariot when he pulled King Mu to the Kunlun Mountains in Heaven?" Alex asked.

Wrong question.

"No, he didn't," said Moli "But you're not King Mu. You're some geeky—some geeky—" She bit her lip and turned red, as though searching for a bad enough name to call my brother. "Book-obsessed, sniveling weakling."

"Hey," Alex protested.

"And I'm not Zhao Fu. I'm Zhao Moli. I actually care about animal rights, and I say my horses and I need rest, preferably at a spa. If you guys want to go kill demons, be my guest. But don't you dare drag me into it. Tīng dǒng le ma?"

Alex conceded with a scowl. "Yeah, I understood you perfectly fine. We'll hunt demons—tomorrow. If . . . that's okay with you, Faryn?"

I shrugged, not wanting to anger Moli more. "We can spare one night. And we need the rest."

Moli tossed her ponytail behind her, a satisfied smile on her lips.

"Remind me not to get on her bad side." Ren looked at Moli nervously.

"I don't think anyone is ever *not* on her bad side," I said.

Moli whipped around, showering me in droplets of rain from her hair. "Let's go. My horses need carrots."

We left the chariots and stepped inside the vaguely fishy-smelling store. The produce sat in rows in the middle of the store: green and purple cabbage, packages of ruby-red beets, bushels of leafy greens. The shelves along the walls contained boxes of healthy snacks, like nuts and dried meat.

A couple of older women picked their way down the line of vegetables and fruits, but otherwise the store was empty. They stared at us and whispered when we entered. Their eyes were glued to Ren, who determinedly looked the other way.

"Do you hear that?" Ren asked, touching my shoulder. "Cindy You. Isn't she great?"

The store speakers played a pop song I'd heard over and over again on the radio but had never liked enough to bother looking up. Maybe Mao had played the song at her banquet.

Like a lot of Chinese artists, the girl had a soft, lilting voice, with a gentle tone that weaved in an out of the instrumentation—not at all like the powerhouse belts of American singers.

"Um, sure?" I hadn't expected Ren to be the Mandopop-groupie kind of guy. He fit the death-metal image better.

157

Ren arched an eyebrow at me, a smile playing on his lips. "You don't have a clue who Cindy You is."

"Nope."

"She's a famous Chinese American pop singer. You should look into her work sometime." Ren pulled out his music player. He flipped through his songs, showing me the titles. They were all listed under "Cindy You." I frowned, wondering why those were the only songs on the player.

"Hey, are you guys coming or what?" Alex yelled. He and Moli already waited at the counter.

They'd grabbed a huge bag of carrots, dried meat, and fruit for Moli, and dumped it in front of a young cashier with dyed blond hair. He'd been speaking in rapid-fire Mandarin on the phone but hung up when we approached him. His glazed eyes sparked to life at the four of us, our clothes dripping water that puddled on the ground.

"Geez. It's raining like Yu Zu is crying his eyes out," the young man said in flawless English. When we stared at him blankly, he clarified, "Yu Zu. God of rain?" He grinned, holding out his fist for Ren to bump. "Dude. Sick hair. Where'd you get it done?"

Ren stared at the fist until the cashier was forced to lower it awkwardly. "The womb."

"The Womb?" The guy's eyebrows, which were also dyed a horrendous blond, shot up. "Is that a new Asian hair salon around here? Man, those things pop out of the ground faster than daisies. A guy can't keep track."

"Is there a hotel where we could stay a night?" Moli interjected in Mandarin.

The cashier blinked. Then he replied in accented Mandarin, "You speak?" His eyes flickered over to Alex and me

"Yes, we speak," I said, annoyed. I was sick of people seeing our lighter hair color and assuming we were foreign to our own language.

So many times, I'd stepped into San Francisco's Chinatown to run errands for Mao, and people would be surprised by my fluency in Mandarin.

The guy looked surprised, and my anger faded to guilt. I'd found his perfect English surprising, hadn't I?

"Cool," the cashier said, shrugging. "There's a nice hotel down the street. Royal Dragon Hotel."

Ren managed to disguise his choke as a hacking cough.

"It's got great reviews on Yelp. Haven't been there myself, but I've heard good things. But—" He peered behind us, as though searching for somebody. "Kids, you aren't lost or traveling alone, are you? Where are your parents? Your family?"

I thought quickly. "Uh . . . o-outside," I stammered, jerking a thumb behind me, "in the ch-chari—uh—car! They're waiting in th-the car. Our mother and father, I mean."

"And grandmother and grandfather," Alex said. "And uncle, second cousin twice removed, pet gerbil—*mrrph!*"

I smacked a hand over his mouth. Why couldn't Ye Ye have taught us how to lie, too?

"Why did they stay behind while you children came in instead?" the young man asked, baffled.

"Our parents are afraid of . . . grocery stores," Ren supplied.

"Grocery stores?" The guy's eyebrows rose so high they disappeared under his hair.

Molly shook her head and gave a theatrical sigh. "Trauma, you know, from living through the, um, the seventies."

The cashier's disbelief was written all over his face. He squinted at us, a question knitting his eyebrows together. *Runaways*, I could see him thinking.

Grabbing our bag of groceries, I blurted out, "Anyway, we have to go. Thanks!"

"That was weird," I heard the cashier mutter to himself as we headed back out.

The rain had subsided into a drizzle. Alex quickly took the lead, his eyes glued once again to our father's notebook. We hurried past barber shops and restaurants filled with hanging ducks.

"You sure he didn't mention anything else about the Royal Dragon Hotel, like maybe a line about horrible old monks or crazy gods?" Moli grumbled. "Sure would be nice if we could get a warning about any danger this time."

"Nah, but apparently the Jade Pagoda is the most highly rated restaurant of—" Alex stopped walking, nearly causing me to crash into him.

At the end of the street stood a well-kept, modern, Western-looking hotel. The sleek, glassy black building of the Royal Dragon Hotel easily stood ten stories high. Red lanterns dangled from the roof and framed a set of revolving doors on either side by.

Businessmen carrying briefcases wandered in and out. The sign that hung above the entrance flashed: ROYAL DRAGON FAMILY WISHES YOU A HAPPY CHINESE NEW YEAR.

"This is more like it," Moli said with a satisfied sigh. "I haven't seen proper civilization in days."

Two bellboys by the entrance rushed around, helping men and women wearing polished business suits park their cars and move their luggage.

We entered to the soothing ambience of soft classical èr hú music. The bellhop behind the counter set down the Chinese newspaper he'd been perusing to reveal the same wide, practiced smile as the other two men.

Ren sniffed the air, a worried look on his face. "Uh, guys?"

But Moli had already stormed up to the front desk.

"We're hoping to book two rooms for tonight. Queen-sized beds. Smoke-free," Moli said.

Ren darted his eyes around the empty lobby. "The odor is getting stronger."

I tried to ignore the prickling sensation along my arms. "Moli, maybe we should leave."

The greeter nodded at Moli, still smiling. "Name and identification?"

"Zhao Moli."

The man typed something onto his computer screen. His smile vanished. "A reservation under that name has already been made."

"What?" Moli cried. "Impossible."

"Let's go."

The man snapped his fingers. The floor opened beneath our feet, and we fell.

CHAPTER

14

A scream had barely clawed its way out of my throat when I landed with a *thud* on a cold stone floor. The other three groaned and cursed. Pain shot up my right side where I'd fallen, but as I tested my limbs, I confirmed nothing had been broken or sprained. Except maybe my dignity.

"Ah, perfect timing."

I lifted my head toward the sound of a silky female voice. In the middle of the huge golden hall with a high ceiling, a woman sat on a cushy-looking red velvet throne, wearing deep-maroon robes. Little pink flowers decorated her hair, stabilizing her tall bun. Two servants fanned her, while several guards wearing red robes lined either side of the hall, spears held at their sides.

Around me, Alex's, Ren's, and Moli's expressions shifted from grogginess to confusion to shock.

"Strange," Ren mumbled. "I don't smell demons anymore. Just . . . bad department-store perfume."

"Nice of you kids to finally *drop* by."

The woman on the throne laughed at her own joke but stopped when she realized she was the only one. She scowled and snapped her fingers. At once, the servants and guards cracked up and held their stomachs, too.

"Who—who are you?" I shouted over the ruckus.

"Chuangmu," Alex supplied, his eyes as wide as quarters. "The goddess we've been searching for. The goddess who helped Ba. Goddess of love, and sleep."

Chuangmu snapped her fingers again. Her servants ceased laughing. She smiled, revealing a row of perfect white teeth. "Very good. I thought the warriors had almost forgotten about us gods, but it seems you've done your homework."

"But why did you drop us through the floor?" Moli squeaked.

"You're young! Walk it off," Chuangmu said with a dismissive laugh. "When I was your age, I could contort my limbs into any position imaginable. I couldn't break a bone if I tried!"

"Yes, but you're immortal," Alex pointed out.

Chuangmu chose to ignore him. "I was already under this entryway, so believe me, it was easier for you to get to me through the floor. So, here we are. Welcome to the Royal Dragon Hotel."

Through a forced smile, I gritted my teeth. Even the gods wouldn't give us a break.

"Our father—Liu Bo—did a favor for you years ago," Alex said, pulling the notebook out with shaking hands. "We're his children, and we need help. Please, can you tell us—?"

Chuangmu put her hand up. "I know who you are. And I remember your father well." A dreamy smile stretched across her face. She flung one arm over the side of her chair, propping up her head. Her opposite leg lay over the other arm of her throne. "Let me guess. You're trying to reach Peng Lai Island in time for the banquet. You think your father might be there." She examined her long, red nail with an exaggerated yawn. "You want me to help you find it."

"Can you?" I asked.

"I don't know why you mortals are so fascinated with the island," Chuangmu sniffed. "That banquet is so stuffy. Those old deities don't know how to have fun—not like we do at the Royal Dragon Hotel." She winked.

Alex nodded absently. "Sure, yeah, fun. But our father—"

"—would want you to *rest*, dears. When's the last time you had a decent sleep?"

At Chuangmu's soft words, my eyelids grew heavy. I hadn't properly slept in days. My limbs felt like they weighed more than a ton of rocks. Everyone else's expression turned droopy as drowsiness stole over them.

"You've made a good choice to stay here for the Lunar New

Year," Chuangmu said. "Four point seven stars on Yelp, and the glowing reviews just keep coming. And since you are the children of Liu Bo, you may stay as long as you wish—as long as you pray to Xi Wangmu and me, in the morning and evening of each day."

Chuangmu swept her billowing sleeves through the air. A huge, glittering golden altar appeared in the space in front of her. Foods like dumplings and Peking duck lay on the table, set between two incense sticks. A golden statue of a familiar large woman—Xi Wangmu—sat behind the table. Beside her altar sat a much smaller one, with a golden statue that bore an uncanny resemblance to Chuangmu. She wasn't among the usual deities we honored at the Society, so no wonder I hadn't recognized her.

I exchanged a look with Alex, who shrugged and got down to his knees. Ren and Moli did the same. A couple of prayers for a night of rest, which we sorely needed after two days of nonstop travel? I guess it was worth it.

"I hope this prayer covers cable, too," Alex muttered to me after we'd finished.

"Don't you know anything?" I whispered. "These places always charge extra for cable."

Something white fluttered through the air. Chuangmu snatched it up and tucked it into her robe. Unless my eyes played tricks on me, her glow grew stronger and rosier. The goddess snapped her fingers at the servant standing on her left.

"You. Zai. Show these warriors to their rooms upstairs. And remember, they're *honored guests.*"

That sharp, predatory gleam in Chuangmu's eye didn't make me feel like an honored guest at all. More like a particularly plump bāo zi. An uneasy feeling settled in my stomach, but I swallowed it down. Ba had trusted this woman. I should, too. I had to, if I wanted to solve the second riddle and "free the fallen beasts."

Zai trembled at the goddess's harsh tone but nodded in obedience. She set down her large leaf fan and beckoned for us to follow. She led the way through a side door, where we entered a great hall bustling with activity.

The inside looked like something out of one those old-timey Chinese period dramas. The architecture looked like it dated back to at least the fifteenth century. Red lanterns hung from alcoves on the walls. A hallway stretched in front of us, lined with white panel sliding doors. People wearing all different types of clothing walked up and down the wooden floors: men who must have been scholars, in fancy, flowy robes and tall, thin hats; women whom I guessed to be workers, in dull white shirts paired with brown skirts worn with age. When they passed us, they pointed and whispered.

"Bet Ba loved it here," Alex breathed.

"It's rare to see warriors like yourselves here," Zai said softly. "There were many warriors back in China. Since Chuangmu moved this hotel to America, we've had fewer and fewer come through. We get plenty of traveling scholars, though. And honored celebrities, like Cindy You."

Ren perked up. "Cindy You?"

Zai nodded. "Jackie Chan came once, too," she said proudly. "Sometimes, but not often, the deities will stay here. The deities' pets are here far more than their owners are."

"Pets?" Alex echoed.

"Yeah, like dragons." Catching the shocked looks on our faces, Zai gave us a small smile. "Don't worry. They're kept on a special floor. And they've only burned the hotel down twice before."

Ren's face turned green. Then I noticed the walls, decorated with colorful tapestries depicting dragons and deities fighting in the land and skies. I thought I heard faint dragon roars in the distance, but when I whirled around, I only saw a girl pushing a huge bin filled with towels.

Zai stopped in front of a big room at the end of the hall and slid open the paneled door. The inside was even more spacious than it looked from the outside. Curtains of beaded dividers split the room into two chambers.

"The baths are around the corner, near the main staircase. There's a training room in the basement. Just take the elevators straight down." Zai scrunched up her nose. "Oh, and bear in mind that Chuangmu has a very strict no-murder policy. I never think I need to mention that one, but then I end up scrubbing blood and guts out of the bedsheets for days, and it's just awful."

On that cheerful note, Zai swung open the door and left.

I was glad to be on Moli's side for once. She bullied Ren and Alex into giving us the bigger room using her "challenge me and die" glare.

Two queen-sized beds framed by tall white canopies sat on opposite ends of the room. There were two nightstands, and a small brown table in the middle of the floor.

Moli claimed the bed next to the window. "Helps me sleep" was her short explanation.

I didn't care. Our beds had actual canopies! Back in the Jade Society, my "bed" hadn't even had a mattress.

I flopped onto the bed, sinking my head back into the pillow, and sighed. It felt like I was floating on a giant cloud. I had to have reached Heaven. A flat-screen TV even sat on the small cabinet across from my bed. I flipped through the channels and heard a horrendous Cindy You cover on some show called *The Heavenly Voice*. I shut it off.

Moli had her back to me. She pulled her hóng bāo out of her pocket.

"So . . . ," I said. What did normal girls talk about? "Have you tried on the . . . makeups . . . lately?"

Moli whipped around, narrowing her eyes. She pulled her sword out of her packet. "There's something I need you to do for me."

Forget trying to have a normal conversation. There was no such thing with Moli. "Word of advice? If you want someone to help you, make it a request, not an order."

Moli's cheeks colored. She took a deep breath. "Will you . . . Big Loser—I mean, Faryn Liu—please train me tonight?"

I blinked, stunned. Moli tucked her hair behind her ear and glared back at me defiantly.

This coming from the girl who'd spent the past few years choosing fancy dresses over swords, and had even called swordplay "the violent, tasteless man's sport." The girl who would much sooner wield a makeup brush than a weapon. The girl who believed, like Mao, that girls belonged in the kitchen, not on the battlefield.

"What? Why?" I asked.

Moli swallowed hard and wrapped her arms around herself. Although she stood taller than me by a few inches, in that moment she looked small and shriveled.

"I couldn't help you guys when Ren went wild in Phoenix. And I don't really want to lie around at some spa while you guys fight demons tomorrow. If I'm going all the way to the island, I need to be able to protect myself—and the people of Chinatown."

"Why the change of heart?"

Moli's eyes slid over to the window, where fireworks painted the dark sky with bright colors. "It's the Lunar New Year, but it doesn't feel like it. Not with all these demons everywhere, and all the empty streets, and . . ." She sighed. "Mao's got her flaws—"

I snorted. "That's an understatement."

"—but she always made sure everyone, even you and your family, had a proper Lunar New Year celebration."

She had a point. Mao's banquet was something everyone looked forward to attending every year.

Moli tilted the blade of her sword back and forth, letting it reflect the light of the fireworks. "If I can't be with my father this Lunar New Year, at least I can protect other families."

"Who are you and what have you done with Moli?" I spluttered.

"I'm acting like I always do," she snapped. "Stop staring at me like that."

"Okay, now you're acting like you normally do." I paused. "Fine. I'll help, but you won't learn nearly enough tonight to fight demons."

"That's fine. If I get in trouble, I've got four horses that will stampede anything to death for me."

Another reason not to get on this girl's bad side.

"But I have one condition," I warned.

Moli's expression soured. "What condition?"

"The mean names you call me and Alex? Erase them from your vocabulary. And stop acting like we're disgusting weaklings who are beneath you."

"That's all?"

Moli looked genuinely confused. A wave of anger rolled over me.

Being treated like an outcast had kept me from doing what I wanted at the Jade Society. It was Mao's excuse to wrap Alex and me around her finger. Moli's reason for breaking up our friendship. Everyone's excuse for ridiculing Alex and me.

Moli thought being nicer was a small thing?

"Okay, consider it done," Moli said quickly.

"Maybe the way you talk to us doesn't mean anything to you or anyone else in the Jade Society," I said, my throat tight with the sudden urge to cry, "but it's always been a cruel sentence to Alex and me. Everything you always took for granted—nice things like friendship and horses—we never got to have."

"Well, at least you never had to go to school," Moli protested.

I stared at Moli coldly until she was forced to drop her gaze to the ground. "That's just one more thing that made me feel like an outcast."

She reached a hand toward her other elbow and looked, for once, uncomfortable in her own skin. "Gosh, I . . . Faryn . . . I never meant to . . ."

I didn't even know why I'd bothered revealing to Moli how much pain all the names and bullying had caused my brother and me. I didn't want to hear her half-hearted apology.

And I didn't want to help the girl who'd been so cruel to me for so long—but Moli learning to fight would definitely help us all out if she was going to keep tagging along on the quest.

"Zai said there's a training room around here somewhere," I said abruptly. "C'mon."

Moli furrowed her brow at me. "C'mon, what?"

"C'mon and I'll teach you how to decapitate things." I picked up Moli's sword, which lay on the ground near her bed, and pressed it into her limp palm.

"What? *Now?*"

"No, after the whole planet is taken over by demons. Of course, now!"

I guess Moli and I had an understanding after all, because after that, she shut up and followed me out the door.

CHAPTER

15

I nearly stumbled over Ren and Alex, who were lying on the floor in the main room of our suite.

"Where're you going?" Alex asked, eyeing Moli's sword.

"Training," Moli said shortly.

"But the banquet's just about to start," my brother pointed out. "You're going to miss all the food. And we're planning to ask Chuangmu again about the second riddle."

I thought longingly of my favorite traditional New Year dishes: Mao's dumplings, the Xiongs' spicy noodles, Ye Ye's nián gāo . . .

No. Focus. "Okay, so here's the plan," I said. "We'll split up to find clues for the second riddle—freeing the fallen beasts. You guys wheedle info from Chuangmu. Moli and I will scope out the hotel to see if we can find anything."

"So make sure you drill that goddess, and save us something good to eat. We're busy."

Moli stepped out of the room, her long ponytail swishing behind her.

"Don't worry. I'll save you a crumb. Maybe," Alex said.

I sighed and followed Moli. "Keep your eyes out for—"

"—fallen beasts," Moli finished. "Got it."

My mind was already whirring, attempting to decipher the second part of the riddle. Which beasts had fallen, and how were we supposed to save them? More important—were they friendly? Did they want to eat us? These things were good to know ahead of time.

I kept my eyes peeled for anything beast-like, but it seemed as though there were strange human-sized creatures at every turn: snakes, lizards, and even rats.

"I'm dreaming, I'm dreaming, I'm dreaming," I muttered to myself. It was the only way I could keep moving forward without freaking out.

We skirted past a pair of female servants who had seized a large, ugly person—no, I realized, a brown toad. He wore a scholar's hat and blue silk coat. He pleaded the whole way as they marched him down the hall, the wooden floorboards creaking under their feet.

"I'll come up with a way to pay the fees somehow. My boss is King Yama. That's King Yama, the ruler of Diyu. You'll regret this!"

"King Yama?" one of the girls said. "Perfect. Tell him Chuangmu niáng niang, our mistress, sends her regards."

Together, the girls unceremoniously flung the toad off the

patio. He screamed curses the whole way down. The servants dusted their hands off and bustled back down the hall as though nothing had happened.

Moli raised her eyebrows at me. "Do you think one of the fallen beasts we're supposed to save is that toad thing?"

Something told me that was a definite no.

"You can jump after him, if you want," I said.

Moli glared at me.

We found two great golden elevators at the end of the hall. A queue of nine or ten people gathered around them. Human scholars and servants. Humanoid creatures who looked like lizards and weasels, wearing fine silk robes. A weasel man caught Moli's eye and winked. The look she gave him could have incinerated steel.

"Okay, if these aren't fallen beasts, then are we sure they aren't demons?" Moli whispered.

I shrugged again. "Sometimes the deities and scholars look more demonic than the demons."

We took the elevator down to the basement. The doors parted to reveal a huge, empty room with walls lined with ancient pieces of armor: silver helmets, bronze chest plates, metal swords. Grass covered the floor beneath our feet. Moonlight shone through a small window at the end of the room. The only sign of modern technology was a small flat-screen TV that hung from one corner of the ceiling. On it, a woman with blue skin and long, black hair reported the weather, holding a mirror in each hand.

"Is this the gods' TV channel?" Moli gasped, her jaw dropping.

I grabbed her arm and tugged her along. "C'mon. We don't have a moment to waste if we want to train, solve the riddle, *and* hunt demons tomorrow," I warned. "Man, we'd better get an interview on a celebrity talk show after going through all this."

Moli's thoughts must've been far away, because she actually snapped to attention and held out her sword.

"When was the last time you picked up a sword?" I asked. Her grip was all off. I rearranged her fingers so her thumb, middle finger, and ring finger gripped the handle.

"Must've been . . . when our fathers used to teach us swordplay together."

I froze. "That was four years ago. I thought you'd forgotten."

"How could I? Those lessons were my favorite . . ."

The memories of our childhood rushed back. Ba and Mr. Zhao sneaking Alex, Moli, and me into the training hall whenever they could. Back then, they'd trained us with wooden sticks that were as big as we were.

I shook my head to clear the memory. "Forget it." I shifted Fenghuang into a spear. Its golden shaft glinted under the moonlight, drawing Moli's wide eyes. "There's no way you'll be close to ready by the end of tonight, and I can't waste time on you. I've got my own practice to do."

"We had a deal," Moli pleaded—her voice surprisingly

more desperate than angry. "No more name-calling. Now you have to train me." She averted her eyes. "Please," she added quietly.

"What was that?"

"I said, *please*," Moli huffed.

I could count on one hand how many times I'd heard such a polite word pass through Moli's lips. I guess she really, *really* wanted to learn swordplay.

"Fine. We'll try this again."

I imagined my grandfather smiling down proudly from Heaven. The idea fueled me to push Moli harder.

An hour later, Moli could block my thrusts almost half the time, and she got in some sharp jabs of her own. I knew it wouldn't be enough to beat a demon—not by a long shot. But at the very least, Moli would last three minutes and not make a complete fool out of herself.

Training Moli stirred an almost-forgotten memory. The two of us at eight years old, giggling and sneaking into the training hall, handling weapons half our size. My throat closed.

"That's all you've got?" Moli asked. She was panting, and her hair had fallen into loose waves around her shoulders.

"I . . . I'll have to show you the rest another time." The promise tumbled out of my mouth before I could stop it.

Moli flashed me a rare smile. "Deal."

She wiped away a sheen of sweat that glistened on her forehead. Disheveled, she reminded me of the young girl who'd once trained with Alex and me.

Something passed through the air between us. Begrudging respect—and regret.

I tugged at the end of my hair. Once, the edges had been ruined when some Jade Society girls had tried out a hair-dyeing experiment on me three years ago. The memory stung like a slap as it resurfaced in my mind. Moli had just stood by and watched as the girls dunked my head in the black liquid. It had gotten everywhere. Up my nostrils. In my pores. Even after the damage had been done, the other girls mocked me until the dye faded into a stain of ugly memories on my hair.

"What . . . happened?" I asked Moli.

"I came two seconds away from kicking your—"

"I'm not talking about training just now. Why did everything change? What happened to *us*?"

Silently, I thought, *And why have you been so mean to me all these years?*

Moli dug the point of her sword into the ground and leaned against the hilt. "After your father disappeared, my bà ba refused to pick up another sword. He couldn't imagine training without his best friend, so he forbade me from training, too. But I—I . . ." Her hand tightened around her sword handle. "I would've loved to have kept learning."

"Ye Ye would have been happy to train you, too, you know."

Moli gave me a smile that didn't meet her eyes. "I didn't know. I guess I was . . . jealous of you."

"Jealous. You. Of me."

"Sure, Mao might've isolated your family, but you got to be different from the other girls. You could train, and you never had to worry about impressing Mao, and—"

"—and I never went to public school, or got to feel normal." Heart hammering, I blinked away furious tears. "Everyone in the Jade Society *hates* me, Moli. Including you."

"I don't, though. And I don't think the adults hate you, either," Moli said quietly. "My father certainly doesn't. I'm sure everyone is too afraid of Mao and those gangsters to speak up."

"That's just as bad," I spat. How could a bunch of adults let one mad old hag and a couple of tattooed meatheads push them around? "And that's why I hate it when you're rude to me and call me names."

"I won't call you those names ever again," said Moli. "And I . . . I'm not proud of how I treated you. If I could turn back time, maybe—"

The sound of screaming from the TV cut her off. The segment, on one of the gods' channels, had cut abruptly to footage airing from a deserted-looking Chinatown filled with boarded-up shops and barren streets.

"Washington, D.C., lies in quiet ruins, thanks to increased demon activity," said the meteorologist. "And the situation on the West Coast isn't much better. Handing it over to me, Leizi, the goddess of weather, reporting live from northern California."

The footage jumped to another scene with Leizi, only now she stood in front of a different Chinatown.

"Thanks, me," Leizi said. "As you can see here . . ."

My pulse quickened. This was a familiar Chinatown, decorated with the red-and-gold colors of Lunar New Year. It was pretty except for the minor detail that demons—humanoid creatures with huge fangs and red-and-black skin—yanked down paper streamers left and right, setting fire to the town.

"That's—" I gasped.

"San Francisco," Moli finished.

We raced to the elevator.

CHAPTER

16

A vaguely familiar Mandopop song played in the elevator. The bellhop, a squat man with a disproportionately large moustache, hummed along to the soft tune, ignoring the panicking kids with him.

"We have to head back to San Francisco," Moli said, waving her sword through the air and slicing off part of the bellhop's sleeve. His expression remained serene. "My father's there."

"Okay, let's think calmly about this—" I said.

"My father is in danger, Faryn! How am I supposed to be calm?" Moli turned on the bellhop. "You! Where's the nearest army? I need it dispatched to San Francisco, stat."

"Army? Haven't got one. We have complimentary herbal tea and eye masks in the lobby, though," the bellhop told us with a bright smile. "Enjoy your stay."

We reached our floor with a *ding*. The doors slid open. Ren and Alex stood in front of us, still chewing on some dumplings. Alex's hand hovered over the elevator button.

"Oh, hey," my brother said. He raised a brown paper bag in one hand. "We were just about to bring you some of this foo— *Whoa*, what're you doing?"

Moli dragged him by the sleeve down the hall. "Vacation's over. We're returning to the Jade Society. Now. San Francisco's in big trouble."

Once I explained what Moli and I had seen on the TV, Ren's eyes widened. "We've gotta go back and rescue your friends, then."

"They're not my friends," I said quickly. "And we can't just abandon this quest. Did you guys find the fallen beasts?"

"No," Alex admitted.

I turned to Ren. "And what about your curse?"

"Some things are more important than that. Like saving people's lives."

I hesitated, even though my head screamed that Ren was right. Nothing outweighed saving people's lives. But what if saving some lives came at the cost of other people's lives?

Ren grabbed my hand. "C'mon."

Shaking my head, I allowed Ren to pull me along. Ye Ye would've been furious to find out I'd even considered abandoning the warriors in their time of need. But I was the Heaven Breaker. I had to fulfill my quest.

We barreled past servants and scholars who gave us disgruntled looks as Moli all but pushed them out of the way. She rounded a corner—and stopped, nearly causing me to run right into her.

"Chuangmu," Moli said, kneeling down.

The goddess wrapped a red robe more tightly around herself as we paid our respects to her on our hands and knees. "Going somewhere?"

Alex stammered, "J-just headed over y-yonder, back to the—"

"Home," Moli interrupted. "San Francisco's in trouble. We have to save our city."

Chuangmu's smile widened, her white teeth glinting in the light. "Surely you can stay a *little* longer, warriors. You've just arrived."

"Yeah, Moli," Alex urged. "Maybe we can stay a—"

"Thank you for your hospitality, but we'll be on our way now." Moli rose to her feet and made to push past the immortal beings.

"In that case, allow me to give you a goodbye present. A hóng bāo of sorts, if you will."

Chuangmu snapped her fingers. Two female servants floated down on either side of the goddess, grasping something behind their backs. The goddess of love pointed a perfectly manicured, blood-red fingernail at us and smiled.

"Seize them."

Before I could process her words or the shock of betrayal, the servants swooped in and bound our hands with rope.

———

Apparently, Chuangmu tortured prisoners by forcing them to watch awful reruns of *The Heavenly Voice*.

"You don't like this show?" The goddess lounged in her golden throne while we knelt at her feet. She pointed her remote up at the four huge flat-screen TVs that hung above her head. A pudgy, middle-aged man with thinning gray hair dodged her remote before it whacked his face. "But this is the highlight reel from season one of *The Heavenly Voice*. Biggest hit in Heaven, you know."

If this was the highlight reel, I hoped no one would ever force me to sit through the bloopers.

"Why have you taken our weapons and tied us up?" Moli demanded.

"My sister and I are the children of Liu Bo," Alex added indignantly. "Liu Bo, the man who helped you. Doesn't that mean anything to you?"

"When you can find your father and bring him to me, I'll let you know."

I gritted my teeth against the sting of Chuangmu's lofty words. "Oh, don't take it personally," the goddess said. "Back-stabbing happens all the time. This is the day and age of moral corrupt—um, I mean, business. And I *am* a businesswoman, after all."

"That's not what it says in *Demons and Deities through the Dynasties*," Alex protested.

"Times have changed. As humans adapt to society's changes, so do the gods."

"But what does you being a businesswoman have to do with us?" I spluttered.

"There is quite a bit of demand for your *kind* in the market right now." The goddess rubbed her hands together. "Especially for a dragon boy. Dragons are very valuable, you know. They are majestic and well-respected creatures."

Chuangmu leaned forward and examined Ren, licking her lips. "What a sweet face. I could eat you up. Or sell you."

Ren's face was flaming red. "I . . ."

A protective feeling surged inside me.

The man behind her frowned. "Not as handsome as me, bǎo bèi."

"Of course. No one is as handsome as you are, my sun and moon." Chuangmu pecked the short, rotund man on his scruffy cheek. He glowed, his smile revealing mossy, bricklike yellow teeth.

I guess this proved love really was blind.

"You're a goddess," Alex said. "Why do you care what's in 'the market'?"

Chuangmu's eyes snapped to him. "Money is power. It

allows me to run this empire and keep my name alive, you stupid boy. Some of us aren't lucky enough to have altars in temples across the world. Some of us are barely remembered by the humans." For just a moment, her expression turned sad. Then her lips curled into a sneer. In two long strides, she knelt before my brother and grasped his chin with her fingers. She appraised Alex like a jeweler would a ten-carat diamond. "Ooh, exotic eyes and hair, but a very distinct Chinese nose."

"What's a Chinese nose supposed to look like?" Alex snapped.

Chuangmu let go of his chin and patted his cheek. "You, boy, are certainly worth a pretty yuán. But you"—the goddess pointed at me—"are worth a fortune, with that powerful mix of Chinese, Greek, Turkish, and Egyptian blood in your veins."

I blinked. "Powerful?"

Nobody had ever called us powerful. Not even Ye Ye.

"What are you saying?" Moli demanded. "The rest of us warriors *aren't* powerful?"

The goddess of love regarded Moli like she was a particularly smelly plate of stinky tofu, and dismissed her by focusing her attention on me. "You are one of a kind, Heaven Breaker. The Greeks, Egyptians, and Turks have produced some of history's greatest heroes. Hector. Odysseus. Nefertiti. Ramses II. Köroğlu. Their blood is your blood. Their power is your power. Engineered with your father's warrior ancestry and mother's mixed blood, you have unlimited potential."

Engineered. My stomach lurched at the word. It sounded as though I were a piece of machinery built to be used and tossed aside.

Even though Chuangmu thought I was powerful, I didn't *feel* it. Had the gods named me the Heaven Breaker just because I had mixed ancestry?

I didn't get it. I'd only ever seen myself as a girl who wanted, more than anything, to become a warrior who would make the Jade Society—and my family—proud. My ancestry shouldn't have anything to do with that.

"Then why wasn't I chosen to be the Heaven Breaker?" asked Alex. "Faryn and I share the same blood."

Chuangmu raised an eyebrow. "You do not share the same blood."

Alex reeled backward as though she'd slapped him.

"Of course we have the same blood," I snapped. "He's my dì di. My little brother."

The goddess of love laughed. "That's very touching. But it doesn't change the fact that you"—she pointed at Alex—"don't possess the powerful blood that your so-called sister does."

Alex fell silent. My rapid heartbeat stole the breath from my lungs.

To my surprise, it was Ren whose expression contorted into one of anger, a flush creeping into his cheeks.

"Stop lying," he snapped.

The goddess's smile faded. "How very rude of you. Your mother wouldn't like it if she heard you speaking to me that way. She's a member of my rewards program. A very loyal customer."

Ren gaped at Chuangmu, his eyes as wide as golf balls. "You know . . . my mother? How?"

"Rumors spread even faster through Heaven than through Earth."

Ren leaned forward. "Can—can you tell me who she is?"

"Nope! You'd get silly ideas in your head. Try to escape and find her. No, it's best to keep you in the dark. I'm sorry about that. I truly am," Chuangmu simpered, fooling no one.

"Let us go!" Moli commanded. I was stunned to see a tear slip out of her eye. "We have to return to San Francisco to save our families."

Chuangmu sneered and rolled up her sleeves. "I'm afraid this is not a negotiation. You will stay right here. If I can't sell you, I can *always* use more mortals to pray for me and build my power."

My body trembled at the thought of being trapped here forever, forced to do this goddess's horrible bidding. No. I couldn't let that happen. A plan took root in my head.

"If it's your home you're concerned about, you need not worry," Chuangmu continued. "San Francisco's Chinatown will fall within the day, if it has not already. Guards, take them to the holding cells."

She snapped her fingers, and the guards closed in on us. I struggled against the rough hands that forced me to my feet.

"Get your hands off me!" Moli snapped, kicking and twisting.

Alex hissed, "You'll regret this."

"No, I don't think I will," Chuangmu said, sitting back in her throne. "Qīn ài de, hand me my quill and prayer note. I have an important message to send to the Queen Mother of the West." Her husband dutifully plopped a small piece of parchment, along with a quill and ink, into her hand. Her quill dashed madly across the parchment, and with a frown on her face she studied her altar of Xi Wangmu.

The guards marched us down a dark, gloomy hall filled with rocky walls and barred cells, as well as the sound of inhumanly low rumbling and snarls. The servants scurrying toward us kept their eyes averted.

As I peered into the cells and saw the flash of huge white fangs and glowing red eyes, I discovered the source of the noise.

Dragons. White ones, green ones, tall ones, short ones. Our footsteps woke them from their slumber. Trapped in the cells, they tracked our movement down the hall with their glowing eyes.

Their whispers crackled in and out of focus like a radio.

Trapped . . . sold . . . betrayed . . .

None of the guards reacted to the voices.

"Do you guys hear that?" I asked. Moli and Alex gave me blank looks, but Ren nodded.

"This is horrible," Ren muttered. "Dragons shouldn't be locked up like this."

With lackluster scales, the magnificent creatures lay brokenly in defeat. I had a feeling no one had prayed to or truly believed in them for a while, either.

"There is no 'right' or 'wrong' in the business of dragon trading," said a guard behind Ren. "Learn well, little dragon. You'll soon join their ranks."

I desperately racked my brain for a way out. Things really weren't looking so hot for us. We hadn't solved the latter half of the riddle. We hadn't freed the fallen beasts. We hadn't even lasted a full night here before getting thrown into jail.

Wait a minute.

Fallen beasts.

I paused at the shocking realization, but a guard behind me forced me forward. I stumbled but managed to stay upright.

The dragons. *These* were the fallen beasts we had to save. And Chuangmu had had them locked up all this time.

How I could I communicate this silent message to the others? Too bad we couldn't telepathically communicate . . .

Except, I could. With Fenghuang.

Of course. I could speak to the dragons, like I'd spoken to

Ren's dragon. Get them to help us, somehow. But first I had to break through the ropes that bound my wrists and reach up for the pin in my hair.

"Keep marching." A guard prodded the small of my back with the blunt end of his spear again. I stumbled into Ren, whose face had gone white. He gazed at one of the smaller holding cells at the end of the hall.

"Those—those are . . . kids."

I peered inside and saw two boys. Familiar—though battered, bruised—boys whose clothes were torn, who'd shrunk into bony, hollow versions of their former selves.

"It's you losers!" Luhao yelled in a hoarse voice.

CHAPTER

17

Luhao's rude outburst was met by utter silence and angry looks.

"I mean, um . . . hello . . . dearest . . . friends," he amended, which just made me shudder. Luhao being nice? I guess the world really was about to come to an end.

Wang lunged forward. With his face pressed against the bars, he blinked at us in disbelief, like we were illusions that might disappear any moment.

How had these two ended up here when they were supposed to be thousands of miles away, back in San Francisco?

Frowning, Ren turned to me. "Do you know them?"

My mouth dried. I didn't want to explain to Ren why Luhao hated us so much. What that said about me.

One guard snickered as he halted in front of the boys' cell. "Seems like you're already acquainted with these prison rats.

Great. You can spend your copious time catching up with each other."

He pulled out a pair of keys and rattled them in the lock. When the metal door creaked open, the guards shoved us into the cold, damp cell. I tripped over Luhao's unnaturally long, spindly leg and fell to the ground, pain shooting up my back.

"Ow," he grumbled. "Stupid idiot."

There was an ugly purple bruise under Luhao's right eye. The scratches on his face and arms had scabbed over, as though they'd been there awhile.

"Don't worry," said a guard. "We'll let you out every morning and evening to pray to our goddesses, Chuangmu and Wangmu niáng niang."

"You can't lock us up in here," Moli snarled at the guards. But they'd already turned their backs. "Do you hear me? I'm—I'm the descendent of Zhao Fu, and a junior national equestrian champion, and—"

My brother coughed into his bound fists. "I don't think that impresses these guys."

Moli slumped to the ground. The guards disappeared down the hall. Four remained behind, two at either end of the hall.

The air in the prison was stuffy, stale—and now, tense. The two boys sat opposite Moli, Alex, Ren, and me. We glared at each other across an invisible line.

I took in the mildew that clung to the bricks, the ants that crawled along the floor. Searching for an escape route, I bit my lip in frustration. How were we supposed to save ourselves *and* the fallen beasts, especially if I couldn't reach Fenghuang, pinned in my hair?

I had to try. I raised my bound hands to grab it. I winced through the burning pain of the rope against my skin.

"H-hey, guys," Wang said.

He attempted what I think was supposed to be a friendly smile. It made him look like he had a stomachache.

"Why didn't you idiots go back to protect San Francisco like you were supposed to?" Moli demanded. "Everything's on fire now. Are you happy?"

Wang's face turned ashy. "Wh-what? Fire?"

"The demons are invading Chinatown right now. I m-might never s-see my father again." Moli wiped angry tears from her eyes. "And it's all *your* fault."

"Ch-Chinatown . . . is . . . is this true?" asked Wang. When we nodded grimly, he fell back against the wall. "No . . ."

Luhao shook his head at Alex and me. "You two have got no one to blame but yourselves for this."

I paused and gave my poor hand a rest. "What? We're hundreds of miles from San Francisco. How's it *our* fault?"

"My father was right. This world—the great nation and legacy of China—is weakening, and the proof is in your mixed blood." Luhao spat out the words, glowering at Alex and me.

My brother stood up. "Say that again."

Rage washed over me. This time, I didn't try to hold Alex back.

"Luhao, stop it," Wang said. "You know that isn't true."

Luhao's sneer faded. "I'm just looking out for you, dude. Aren't you angry? You were supposed to be the Heaven Breaker. *They* took all that from you."

"They couldn't have taken something that wasn't mine in the first place," Wang said shortly.

Luhao's shoulders drooped in defeat.

"Okay, I'm a little lost," Ren whispered in my ear. "How do you know these guys, and what in Diyu is going on here?"

"Uh . . ." I said intelligently. In my defense, I was too busy still struggling with my bound hands to reach Fenghuang to bother analyzing all my childhood trauma for Ren, too.

Alex got up right in Wang's face. "More importantly, how'd you two end up here? Thought you were gonna go home and become some big-shot actor, Wang."

"Um . . . we got . . . lost?" he offered.

Luhao straightened his back. "No, we didn't. We rode our flying horses to get here on purpose. We knew we had to beat you idiots to the island, and once we did, the gods would *have* to see *we* were the best warriors for the job. Did you really think we would let you two and that horse-obsessed idiot take all the glory?"

"I am *not* horse obsessed," said Moli "I just have a healthy admiration for them."

"What glory?" asked Wang. "Your brilliant plan has only gotten us locked up instead."

Luhao's face reddened. "At least I *had* a plan to do *something*. All you wanted to do was stay behind in San Francisco cleaning up after demons' messes while these guys got to go on a cool quest."

"And now that your plan to do *something* has gone so well, we get to clean up our own mess while San Francisco is up in flames!" Wang spat. Luhao squared his shoulders, but his body trembled. "In case you haven't noticed, a goddess hoodwinked us. We've been squatting in this miserable cell for days."

A long, tense silence followed, broken only by the guards' shouts of laughter. At first I thought they'd come to ridicule us, and I was about to drop my hands to act like I hadn't been trying to escape for the past ten minutes. But they'd congregated at the opposite end of the hall from us and were playing Chinese poker, laughing and shouting with way too much enthusiasm. Nobody should be that happy while playing a game.

"The guards aren't paying attention," I whispered. "This is our chance to escape."

"Except there's no way out of this prison." Wang thudded his head against the wall. "Even the dragons can't break out."

Dragons. I felt like an idiot. Wang and Luhao had distracted me from talking to the dragons like I'd planned.

I *would* break all of us free. With this thought and one huge breath to fuel me, I twisted my shaking fingers into an excruciatingly painful position—and plucked the pin out of my hair.

After making sure all my fingers were intact, I said, "Ǎn ma ne bā mī hōng!"

Luhao yelled at the sight of Fenghuang shifting out of what appeared to be thin air.

"That's—that isn't—?" Wang spluttered.

"Fenghuang," Alex supplied. Pride flickered in his eyes. "That's my big sis, the Heaven Breaker, and the *real* master of Fenghuang."

"Alex . . ." I couldn't stop a smile from spreading across my lips.

"I've solved the riddle—the dragons are the fallen beasts," I informed everyone. "And I'm going to use the power of this spear to break out the dragons. As the Heaven Breaker, I command them, so they'll help us fly out of here."

Surprisingly, no one protested. Everyone only stared at me—and the glowing weapon in my palms—in awe.

"Geez, the gods messed up badly. Some Heaven Breaker you are," Luhao muttered loudly. Alex kicked him. He grunted and swore.

"Shut it," Alex snarled. He nodded at me, his face steeled—with pride.

My brother believed in me. I squeezed my eyes shut

and concentrated on communicating with the dragons. *The Heaven Breaker is here. You have the power within you to break free of your chains, so do it, and help us escape!*

"F-Faryn," Ren whispered. His eyes flashed blue, then black, then back to blue. His body shook. It took me a moment to process what was happening. The dragon inside Ren was responding to the pull of Fenghuang.

Master. The voice of Ren's dragon dropped into my head. *Let us help you.*

"Whoa. What's his deal?" Wang asked, blinking as he noticed Ren shaking.

I recalled the dragon's words to me in Phoenix: whenever Ren transformed, he lost some of his humanity in the process.

"No," I said sharply. "Not you. Go back."

Snarls echoed in the hall as the dragons awoke, some of them banging their bodies against the cages.

"S-something's wrong," Wang stammered.

Alex and Moli looked at each other nervously.

"Ren?" Moli whispered.

Ren's flashing eyes snapped to mine. *Please, Heaven Breaker. Give me the word.*

"I'm sorry," I said, and then filled my voice with more force. "As your master, I forbid you to emerge."

I held my breath for one, two, three heartbeats—until Ren's body stopped shuddering. He blinked, his eyes now back to their usual colors.

But there was no time to waste on relief. The guards began shouting. The other dragons' rumblings grew louder.

And their voices, so many voices, clouded my head, drawing power from the presence of Fenghuang. It had worked. In the shuddering of my weapon, I *felt* their strength return to them, emboldening the dragons who'd been trapped and powerless for so long.

It's the Heaven Breaker.

Must save master.

My mind clouded with a haze of panic, I did the only thing I could think to do: pray. *Please, dragons, help me break us out of this prison.*

The energy thrumming in Fenghuang grew so powerful that I almost dropped the shaking shaft. Instead, I aimed my spear at the white dragon in the neighboring cell. As a burst of golden light surged out of Fenghuang to zap the dragon, the creature grew in size. Metal screeched as its claws tore through the bars of our prison, showering us with dirt and dust.

Everyone in the cell screamed.

"D-d-d-d-d-drag—" Luhao stammered.

"Hey!" shouted one of the guards. "Alert Chuangmu niáng niang. Don't let the beasts and prisoners escape!"

The white dragon fixed its red eyes on me.

I swallowed back my terror and said, in the loudest, steadiest voice I could muster, "As your master, I command you to cut our ropes."

The dragon shot forward. I screamed. The dragon opened its jaws and snapped them down, tearing through my ropes in one clean movement. Everyone in the cell screamed as it tore their ropes, too. Then the dragon slammed against the bars and burst through them. As if encouraged by the white dragon, the other dragons began thrashing against their cages.

Heart hammering, I rubbed my numb hands against the backs of my legs to try to return the feeling to them.

Wang examined his unbound hands, stunned. Luhao swayed on his feet and looked close to fainting.

"Move it," Luhao yelled at his friend as he scrambled through the rubble that had been our prison door. "What're you waiting for?"

Moli whipped her sword out of her hóng bāo. Ren ran with his crossbow in front of him, shooting to disable the guards running toward us. Some fell back, but more kept coming.

"This way!" Wang waved for the rest of us to follow Luhao. "Look out!"

Wang pushed Alex out of the way as a chunk of ceiling thudded to the floor where my brother had been standing moments ago.

"Th-thanks," Alex panted, sounding uncertain.

"Thank me later. Run!" Dodging falling debris, Wang grabbed my brother's arm and yanked him along after Luhao.

The caged dragons roared and bucked against the bars of their cells. *Freedom*, they cried. *Escape . . . so close . . .*

A guard grabbed at my ankle, but I shoved him away with Fenghuang. Wang had disappeared. Alex and Moli had engaged guards in combat and fought their way over the rubble. Moli held up surprisingly well—probably because Ren, who was running beside them, knocked down a guard with each arrow he shot.

One by one, the dragons flew out of their cages—so many that the hallway couldn't contain them. The dragons bucked against the ceiling. The rocky walls cracked. The floor shook. Alex shoved Moli out of the way right before a chunk of rock fell onto her head. The two stopped under a huge piece of rock crumbling from the wall. Moli screamed. By the time the nearest person—Ren—turned around, it was too late.

"No!" I shouted. "Dragons—save them!"

Instantly, the white dragon swooped in and snatched up the two of them, along with Ren. The boulder crashed to the ground where Alex and Moli had been a heartbeat before.

Right behind the white dragon was a horned blue one carrying Wang and Luhao, who were screaming their heads off while simultaneously chucking rock after rock at the guards. Considering the speed at which they were flying, they had really good aim and knocked down at least a quarter of the guards.

The dragons flew down the hall, rousing the other dragons, who screeched and leapt into flight after them.

Follow us, the white dragon commanded.

"Don't let the warriors and dragons escape!" came Chuang-mu's shriek. With a swoosh of air, the goddess hovered on her cloud at the end of the hall, commanding her men forward with a great sweep of her arm. Her hair had fallen into a frazzled mess around her shoulders. "One of those dragons is worth more than all you idiots combined. Catch them, or I'll have all your heads on pikes!"

I sprinted faster, arms pumping madly. Then I felt claws encircle me and lift me into the air. Screaming, I looked up at a scaly red underbelly.

Relax, Heaven Breaker, the dragon said. *You're in good claws.*

Alex and Moli yelped as their white dragon pummeled the wall that separated us from the outside. His snout beat against the rock, crumbling it, but at this rate, Chuangmu and her guards were going to catch up.

"Pathetic!" Chuangmu's shrieks bounced around the tunnel. "If you useless guards don't catch those kids, you're all going to pray to me a thousand times today!"

The idea of praying to the goddess of love must've been less inviting than standing up to a bunch of dragons, because the guards yelled and renewed their charge toward us.

"Dragons, break down the wall!" I yelled.

The swarm of dragons moved as one unit. They crashed their heads against the wall. Three guards rushed at me from behind. One of them got close enough to slice his sword at me, and I didn't duck away in time. Pain shot down my forearm as the guard drew his sword back triumphantly. I swore.

But before he and the other two could finish the job, Wang yelled, "Over here, pea-brains!"

The guards looked. It was a mistake. Three fist-sized rocks flew at their helmets, knocking them out in one blow.

Before I could thank Wang and Luhao, a voice seized my mind. The voice of a deity, responding to my prayer—at long last.

I grant you the power to escape, Heaven Breaker.

A bolt of golden light shot out of Fenghuang's crystallized point. The light slammed into the guards and threw them against the wall the dragons had been breaking. The force of the guards' bodies cracked the wall, which gave way with a resounding crash.

"No, the other deities shouldn't be helping you brats escape! They're supposed to be on *my* side!" I heard Chuangmu wail.

Shouts of panic echoed in the ruined hallway. I glanced behind me to see that the ceiling was caving in, chunks of it dropping onto the guards behind us.

I screamed and closed my eyes as the dragon shot forward. We tumbled out of the prison and into the crisp, cold air.

CHAPTER

18

I opened my eyes, but that turned out to be a mistake. Tiny toy houses lay far below us. My heart leapt with fear. I looked forward instead, facing the colorful beasts that surrounded me. Dragons twirled and flew through the air, reveling in their freedom. Their joyous roars clamored in my head.

Then they stopped and turned in midair. I watched with wide eyes as the tall black building—Chuangmu's realm— crumbled to the ground.

A few lucky guards escaped and raced out of the rubble on a cloud. But Chuangmu hadn't joined them.

I gulped. Any moment, she'd emerge from the building, spot us, and give chase. But when the dust cleared, the goddess of love was nowhere to be found.

The blue and white dragons drew even with my red dragon. Sitting in front of Alex and Moli on the white one, Ren asked, "Is Chuangmu . . . ?"

"No idea," Alex said.

A horrible thought occurred to me as I gazed at the ruined hotel. The chariot. The horses. We'd left them behind.

As if she'd had the same thought, Moli let out an ear-piercing whistle. For a long, heart-stopping moment, nothing happened.

Then something shot out of the building. Several some-things, I realized as they flew closer. Our empty, horse-drawn golden chariot. And two other horses, belonging to Wang and Luhao.

"That hotel had the worst noodles I've ever eaten," Wang said with a shudder.

Both boys leapt off the blue dragon and onto their horses. Wang buried his face in his black steed's neck. He looked so happy that I couldn't bring myself to hate him, even though his friends and family were all jerks.

The golden chariot hovered below me. The dragon's claws released me, and I dropped into the back seat with a *thud*. The horses jolted forward. With two more *thud*s, Moli and Alex landed in front of me.

"Good horses," Moli gushed, wrapping her arms around the two closest ones.

Wang took a deep breath. "We're going home. It's time we returned to the Jade Society to protect our families, like we should have been doing all along."

"Oh, give me a break," Luhao said. "I never thought you were such a coward—"

"This isn't about being a coward or not, Luhao," Wang said sharply. "We've heard the guards talking about the destruction out there. Our people need us. Your family needs you."

Luhao hung his head, his gaze fixed on his horse's brown coat.

"*We* should go back, too," Moli said, raising her eyebrows at me.

Maybe the right thing to do would've been to go home and protect the people of San Francisco. I had no love for the people of the Jade Society, but if they were in trouble, abandoning them during the Lunar New Year, when the demons were strongest, was a jerk move.

But Wang shook his head. "You four finish what you meant to do. The two of us have been training our whole lives to fight demons. We're ready." He drew himself to his full height. "If you really want to protect the people of Earth, go to the banquet. Become the gods' general." Wang gave me a fierce smile. A nod of respect. "Lead the Jade Emperor's army against all the demons. That's something only you can do, Faryn. *Falun.*"

I blinked, stunned. "Wang, I . . ."

"I believe in you, Heaven Breaker."

"So do I," said Alex. For a moment I was touched, and then he added, "There's no way you could fail with such an amazing brother by your side."

After a moment of hesitation, Luhao nodded, too. "You idiots better not die before I get to destroy you."

Well, Luhao still needed some work in the niceness department, but this was progress. I returned his nod. The other warriors didn't think I was a fraud. I could do this, after all. I was worthy enough to be the Heaven Breaker.

Moli swallowed hard. "Promise me . . . promise me you'll protect my father." Her eyes glistened. I wasn't used to seeing Moli ask anyone for anything.

"Course," said Wang. "We'll protect Zhao shū shu and all the others. That's what warriors are supposed to do. Right?" Wang raised his fist toward Luhao, who bumped it.

The two boys turned around and shot off into the distance. Their horses picked up speed, plunging through the puffy white clouds. Then they were gone.

Alex stared after them with a strange look on his face. "Sometimes those guys can be all right."

Moli gasped, her mouth falling open.

My brother waved a hand in her face. "Um . . . I'm shocked that they can be decent, too, but are you okay?"

When Moli still didn't respond, I pinched her arm. "Hello?"

It was another good fifteen seconds before she seemed to come back to herself.

"Longma. He's in trouble." Dread crossed Moli's face.

I gave her a strange look. "Yes. Longma's gone MIA. You're stalking him hardcore. We've established this."

She shook her head, tugging at the end of her ponytail. Her lost, uncertain look reminded me of a Moli I thought had long since disappeared—a younger girl who once trusted me enough to confide her greatest fears.

"I—I had a vision just now," Moli confessed.

"A vision?" Ren interjected.

"Ever since the Lunar New Year started, I've had this connection with the horses. I can feel when they're tired or sad, you know?"

"So can I," I said. "It's called using your powers of observation."

Moli's scowl deepened. "I know what I saw. I had this vision of Longma. H-he was in pain. He was chained to the floor in this dark, horrible shed. And we need to rescue him. Now." Moli settled herself behind the horses.

"Wait," Alex said, raising his hand. "Let's assume, for a moment, that what you saw was real."

"It *was* real!" Moli insisted.

"Just where did you sense him?"

"I . . ." She shrugged helplessly. "Somewhere to the east."

"Somewhere to the east?" I repeated. "East, like New York, east? Or east, like China?"

"Just—east. Can we figure it out on the way? We have to go." Moli yanked on the horses' reins. "Jià!"

The jerky movement knocked the breath out of me for a moment. "H-hold on. We should figure out the third riddle before—"

"Third, find the city in quiet ruins and reclaim a lost

treasure," Alex interrupted, his eyes glued to the notebook again. "There's nothing about a 'city in quiet ruins' in Ba's notes."

He looked as unnerved as I felt by the fact that our father's notebook couldn't help us this time.

But the phrase that had caught my attention was a different one. "Reclaim a lost treasure . . ."

Could it be possible that Longma was the "lost treasure"?

"We're probably supposed to go to another Chinatown," Ren suggested. "There are a bunch of those on the East Coast. Moli's right. We should head there."

"Thank you," Moli said, giving him a rare smile. It vanished when she turned to Alex and me. "Can we get moving now, since neither of you have any brighter ideas?"

I nodded. "I agree. I think Longma's the lost treasure. I mean, have any of us lost anything important to us?"

"Besides our father and grandfather, and possibly our home, you mean?" Alex interjected bluntly.

Okay, I should have expected that.

As the other two shifted awkwardly, Alex sighed. "Okay. You're right. Longma is our best lead, too. East it is, then. But we still need to pick a Chinatown—what about the other part of the riddle? The city in quiet ruins?"

"Oh, right," I said. "That's easy."

"You've figured it out?"

"No, I mean it's easy because *you're* going to figure it out," I clarified, flashing my most winning smile.

Alex grumbled and crossed his arms, but he didn't offer any further suggestions. In fact, he looked sullen. I knew my brother well enough to recognize when he was bottling up his emotions.

"Are you okay?" I asked Alex.

"Fine," he muttered.

"Okay," I said.

There was a moment of silence.

"Fine! Since you're pestering me so much, I'll tell you what's bothering me," Alex snapped.

"I didn't *pester*, I just asked one question—"

"*I'm* the one who's been using Ba's book to help us figure out the riddles, okay?" He waved the book under my nose, whacking me with a sharp corner. I winced. "I mean, fine. You helped in Chicago. But I guess I just . . . I don't know. If you guys can suddenly solve everything without me, I feel kind of useless now."

Alex was so smart for his age that it was easy to forget he was just another kid like me. Suddenly, a wave of guilt washed over me. "Sorry. I guess I—we—didn't realize you felt this way . . ." I managed a weak smile. "And we can't solve everything without you, by the way. We wouldn't have gotten here without you. Plus, like you said, we don't even know if we're right about where Longma is yet . . . or even if we are, which East Coast Chinatown is the right one."

As soon as the words left my mouth, I wanted to shove

them back. When had I become this gross, mushy older sister?

The slight upturn in my brother's lips told me that even if he wouldn't admit it, my words had appeased him. "Yeah, whatever."

I rolled my eyes. "So, genius, how would you solve the riddle?"

Alex paused. Then, grudgingly, he admitted, "I don't know. I guess I was thinking that the lost treasure was . . ." He shook his head. "Never mind."

"Alex. Tell me."

"You'll think I'm being stupid."

"I won't. I promise.

Alex sighed, avoiding my eyes. "Fine. Ba wrote about a Chinatown in the east. Washington, D.C.'s Chinatown. It's where . . . he met our mother. 'A woman as fierce as she was beautiful, with a heart of gold. I couldn't help but fall in love with her.'"

I wondered how many times my brother had read those lines to himself, over and over again, perhaps running his finger down the page so much that it had begun to weather.

I fell back in my seat, stunned, and swallowed the lump in my throat. Our mother. I'd only ever seen one picture of her. The idea of finding the town where she'd met Ba—suddenly, it seemed more important than anything in the world. Even more important than the immortals' banquet.

"I guess I just thought . . . maybe . . . ," mumbled Alex.

"That our mother's family might be 'the lost treasure'?" I supplied. "That they'd be in that Chinatown?"

His eyes were bright. With hope or tears, or maybe both. "Ba, too. He could be here."

When I hesitated, Alex's shoulders fell, and he dropped his gaze. "Never mind. You don't have to listen to my stupid idea."

A sudden memory struck me. Hadn't Leizi, the weather goddess, been reporting about D.C. on the television back at Chuangmu's hotel? How had she described the city's current state?

Lying in quiet ruins.

"It's *not* stupid," I said. "Alex, you're right. I saw a report back at the hotel—they said D.C. 'lies in quiet ruins'! That has to be right, doesn't it?"

"Yes," gasped Moli. "I remember that report. And—and something's telling me Longma's there, too!"

To my surprise, Alex just shrugged. "I don't know. But if you think so, Faryn, it's probably right—you're the Heaven Breaker after all. It's better that you're in charge and forget all that stuff I said about being the riddles expert."

"But, Alex, you *were* right, so—"

"No, really, it's fine."

"To D.C., then?" Moli interrupted.

I fell silent, unsure what to say, certain that my brother and I were barely speaking the same language anymore. What had changed? He'd seemed so proud of me, even just now in the dungeon. Ye Ye would have been able translate for us. But he was far away from us now, too. And without Ba and Ye Ye, Alex was drifting further away from me than ever.

Ba, why did you have to leave us all those years ago? Had my father's duty really been worth more to him than his children? The thought weighed heavily on my mind.

Pushing past me, Alex squeezed into the spot next to Moli. "Let's get going."

Goaded by Moli's shouts, the horses tore across the sky after the dragons, picking up speed as they went. Alex began to boss her around with directions, and strangely, she actually let him do it. She even gave my brother a turn guiding the horses. But after the chariot veered violently to the right, Moli snatched the reins out of Alex's hands despite his protests. She smacked him. Even then, he managed to bring a tiny smile to her face.

I felt a twinge of jealousy, to see them get along so well. But, maybe it was best to give my brother some space if we were going to make it through the rest of this journey intact.

I looked over at Ren, who absentmindedly stroked his crossbow.

"You're an awfully good archer," I said.

"Oh. Uh. Thanks."

"Where'd you learn how to shoot?"

Ren gave me a sheepish look. "I told you Mr. Fan owns an

antique weapons store, right? Huge weapons guy. Sometimes I'd sneak his crossbows down to his basement and practice shooting at the dartboards."

That was like me saying I'd learned swordplay after swinging a baseball bat a few times. "Ren, you have a natural talent."

His face fell, as though I'd insulted rather than complimented him. "I wouldn't call it that. Mr. Fan always said the crossbow was for sissies. Real men fight with swords."

"That's silly. Who cares as long as you've got the upper hand in a fight?"

He gave his weapon a dismal look. "I want to make my father proud, though. Even if I'm cursed. Mr. Fan said my father was the greatest swordsman he ever knew."

My breath hitched. "Was your father a . . . warrior?"

"Nah. He was a businessman. My father traveled a lot. He met *her* on one of his travels." Ren pulled something out of his back pocket: a small, weathered photograph. The young woman's beauty hadn't faded with the age of the picture. She smiled up at us through waves of long, black hair, her almond-shaped eyes twinkling with mischief. "That's my mother."

"She's beautiful."

"Of course. Where do you think I get my good looks from?" Ren threw me a grin, and suddenly, the resemblance he had to his mother was shocking. "It'd be nice if I found my mother before the Lantern Festival. Get to spend our first Lunar New Year together."

"You're sure she's alive, then?" I asked, and immediately wished I could take the insensitive words back. "I'm sorry—"

Ren shook his head with a small smile. "I don't know, but I've got to tell myself she is."

For a long moment, I didn't speak. When I finally found the words, I said, "Maybe we can find another temple and pray for the gods to reunite you with her."

No response. Yay for Faryn's sucky suggestions.

I looked over at Ren—only to find him fast asleep. His white hair flapped in the breeze. I'd never seen him look so peaceful.

We rode on for a few more days, strong winds and rain clouds delaying our progress. But we pressed forward, and the dragons followed closely behind. Just like before, we took turns sleeping in shifts.

I knew I needed to prove myself, so I didn't want to take another shortcut and pray to the gods for teleportation. Besides, something told me that had been a one-time thing.

Even with the weather delays, there was still a week until the Lantern Festival. We were making good time. But we'd gone through our supply of beef jerky and trail mix, leaving me cold, miserable, and hungry.

So when Alex turned around and said, "Jiě jie," in a sickly sweet voice, I had no patience. Alex never addressed me with honorifics, except for that one time I sat on him and refused to get up for hours. Besides, wasn't he still mad at me for solving the third riddle?

"Jiě jie," my brother repeated, "can I see your spear for a second?"

"No."

"Why?"

"Because I said so. Besides, you couldn't carry it even if you tried."

My brother's face fell. "I'm not weak."

"Alex, I didn't mean it like that. Of course you aren't weak. But literally nobody can carry Fenghuang except me."

He sat back and huffed. "It's not fair. You get this awesome weapon, and I'm stuck using a plain old sword."

"How can you say that?" I demanded, my guilt morphing into anger. "That sword belonged to Ba."

My words must have struck sense back into Alex, because he fell silent. For a moment. "When Chuangmu said we don't share the same blood ... do you ... I mean ..." He swallowed. "Sorry. I just wanted to use Fenghuang. To check. That we're, you know ..."

"You don't have to check anything," I said fiercely. "You're my brother. Obviously."

But Alex's expression remained uncertain, and his eyes grew red-rimmed before he ducked his head. He couldn't really believe Chuangmu's words. Could he?

"I mean, it *would* explain a lot," said Alex.

"Alex, we're tired and not thinking straight. Don't worry about it. Really."

I flashed him a weak smile, out of desperation to connect with the brother whom I'd once understood as well as myself.

Alex nodded, though he still didn't look too convinced. "Guess we'll find out when we find Ba and ask him. He'll have a *lot* of explaining to do."

"Yeah," I said. *If we even find him*, I didn't add.

"He left us, his precious children, with Mao and her horrible cronies," Alex went on.

"To hunt demons," I pointed out. "It was his duty."

Alex whirled on me. I probably should've kept my mouth shut. "Sure, demon hunting is important and all, but we're his kids! How can duty be more important than—"

The chariot jerked and dipped downward, stealing the words from Alex's mouth. The horses pulled us through a cloud, and the mist forced me to close my eyes.

"We're getting closer to Longma!" Moli shouted. As if she thought he'd actually hear her from up here, she added, "Longma, where are you?"

When the chariot leveled, we spotted a green sign far below that read: WELCOME TO WASHINGTON, D.C.

"Hey, look down there," Alex shouted, pointing at a rectangular white building below. He seemed to have forgotten about his anger as he flipped through Ba's notebook. "I think that's the entrance to Diyu—wait, no, that's just the White House. Never mind."

We soared above the rooftops after the dragons. Tall, glassy buildings, fancy shopping malls, and bustling restaurants lined the streets. The horses led us into the heart of the city, where traffic itself was a demonic beast. Stationary cars lined the streets from the Capitol Building to the Washington Monument. Drivers leaned out windows and shouted at each other. It looked worse than trying to get into a department store on Black Friday.

The dragons coasted above the city, streaks of red, blue, white, green, and yellow that weaved in and out of the skyscrapers.

The red dragon halted in midair. Then it dove. The horses followed it, spraying our faces with the mist from the clouds. Here, there were no reporters in the streets, just pagoda-shaped buildings that marked another Chinatown. The dragons circled a small, derelict-looking tan building from high above.

They kept a careful distance from the city, snorting and shaking as if they didn't want to get any closer.

The red dragon looked me square in the eye. *A great evil that has not stirred for centuries lies down there.*

A shiver ran through me, and my heart rate sped up. If even the dragons were frightened, exactly what lay in store for us?

I guess I'd find out. Steeling myself, I commanded, "Go, dragons. You're dismissed. I'll only call if I need you."

Good luck, Heaven Breaker.

The dragons shot back in the direction they'd come from.

Great. What was I, a one-woman demon-slaying service?

Moli brought the chariot down on a street just outside Chinatown. She stopped us in an empty parking space. "Keep your eyes peeled for Longma. He's here. I can sense it."

"And Ba," Alex added, but only loud enough for me to hear. "Maybe."

My heart leapt into my throat. But there was no sign of our father—or anyone—nearby.

"There's something else here." Alex's words, combined with a gust of wind, sent shivers down my spine.

"This isn't right," Moli protested. "Why is this Chinatown so deserted, too? It's the Lunar New Year, for crying out loud. Did those strange attacks we saw on TV do all this?"

The wind blew harder. The horses snorted and stomped their hooves. A piece of paper flew up from the ground and into Ren's face. He spluttered and peeled it away.

Again, I couldn't shake off the sense that someone—or something—was following us. The hairs stood up on the back of my neck. My skin prickled. But there was nothing, nobody, in the vicinity.

We disembarked from the chariot. Everyone drew their weapons. I clutched my spear in front of me, ready to strike at the first sign of danger. Chinatown reeked in a familiarly foul way—like King Yama's unwashed tighty-whities, maybe.

Ren grabbed my arm. "Do you guys smell stinky tofu and pickle juice, too?"

"Worse," said Moli. "I smell knockoff Chanel."

A rock clattered behind us. I whirled around and pointed my weapon at the source of ancient evil—a little old lady in a sun hat, carrying a grocery bag in her right hand and pushing a walker with her left.

The others sighed in relief. I lowered my weapon.

The old woman smiled through crooked teeth. "My, what beautiful creatures. It certainly is Year of the Horse." The woman drew closer, and I saw that her shopping bag was filled with oranges. "You're deities, aren't you?"

We looked at each other, unsure how to break it to a sweet old lady that we were just as mortal as she was. But the woman took our awkward silence as confirmation.

"I knew you'd come to save this town one day," she said, clapping her weathered hands together. "Everyone tells me the youth are beyond saving, but I know better. I've prayed and brought offerings to the deities every day for sixty-eight years."

Alex said, "That is . . . a lot of food."

Moli placed the woman's hands into hers. "We, the deities, greatly appreciate your loyalty."

"What was that you said about saving the town?" Ren asked.

The old woman cast her gaze toward the ground. "Oh, it's awful. Gangs control every street, rallying around a powerful leader named the Red Prince."

Alex frowned and squinted. I recognized the look of concentration as one he got whenever he was trying to remember something. "Red Prince. That sounds familiar."

"Word of his deeds has traveled far and wide." The old woman shuddered. Then her grimace transformed into a smile as she pulled four oranges out of her bag. "Please, take these as my thanks in advance for saving this town. Oranges are especially good for rejuvenation in the New Year."

My stomach rumbled. I hadn't eaten anything in over a day. The plump oranges practically begged me to eat them, but I hesitated. "Why are *you* here, then, if the Red Prince and his gang have been terrorizing the town?"

Before the old woman responded, Moli and Ren each took an orange, ripped off the skin, and bit into it eagerly.

"No!" Alex and I shouted at once, knocking the fruits out of their hands.

"Why are you . . . ?" Ren didn't even finish the question before collapsing onto the ground. Moli gasped—and she, too, fell over.

"You evil old woman!" Alex yelled.

The woman gave us a twisted grin and rolled up her sleeves. "That's Red Prince to you."

Alex whipped out his sword. I pointed Fenghuang at the

woman. I had to do something—knock her out, steal her false teeth, anything. My fingers tugged the hóng bāo and Ye Ye's slip of paper out of my pocket, my last resort.

But then a blunt, painful force slammed into my head from behind. As the world spun around me, the spear fell out of my trembling hand and clattered onto the ground.

"I'll take that, thank you very much," said the old woman. She shrunk to the size of a child and leaned down to admire the golden weapon.

Before I lost consciousness, I blew on the prayer note using the remainder of my breath. *Come to Washington, D.C.'s Chinatown, Wenshu and Ye Ye. We're in big trouble.*

The world swam before my eyes. Then they shut, and I fell into a deep slumber.

CHAPTER

19

In my sleep, I cycled through many dreams. In the first, Mao supervised me while I strung paper lanterns from every roof in the Jade Society. Then she turned into the nián, burning the place to the ground and ruining all my hard work.

In the second dream, Ren and I were at a Cindy You concert. I was probably the least excited one there—and he the most. He wore a Cindy You shirt, hat, tattoo, and waved a Cindy You bobblehead through the air. Halfway through her hit song "One Thousand Lives," Cindy You turned into a hú lì jīng, like Wendi Tian, onstage. That made the fans scream harder.

In my third and longest dream, I was hovering outside a window in a great white castle, gazing upon . . . Ye Ye, hunched over and reading a scroll at a wooden desk. But he wasn't the Ye Ye I remembered—not the old, tired grandfather who'd lost most of the light in his eyes. This Ye Ye resembled the portrait of my father. He was much younger and had short black hair, a strong jawline, and a much sturdier physique.

Tears stung the corners of my eyes. My grandfather was doing well under Wenshu's care, just as Guanyin had said he was.

I reached out to knock on the window—and squawked.

Staring back where my reflection should have been was a brilliantly red bird with an enormous wingspan, long legs, and a peacock tail. A fèng huáng, the namesake for my spear. Shocked, I squawked again. I was a bird, and my grandfather was young and alive. This was definitely a dream.

Ye Ye glanced up from his scroll. His exhausted, bloodshot eyes looked hollow, but when they met mine, they flickered with recognition.

I tried to call out. *Ye Ye, it's me. Your granddaughter. I'm in trouble.*

Except it came out as: "Squaaaaaaaawk!"

Ye Ye rushed to the window and yanked it open. I tumbled onto a nearby desk and spilled a potted plant. My grandfather untied something from my foot—a note. The prayer note I'd sent him. He unfolded it, his eyes racing across the paper. When my grandfather finished reading my prayer, he crumpled it up and threw it into the trash can.

"Sūn nǚ er," Ye Ye said. "I promised you I would come save you, but I cannot."

What? "Squawk?"

Ye Ye's voice was choked with regret, and my stomach

225

dropped down to my toes. "Wenshu is—not the deity I thought he was when I pledged myself to him as his disciple." Remembering Wenshu's harsh words from before, I couldn't help but agree with Ye Ye's apprehension. "He will not be happy if he knows I've come to your aid."

Please, Ye Ye. You're the only one who can save us. "Squaaaaaawk!"

Ye Ye stared at my thrashing form, uncomprehending. I guess he didn't speak Panicked Bird.

A loud knock echoed in my grandfather's room. His eyes darted to the door. "Be brave, Falun. I cannot save you, but you are strong enough to save yourself and your friends. Now— wake up!" The urgency in Ye Ye's voice increased. He began shooing me out of the window. "You've slept far too long. If you don't wake up now, the deadline for the immortals' banquet will pass."

My heart lurched. We'd only been gone for a week. What was my grandfather talking about?

"The Red Prince put the four of you under a sleeping curse. There's only one day left until the Lantern Festival." The knocking grew louder and more insistent, accompanied by muffled words I couldn't hear. "You must wake up, and when you do, use your spear. But do not let it control you. Is that clear? You must not let Fenghuang control you."

The knocking grew louder, accompanied by a deep, slow voice. "Liu Jian, have you finished memorizing the Lotus Sutra?"

"N-not yet!" my grandfather shouted, a bead of sweat rolling down his face.

Something wasn't right. Ye Ye shouldn't look this panicked about studying under the god of wisdom.

"Liu Jian," called that same slow voice, "I thought I made it clear that you are forbidden to contact outsiders."

My grandfather shooed me out the window. Before shutting it, he told me, "There's no time to explain. I must go. Remember what I—"

A bang interrupted Ye Ye's words. And then I woke up, gasping, to find myself lying on a scratchy bed of hay. And feeling very, very human.

Reality slowly returned to me. The only light in my musty surroundings came from an open door in front of me.

I blinked, my eyes adjusting to the harsh light. I heard Ren, Alex, and Moli stirring.

"Whooza?" Alex murmured. "Ye Ye, it's still dark out. Let me go back to sleep."

An unfamiliar boy's voice broke the quiet. "Oh, good. You're all awake. Just in time to help me prepare for my Lantern Festival feast."

Framed in the doorway was a child who looked about nine or ten years old. He had three bushy patches of hair, one in the left, right, and middle of his shiny, bald head. The boy wore a red-and-gold vested shirt and skirt under a flaming red cape. He held a red spear in one hand.

Behind him stood demons who looked like Mafia hit men. They wore shades and leather jackets. The stench rolling off them was unbearable. Stinky tofu, pickle juice, gym clothes, Tiger Balm. Beside me, Ren gagged and shifted closer.

The grogginess vanished from my head when I saw the golden object the men struggled to lift onto their shoulders: Fenghuang.

"Who are you?" I demanded.

"The greatest demon lord to walk this Earth."

Following his boast, the boy stepped closer to us, a smirk on his face.

"Give me back my spear."

I tried to sit up but found I couldn't. A sharp pain encircled both of my wrists and ankles. My skin burned as it scraped against rope.

"No, I don't think I will." The demon lord reached out a hand and gripped Fenghuang. He yanked—and stumbled, nearly losing his balance. Fenghuang fell off the men's shoulders and onto the ground. "Why is this thing so heavy?" snapped the Red Prince. He kicked it and then yelped in pain.

"I'm the only one who can lift it," I said, unable to resist being smug.

"The only *human*. I'm an immortal, you brat," spat the demon lord.

"Maybe you're just weak," Moli retorted.

Flames danced in the Red Prince's pupils and from the tip of his spear.

My brother coughed. "Moli, maybe we should be a little nicer to the fire dude."

A low rumbling noise drifted into my ear. I looked over at a dark corner, my heart pounding frantically. There was a creature with us, tucked away in shadow. Was it friend or foe?

"Untie us right now, little boy. We don't have time for this. We're looking for something important. And my father is waiting." Moli growled at the Red Prince. In a sickly sweet voice, she added, "If you let us go, I'll even fix your look for you, honey. Your mama really did a number on that hair of yours."

"How dare you insult our demon lord, the Red Prince! His hairstyle is goals," shouted one of the Mafia-looking demons. He pulled out a sword, but the Red Prince held out a hand and shook his head.

"Wait! Red Prince. I know where I've heard of you." Alex gasped. "You're from *Warfate*. One of Sun Wukong's greatest adversaries."

My brother's words stirred my memory. Ye Ye had loved telling stories about the protagonist of the video game—Sun Wukong, the Monkey King, who had waged war on all of Heaven with his gold-banded cudgel, Ruyi Jingu Bang.

I had no idea how powerful the Monkey King was in the video game, but the fact that Alex had called the Red Prince one of Sun Wukong's greatest adversaries wasn't a good sign.

The demon lord's smile widened. "Sun Wukong? *My* adversary? Do you hear that, men?" The Red Prince laughed, and his followers joined in. The demon lord's smile dropped. "Now shut up." The men quickly obeyed. "Sun Wukong isn't even fit to shine my shoes, especially since he's lost Ruyi Jingu Bang. He's powerless."

Trying to calm my racing heart, I assessed the situation. Fenghuang had been taken from me. I'd already used up my prayer note.

As they were arguing with the men, I saw Alex, Moli, and Ren struggling to reach for their hóng bāos and weapons in their pockets.

I felt for my own hóng bāo. I stretched my fingers as far as they could reach, the rope biting into my skin and threatening to leave burns. They barely grazed the edge of the packet. I pulled, willing myself not to wince from the pain.

I kept my face neutral as the Red Prince continued listing all the ways he was better than Sun Wukong. ". . . And so what if he's got a stupid stick? The flames of my samadhi fire can consume anything—even water."

"That sounds, um," Alex said, "most impressive and villainous of you."

"Isn't it? Would you like to see?"

"Keep your stupid salami fire to yourself," Moli snapped.

"It's *samadhi* fire!" the Red Prince roared.

Ren's face turned red, though I didn't know if it was from anger or the exertion of trying to extract his weapon from his hóng bāo.

After ages of slow, painful work, the hóng bāo opened beneath my fingers. I grasped Ye Ye's gift—the hilt of a pocketknife. Careful not to accidentally cut my fingers, I sawed at the rope.

The demon lord had turned around to yell at his men. Moli sat up straight, her body still. The look on her face was stricken. Her eyes met mine, and she mouthed a word: "Longma."

I was worried about the poor horse, too. But we'd been tied up by a demon lord, and all she could do was think about Longma?

"I hope you idiots are prepared for a feast tonight," the Red Prince was saying. "It'll be a nice warm-up for the real banquet tomorrow—when we ambush Peng Lai Island."

I nearly yelped but caught myself just in time. The demons whooped with glee. If we didn't stop them, they were going to wreak havoc on humans *and* immortals.

Alex, Moli, and Ren followed the motion of my arm. They nodded. Their hands grasped their hóng bāos behind their backs. I eyed Fenghuang where it lay on the ground in front of the demons' feet, calculating the distance I had to cover to run to it.

"On my count," I whispered. "Three, two . . . one!"

I tore through the last bit of rope with one vicious slice, freeing my hands. The demons yelled as Alex and Moli slashed through their rope with their swords, Alex helping release

Ren a second later. I moved on to the ropes that bound my legs and lunged to pick up Fenghuang.

"Hey!" The Red Prince stumbled back. His henchmen threw their hands over their eyes to shield themselves from the bright light. The spear's glow transferred to me and traveled through my whole body. A white-hot sensation ran down my arms and legs.

A snarl twisting his face, the demon lord thrust his red spear at us.

"After them!" he ordered his men.

The gangster groupies roared and surged forward, but their movements seemed slow and clumsy. I sent a silent prayer to the gods. Strength surged through me, a burning sensation so powerful it nearly swept me off my feet.

I swept my spear in an arc and knocked the demons down in one wave of gold. They yelped, their swords clattering to the ground.

The demon lord stepped over the groaning men on the floor as though they weren't there. "Cute trick," the Red Prince sneered, holding out his palms, "but nothing stands a chance against my samadhi fire." Flames burst from his palms and outlined his body.

"Samadhi fire." Alex's voice was already choked from the smoke. "M-most powerful fire in the w-world. Run!"

"There's nowhere to go," Ren shouted. He shot off arrows left and right, each one meeting its mark with a shriek of pain from its target. I couldn't imagine how he could see through the smoke.

Alex grabbed my hand, pushing Moli and Ren along as we scrambled to the opposite end of the shed to get away from the flames. The Red Prince's laughter grew with the size of his flames. He threw ball after ball of fire, which I blocked with Fenghuang, at us. The glow of the spear itself repelled the samadhi fire and shielded us, but I could see it weakening with each blow.

"We can't keep blocking forever," Alex said.

Already the smoke that filled my lungs made it too difficult to breathe, let alone hold off the Red Prince's attacks. Fire jumped and spread onto the walls around us. The samadhi fire ate away at the hay hungrily. We backed up against the far wall until there was nowhere else to go.

A flame leapt up and licked my hand. Pain, scorching hot, seared through my arm, and I couldn't help but scream. In my desperation, I said a silent prayer. *Help us! How do we get out of this mess?*

Do not fret, Heaven Breaker. That familiar female voice entered my mind once more. *There is one cure for the samadhi fire: rain from a Dragon King. The son of the Dragon King of the West Sea, Ao Ji, is by your side. Awaken him. Bend his will to yours.*

By "son of the Dragon King of the West Sea," could she mean Ren? I didn't like the sound of that. And come to think of it, that didn't make any sense. Ren was already awake, albeit choking and half-dead from the smoke. Plus, hadn't he been cursed by the Dragon King of the *East* Sea, Ao Guang?

My hands shook. I could no longer hold Fenghuang steady. A blur of red and gold showed me the Red Prince was advancing, homing in for the kill.

To my left, I heard a choke from Moli. "Longma!"

At first I thought she was hallucinating. Flashes of her life reeling through her head, that sort of thing. Then a sound rose above the roar of the flames—whinnying and snorts.

Through tear-soaked, blurry vision, I spotted a skinny white horse. My brain leapt back to the animal noises I'd heard earlier.

Longma had been trapped here all along?

A new voice entered my head, lower, and male. *Five hundred years I've been a horse, waiting for the Fenghuang's presence to ignite. I, Yulong, third Dragon Prince, have come to serve you—and break my father's curse. Free me, Heaven Breaker.*

Instinct told me what to do. *I give you permission to transform and help me.*

Longma's hooves morphed and lengthened into blue claws. His body shot up and quadrupled in length, turning scaly and serpentine. His head was the last to transform, turning the horse's muzzle into the whiskered, ridged face of a dragon.

In transforming, Longma—no, Yulong, the third Dragon Prince—busted the roof. Dust showered on us. The Red Prince dove out of the way as a chunk of ceiling plunged down. The walls collapsed, eaten away by the fire. Fresh air rushed into my lungs, but only momentarily. Moonlight poured through the ruined building.

"No, you stupid animal!" screamed the Red Prince, emerging from the rubble unscathed. He stamped his foot and spear on the ground, glaring up at the dragon. "I wanted white-horse meat for the Year of the Horse. If you don't want to die, then make yourself presentable on a dinner plate!"

The demon lord sucked in a deep breath, and I saw flames forming in the back of his mouth.

Yulong roared, tilting his horned head skyward. *Father, the great Ao Ji, bring forth the rain. Powerful enough to purge Chinatown of this evil.*

As I raised Fenghuang to shield against another blast of the Red Prince's fire, a column of water shot out of Yulong's mouth. The speed of the water alone was enough to cause me to stumble away.

The Red Prince's fire had barely left his mouth before the water pushed him back. He flew through the air with a scream, his body slamming against a distant building and falling to the ground.

I breathed a sigh of relief. Looked like the demon lord wouldn't be in shape to ambush banquets anytime soon.

But there was no time to relax. The rain fell in unforgiving sheets, pounding my body so hard I clenched my teeth. The Red Prince's henchmen screamed with pain.

Master, we must get out of here, Yulong roared. Far from seeming pleased with himself, his eyes were stricken with terror. *My father must be angry. His rain is too powerful. This Chinatown is ruined. We must abandon it.*

As though she'd somehow sensed Yulong's thoughts, Moli whistled. Within seconds, the golden flash of a large flying object tumbled out of the gray clouds. Soaring high above our heads was our driverless chariot, pulled by four drenched horses. With the sound of horses neighing and a gust of harsh wind and rain, the chariot swooped down.

Someone grabbed my hand. Ren. "Get in!"

The rain was falling too hard and fast. It pummeled our intertwined fingers until they were forced to separate. Ren shouted. His cries grew more distant. The rain poured down harder. Faster.

The rain was going to consume me. I would die where I stood, unless . . .

"D-Dragon Prince," I spluttered through the pouring rain. "S-save your master!"

Something thwacked my body, and I flew through the air. I screamed as I landed on a large, cool, and bumpy surface, the fall knocking the breath out of me. I grappled around wildly for something to cling to and managed to wrap my legs around the length of a thick, scaly body, my free hand closing around a thin, leathery white line that whipped past me in the rain.

I shot upward into the sky, my skin on fire, praying the pain would end.

CHAPTER

20

After a while, the downpour lightened to a drizzle. I peeked an eye open—and screamed. Scales. Blue scales in front of and beneath me.

Ow! Yulong protested. *Watch the whiskers. The ladies love them.*

I relinquished my death grip on his whisker. I wish I could've produced some snappy comeback for the horse-turned-dragon, but really my thoughts were something closer to: *AaaauGHHHaaaauGHHH!*

The chariot streaked below us, with Moli standing at the front, commanding the horses. Even though we'd just lived through a hurricane from hell—probably literally—the wind up here seemed to love Moli. Her black hair had fallen out of its ponytail and billowed behind her like it thought it was in a shampoo commercial. My hair probably looked like it had lost a duel with a Weedwacker.

Yulong roared with glee. *This feels good. Being cursed as a horse gave me horrible knots in my hair.*

I had so many questions for the dragon. "Are you the lost treasure? Did you know we'd come to D.C.? And why were you a *horse* for so long?"

Lost treasure? Maybe, answered Yulong. *Guanyin told me that once I made it to this Chinatown, the way back to my family would become clear. At first, I thought she'd deceived me. But when you showed up, Heaven Breaker, I realized what she meant was that in order to find my own family, I had to help you complete your quest first.*

"Okay," I said, struggling to process all this information. "That still doesn't explain why you were a horse for so long."

No response except a snort from Yulong. I guess I'd hit a touchy topic.

"And if you're a dragon, how come I couldn't sense you before?" I added.

My father's curse is powerful. I was shielded from your powers.

Of course. It would've been too easy if we'd found Yulong earlier. The gods really liked toying with warriors.

"H-hey, we can't leave just yet. What about Ba?" Alex's voice reached my ears, faint over the wind. I looked down at the chariot and saw that he was waving his arms as if flagging down an airplane, trying to get our attention. "Tell the dragon to go back. We have to find our family!"

Your family is not in that Chinatown, Yulong said. *The Red Prince chased out all the inhabitants.*

"Then where can we find our family?" I demanded.

I do not know. But the deities at Peng Lai Island will.

"Where's the dragon taking us?" Alex demanded.

"His name's Yulong," I shouted. Then I turned back to the creature I was riding. "And now that we've completed this quest, as the Heaven Breaker, I order that you take us to the island."

Yulong shot through the sky at breakneck speed, the chariot following close behind. I closed my eyes and clutched my spear in a tight grip, so the wind didn't tear it out of my hands. The dragon wouldn't stop whooping with glee in my head.

Yulong slowed after a while. I dared to open my eyes again. We'd reached the shoreline of a vast, sparkling body of water that seemed to sprawl on to the edge of the Earth. The Atlantic Ocean.

Exhilaration swept through me. The wind whipped my face as Yulong dove toward the water. He righted himself millimeters before breaking the surface. His great white underbelly skimmed the waves, the spray of mist hitting me in the face and dampening my clothes.

My heart felt like it could burst with fear and joy. I'd never felt so alive.

Yulong's voice returned. *Take out Fenghuang, Heaven Breaker.*

I obeyed with difficulty, leaning forward to keep my balance as the wind threatened to knock me off the dragon. Fenghuang's glow radiated with heat. Its crystallized point skidded along the surface of the water, and the waves churned more violently than ever.

My breath caught in my throat. Wave by wave, the ocean lit up with a dazzling golden path that stretched before us, ending somewhere far beyond the horizon.

Yulong shot along the path, increasing his speed until I was forced to close my eyes. We flew through the night, and I dozed in and out of sleep—until the dragon prince lurched to a stop and bobbed on the surface of the water.

We're here, master. This is Peng Lai Island.

The water beneath us looked different. It was a clear, crystal blue, untouched by human pollution. It stretched on forever in all directions.

And then the island before us. The sand on the shores led us to a huge redbrick wall that spanned the entire length of the island. Beyond the wall I could see the sparkling lights of a great metropolis—in the middle of the sandy shores.

With wobbly legs, I disembarked from Yulong's back and stumbled in the sand. The horses came to an abrupt halt, spraying sand all over me. Moli, Ren, and Alex got out of the chariot.

"Fenghuang," Ren murmured. I thought he was referring to my weapon for a moment before realizing he was studying a pair of red birds that soared into the city. The spear's name-sake. "This is Peng Lai Island?"

"Ah," said a familiar male voice from behind. "The deities have done some renovating in the last five hundred years."

I turned toward the voice. A boy a little older than me, with the greenest eyes I'd ever seen, stood there. He walked toward us over the surface of the water. He wore green cháng shā, an outfit of a matching long-sleeved shirt and pants, embellished with intricate gold designs.

Moli gaped at Yulong. The former horse looked up at her with innocent eyes, as though expecting sugar cubes or carrots.

Instead Moli scowled. "I liked you better as a horse."

Yulong's shoulders drooped. "Really? I thought . . . once my father's curse lifted, you'd be . . . I mean, you'd want to . . ."

He scratched the back of his head and blushed.

Ren's shoulders shook as he held back a laugh. It *was* pretty comical: the idea that Moli's horse had been harboring a secret crush on her all along.

Moli's mouth dropped. "What? No way! I mean, you're a . . . and you were . . . my horse, and . . ."

Yulong cut off her horrified babbles by raising a hand. He closed his eyes and sighed. "I get it. No matter how hard we try, we could never work out. You know that I'm too good for you. I am a prince, after all, and you're a lowly mortal."

The bewildered look on Moli's face told us that wasn't what she'd been thinking at all. "What? Longma—I mean, Yulong—"

"Say no more, Zhao Moli. Our star-crossed love simply isn't meant to be in this lifetime. But in another, I pray our stars will align."

Yulong blew her a kiss.

Moli looked like she wanted to cry or gag. "Lost treasure," she mumbled. "Lost treasure, my butt."

My brother glared at Yulong and shifted closer to Moli. Ren had doubled over in silent fits of laughter. I patted his back, unable to suppress my own grin, even though I felt kind of bad for Moli, too.

"What's his deal?" Yulong nodded at Ren.

"He is, um . . . oh, uh, it's almost time for the banquet!" Pulling Ren along with me, I rushed up to the wall.

Ren had recovered by the time we arrived in front of two guards blocking a circular door in the wall. The men, dressed in bronze armor and holding matching black spears, crossed their weapons in front of us. The message was clear. We weren't allowed in.

The Dragon Prince appeared beside me, giving the guards an annoyed look. "It's me, idiots. Yulong. Third and favorite son of Ao Ji. My father's in there. Let us through."

The guards relaxed their stances but not their weapons. "Oh, Yulong," said one with a nod. "You're just in time. The Lantern Festival is about to start."

The other guard eyed us warily. "We haven't seen you in centuries. What kept you away for so long?"

Yulong scowled. "I, uh . . ."

"He was horsing around," Alex offered. Ren burst out laughing, and even Moli stopped sulking to crack a smile.

Yulong's face turned bright red. "That is *not funny!*"

"Who are these mortals?" the unsmiling guard asked. "And how did they even get here?"

"Dragons," I blurted out. "Lots and lots of dragons."

Alex elbowed me. "The guards are testing us. This is where we fulfill the last part of the riddle."

"Right," I said. "Which is . . . ?"

He sighed and rolled his eyes. "Finally, prove the tests have been fulfilled to gain entry to Peng Lai Island."

"What are we whispering about?" Moli whispered. Ren and Yulong leaned in, too.

"We're trying to decide how we're supposed to prove that we've fulfilled the tests," Alex explained. "Maybe we just present them to the guards in order."

"Present what to them?" Ren asked.

"You," Moli said in a *duh* tone of voice. "And you," she added with a nod to Yulong.

Ren pointed to Yulong, and then at himself. "U-us?"

"You and all the other dragons." She patted Ren on the shoulder, and added, "Try to look a little cooler than that," and, pulling him by the hand, swaggered over to the entrance.

"What does she think she's doing?" Alex spluttered, but he looked more awed than angered.

Moli tossed her hair over her shoulder, which did nothing to impress the stone-faced guards. "We've fulfilled the quests."

"Are you the Heaven Breaker?" one of the guards asked.

"Excuse you," said Moli, "I'm *way* cooler than—"

I interrupted her with a throat-clearing cough. "Moli, I can handle this."

Moli sniffed and folded her arms across her chest.

"I'm the Heaven Breaker, come to claim my place as the Jade Emperor's general," I announced. I was grateful that my voice didn't crack despite the fact that I'd never been more petrified in my entire life, not even when Mao discovered that I'd been the one to switch out all her ketchup for hot sauce when I was nine. I still maintain that that masterful prank was worth the punishment, though.

As I spoke, the glow around Fenghuang grew brighter than ever before. And somehow, I knew what to do to prove I'd passed the Jade Emperor's tests of valor.

Dragons, come to me. The Heaven Breaker commands it.

Out loud, I declared, "First, we found the city named after the Empress—Phoenix—and rescued the animal named after the Emperor—the dragon."

I turned around, meeting Ren's eyes. His eyebrows were scrunched together, but he stepped forward and gave the guards a nervous smile and half-hearted wave. "Hi."

Then I said, "Second, we traveled east to the city of the goddess who brings sleep, to free the fallen beasts."

At these words, the spear grew so hot under my hands that I could barely stand to hold it. I gritted my teeth. As the seconds passed, each one lasting an eternity, the atmosphere grew tenser.

Then, from up above came a great rushing noise. I inhaled sharply in relief. The dragons we'd freed from Chuangmu's prison flew in circles high above us.

Turning back to the guards, I continued. "Third, we found the city in quiet ruins and reclaimed a lost treasure."

Moli pushed Yulong forward with a proud smile. "That's my horse—I mean, cursed dragon prince, now un-cursed. It's complicated. You know how it is."

The guards exchanged questioning looks, clearly not "knowing how it is."

"It seems the Heaven Breaker has fulfilled her quest," one murmured to the other.

"Not yet," said the other. "There is one more riddle that the Heaven Breaker herself must solve in order to gain entrance to the island. This time, you may not receive help from your friends."

"Seriously?" I groaned under my breath.

Alex slapped his forehead. "Great. We're all doomed."

"Hey," I protested. I'd helped him solve riddles. I wasn't *that* hopeless.

"Don't worry. This riddle is more straightforward," said the guard, beckoning me closer. I gulped and stepped toward him, and he spoke into my ear. "What is the most important quality that the Heaven Breaker can possess?"

I could've cried with relief. This was easy. Ye Ye had said it himself, hadn't he, with one of his last breaths? A warrior always puts others above himself or herself.

"Take your time, Faryn," Alex called. "A few deep yoga breaths always helps me—"

"I've got it," I blurted out. "It's—"

But then the word *selflessness* got caught somewhere in the back of my throat. The question had been phrased oddly, I realized. The guard had asked specifically about the Heaven Breaker. Not warriors.

As the Heaven Breaker, master of Fenghuang and dragons, the most important and consistent thing I'd done was not being selfless, but praying to the gods for power. The answer came to me, almost as though someone had whispered it in my head.

After a long, drawn-out moment, I said, "Obedience to the gods."

Neither guard said anything. I took a deep breath and hoped I'd gotten it right. Even though responding with "obedience to the gods" left a bad taste in my mouth, that had to be the right answer.

Right?

The two men bowed their heads and stepped aside, and I exhaled.

"Good job," Moli said, fanning her face. "But next time, don't leave us hanging in suspense and get to the answer a little quicker, will you?"

"I would've gotten that answer quicker," Alex said smugly. I rolled my eyes at him.

Yulong stepped through first. Moli rushed toward the entrance next, but the guards stepped back in and crossed their spears together in front of her.

"Hey, what's the big idea?" she snapped.

"Our orders are to let only the Heaven Breaker pass. No other mortals are allowed to attend the Lantern Festival banquet," responded the guard on the right.

"They're all with me," I said. "I couldn't have done it without their help." The guards at least had the decency to incline their heads as if in shame. "If my friends don't go in, I don't go in. See how the Jade Emperor likes that."

"Faryn, are you serious?" Ren muttered. "You should go. You *have* to go."

Alex stepped forward. "If she doesn't wanna go, can I go in her place?"

"Alex!" I hissed.

"The Jade Emperor has ordered that the Heaven Breaker *and* all her companions may enter the banquet," called a voice from above.

A familiar deity floated down toward us on a cloud—Nezha, the Third Lotus Prince. My heart rose at the sight of him. He wasn't riding his pí xiū today. He'd changed into a cháng shā like Yulong's, though his outfit was a red-and-gold tribute to the New Year. The guards knelt as Nezha's feet touched down to the ground, and we followed suit.

"Nezha," the guards murmured.

"Let the mortals in," Nezha commanded.

"But the Jade Emperor—" one protested.

"—has sent me to pass along his latest order," the boy god finished. "I suggest you don't try to defy it."

The men's spears fell to their sides, and they stepped aside from the entrance. One of the guards commanded, "Fine, but the horses stay out here."

"No way," Moli snapped. "It's the Year of the Horse. My horses should be, like, guests of honor."

Nezha raised his spear threateningly, flames leaping off the tip. The guard paled.

"She's right, you know," the other guard told his friend with a shrug.

Reluctantly, the guards let us and the chariot through. Skyscrapers glimmered in the distance, and joyous shouts filled the streets. We stepped into the realm of the immortals.

CHAPTER

21

Peng Lai Island should've been named Peng Lai City. The streets were paved with bricks of gold. We were surrounded by both modern skyscrapers and rustic temples, the buildings bedecked with the red-and-gold Lunar New Year decorations. Huge winged beasts soared through the air, crossing paths with phoenixes and other strange birds that dangled hóng bāo in their beaks.

I couldn't help but feel awed as I took in my surroundings. I'd actually done it. I'd completed my quest, and I'd made it.

Gods and goddesses floated from place to place on clouds, shouting greetings to Nezha and Yulong and giving us curious looks.

"Did the Jade Emperor really tell you to tell the guards to let us all through?" I asked Nezha.

Instead of responding, Nezha dragged us onto one huge cloud.

"Whoa!" When I nearly stumbled, Ren caught me. My skin tingled where his arms had wrapped around me. I quickly pushed away to stand on my own feet.

"That's where the banquet's being held—the palace of the eight immortals," Nezha shouted over the excited chatter of the gods and goddesses.

In the distance, an enormous palace rose above the skyscrapers. Golden turrets shot out of the top of the building, climbing up as if trying to reach the stars. High above, fireworks shot up into the night sky, showering the city with bursts of color.

"This place is huge," Ren observed, mouth open with awe.

"It can't compare to Heaven," Nezha said, "but it's nothing to sneeze at."

He twirled his flaming hoop through the air, setting a passing deity's skirt on fire.

"Sorry, Xiangu!" Nezha called up as she huffed and shot water out of her palm to put out the flames. He turned to us. "That's He Xiangu of the eight immortals, who are hosting the banquet tonight. She's rather temperamental."

"I heard that!" the goddess called, scowling. Then her eyes landed on Yulong, and she smiled. "Yulong. Wonderful to see you again. It's been too long."

She hurried away, weaving in and out of the other deities.

Nezha winked. "Anyway, the magnificence of Peng Lai Island—it's all thanks to the loyalty of you humans."

Ren blinked. "Huh?"

Was that why Nezha had helped my friends pass through the entrance? Because the gods wanted to use their power? I couldn't help but think back to the way Guanyin and Nezha had both defended us, even against another god, Wenshu.

The boy god definitely had an ulterior motive. The question was—was it a good or a bad one?

As we flew over a sleek black building, Nezha pointed his spear at a thick, long, transparent chute that connected the building to the ground. Small slips of white paper shot through it. "See those pieces of paper?"

"Prayer notes," I blurted out.

The god nodded. "Those are prayers of thanks from the humans. The ones given to individual gods seep into our life forces, giving us greater power and longevity. The ones that aren't directed to specific deities come up through the chute and power the whole city. The reason we've got so many lights and fireworks for the Lunar New Year is because all the prayers are flooding in during the holiday."

Every prayer of thanks I'd ever given the gods—a *lot*—had kept this flashy city running. My mind reeled.

"What about other kinds of prayers?" I asked. "People asking the gods for help?"

Nezha jabbed his spear toward a white building in the distance. "Those prayers are sorted and sent to the specific god in question at the mailing system, the UPS."

"UPS?" Moli spluttered.

"United Pí-xiū Service." A line of huge winged lions, like the ones Nezha rode, flew out of the building. The beasts shot up, gripping brown bags stuffed with notes in their claws. "Once those prayers are fulfilled, the gods earn greater power. Influence over mortals. It's what keeps us alive."

"So you gods are getting rich off us?" Alex asked in disbelief.

Nezha paused, rubbing his chin. "Well, when you put it that way . . ." He grinned. "Definitely. Feel free to pray as you'd like up here, by the way. You've entered one of the realms of the immortals. All you need is this"—Nezha tapped his head—"to send us prayers telling us how amazing we are."

I looked behind me to see how Moli was taking this news, but she was barely even paying attention. There was a stormy, angry look in her eyes—even angrier than usual.

"Something wrong?" I asked.

For a moment, I thought she was going to snap at me to mind my own business. Instead she sighed. "Just . . . feel like I lost a friend, I guess."

I followed her gaze to Yulong, who was walking alongside Nezha. "Oh."

I didn't know what to say. I guess Ye Ye had forgotten to teach the "How to Give Your Frenemy a Pep Talk after Her Beloved Horse Turns into a Dragon Prince" segment of his training.

"Sometimes . . . friends change . . . literally," I said. "It sucks, but you have to know when to let them go. Besides, there's always room for new friendships."

I nodded toward the four horses in front of her.

"Don't try to be all Confucius on me, Faryn Liu. It doesn't suit you," Moli scoffed. Then she smiled, just a little. "But . . . I guess you do have a point. And sometimes, it's nice to make things right with old friends, too."

"Thanks, Moli." I smiled. Maybe there was hope for me and Moli to go back to the way things were.

She tugged at the horses' reins to coax them forward. They seemed unimpressed by the city around us and kept wanting to turn back.

"Yulong," said Nezha, flames dancing in his eyes. "Your father has been eagerly awaiting your return."

"My father cursed me and cast me out of the palace in the first place," Yulong said bitterly. "He's probably itching to test out his latest curse on me."

"Don't speak so ill of your father at the banquet tonight," Nezha warned. "There's been bad blood between many of the deities lately. The last thing you want to do is stir up more trouble in front of the Jade Emperor."

"Speaking of the Jade Emperor," Yulong said slowly, "I've been meaning to ask you something about him. As a horse, I overheard many rumors. One of them is that the Emperor's got a powerful new weapon he's hoping to unveil at the—"

"Shhhhh." Nezha looked right at me, the flames in his eyes

a warning to stop listening. I blushed and looked away. Nezha and Yulong spoke in lowered voices.

"Hey . . ." Ren poked my shoulder. He pointed at a tall billboard above our heads. It showed a young woman with hair as short as mine, smiling and holding a microphone. The sign read: NO BANQUET INVITATION? NO PROBLEM! COME TO MISS CINDY YOU'S CHŪN JIÉ WǍN HUÌ: TONIGHT AT PENG LAI HALL.

Chūn jié wǎn huì, or Spring Festival Gala, was the annual performance held to celebrate the Lunar New Year. At least, that was what we did in the human world. I didn't know the gods celebrated the Lunar New Year with a gala, too.

Ren squinted at the billboard. "I've seen that woman before."

"Duh. That's Cindy You."

"No, I—I've only recently gotten into Cindy's work, and I haven't seen a picture of her before. She looks—she looks so . . . familiar." As we drew farther from the billboard, Ren shouted, "Guys, wait!"

Nezha stopped, and the momentum of our cloud stopped with him. The deities around us pulled ahead. "What's wrong? We're going to be late to the banquet if we don't hurry."

"This will just take a minute." Ren grabbed my hand and stepped off the cloud. A new one formed beneath us, drifting us closer to the billboard.

"Humans. Can't take them anywhere," Yulong muttered.

I stood with Ren, hovering in the air and squinting up at the billboard. Cindy You was a mortal singer—right? But the gods had invited her to their realm of immortality.

Suddenly I felt ticked off. To score an invite to the Lantern Festival banquet, I'd had to slay demons and escape crazy love goddesses. All Cindy You had to do was be herself?

Someone coughed. "*Psst.*"

I dropped my gaze to a crouching figure. The person wore a tattered blue gown with a wooden belt tied around the middle, and only one weathered brown shoe, with hair tied up into two small high buns.

"You're a strange-looking one. Mixed blood?" the person guessed. "Interesting. Never seen your kind up here before."

Frustration twinged in my gut. Another person who couldn't see past the way I looked.

"Ah, I see I've offended you, but I meant no harm by the question," the person said. "I'm nonbinary. I go by 'he'—for now." He waved something under my nose—two tickets, his black eyes glittering as they passed over Ren and me. "You two are on your way to the banquet, aren't you?" When we nodded, he shook his head. "Better that you don't go. The real fun is going to be at the Spring Festival Gala. And did I mention there's going to be food, too? Fun food, like chicken feet. Not that hoity-toity fancy stuff they'll feed you at the banquet."

Ren extended his arm for the tickets. I stepped in front of him. "Sorry, but we don't have any money."

The person smiled and blinked long eyelashes. "Oh, but these tickets only cost one measly prayer!"

"Bye." I tugged Ren away. It was like hauling a boulder.

"Fine," said the stranger. "You drive a hard deal. Two tickets for the price of one." The stranger indicated a brown basket that sat beside him, filled with incense sticks and Choco Pies. "Just one prayer to me, the majestic Lan Caihe, and the tickets are yours." The god bowed his head, as though expecting a shower of praise.

I blinked. "Um . . . who?"

The stranger looked miffed. "I'm one of the eight immortals. The best one. Me, Lan Caihe."

"Never heard of you," I said. He glowered.

"If you're one of the eight immortals, shouldn't you be hosting the banquet?" Ren asked.

"I hate banquets." Caihe shuddered. "Ol' Tieguai—that's one of the other eight immortals, looks like me, but less handsome—has been running this concert with me every year for the past hundred years. All the young deities love it. They don't even want to attend that stuffy banquet anymore." He frowned. "Besides, the banquet's only fun if you're a major deity and rake in the prayers. Not much to brag about when most of the humans don't even remember who you are, let alone remember to send their prayers."

My stomach sank. "Oh. Sorry about that."

Before I could stop him, Ren grabbed two incense sticks

and a Choco Pie. He knelt down in front of the god. I joined him. Ren darted his eyes toward me, the corners of his lips lifting into a small smile.

As we prayed, Caihe smiled and hummed a tune under his breath, one of Cindy You's songs.

When we finished, Caihe beamed and handed us our tickets. "Wonderful. Enjoy the show."

As we floated back to the others, Ren cast one more puzzled look back at Cindy You's beatific smile, as though still trying to place where he'd seen her.

"You know we can't go to Cindy You's concert," I said softly.

"Yeah." His smile faltered, but then he brightened. "But maybe if the banquet ends early, we could catch the end of her concert together."

My heart leapt. I blinked, feeling flustered but not knowing why.

Ren blushed and stuffed the tickets into his pocket. "Hey, we're way behind the others," he said, grabbing hold of my hand and pulling me toward the golden chariot that was disappearing in the crowd.

When our cloud caught up with the others, Moli and Alex both stared at Ren's and my intertwined hands. Moli's lips twitched into a knowing smile, and I dropped Ren's hand like it had burned me. I couldn't look in his direction.

"All right, kids. Welcome to the palace of the eight

immortals," Nezha said. The cloud disappeared beneath our feet as we descended onto solid ground. "Don't feed the animals. They get stomachaches after eating too many warriors."

Nezha took us to the edge of a tall bridge that stood above a river with the clearest water I'd ever seen. The surface sparkled under the light. Moving with the crowd of other deities, we crossed over to the palace.

There was a large courtyard in front of the doors. As we walked through it, I spotted ordinary creatures like blue jays, along with familiar plants such as lotuses. Butterflies and dogs chased each other in the garden. A pair of deer roamed, picking at the vivid green grass beneath their hooves.

I also saw strange creatures that could have leapt straight out of the pages of *Demons and Deities through the Dynasties*: Qí lín, a creature with the body of a horse covered in scales and enveloped in fire, with a single horn protruding out of its dragon head. A few white tigers that had stretched out lazily along a bed of rocks watched us curiously as the deities passed by, forming a line to get into the palace.

I heard shouting ahead. A man guarding the palace gates kicked a deity out of the long line. Then another. And another. The disgruntled deities flew off, the exploding fireworks lighting their way out.

"What's going on?" Ren asked. "Why is everyone getting kicked out?"

Nezha sighed. "There isn't enough space in their palace, so

the eight immortals invite only the most distinguished deities to their annual Lantern Festival banquet. Usually it's the same old crowd. Me, of course. Then the Jade Emperor, his wife . . . you get the drift. But of course, every year a bunch of the minor deities try to sneak in." Nezha paused. "Speaking of invitations—I almost forgot."

He reached down the back of his cháng shā and produced three golden envelopes sealed with the sticker of a dragon's head, handing one each to Alex, me, and Yulong. My name was written in red lettering at the top. I pried open my envelope to reveal a simple white postcard.

Dear [insert annoying warrior's name here],

Congratulations on all the demons you've slain in your journey. To celebrate your achievements, we, the eight immortals, would like to cordially invite you to the Lantern Festival banquet.

Please present this invitation to the guard. If you fail to show proof of invitation to this banquet, you will be promptly eaten.

Note: if you have died an unfortunate death, please do not feel obligated to attend this celebration.

Regards,

He Xiangu, Cao Guojiu, Li Tieguai, Lan Caihe, Lü Dongbin, Han Xiangzi, Zhang Guolao, and Zhongli Quan

My head spun trying to keep track of all the names.

Yulong leaned in and whispered, "Don't worry. I've lived for thousands of years, and I can never remember their names either."

"Aren't you forgetting something?" Moli asked, folding her arms over her chest. "What about invitations for Ren and me?"

"Ah." Nezha gave them both an apologetic look. "The Jade Emperor only gave me two invitations for mortals: the Heaven Breaker and her plus-one."

"What?" Moli snapped. She looked on the verge of explosion. "Listen, I've traveled thousands of miles. I'm starving and thirsty, and so are my horses." The horses drooped their heads as though in agreement. "It's the last day of the Lunar New Year. My entire family is on the other side of the country. My horse turned into a stupid dragon."

"I was a dragon first," said Yulong.

"I dragged these two across the country just so they could eat some food," Moli added.

"Hey," my brother protested.

She whirled on Nezha. "The least you can do, *Third Lotus Prince*, is let me into the stinking ban—"

"Moli." To everyone's surprise, Ren cut her off. "It's okay. I know where we can get good food and good music."

Moli's eyes widened. "What?"

"Cindy You's concert." Ren raised two tickets in his hand. He didn't look at me. For some reason, that made my heart sink.

Moli grabbed the tickets. "Free music *and* food? Score." She paused. "But weren't you supposed to speak to Ao Guang about your curse?"

Ren swallowed, his eyes falling to his feet. "Maybe another time."

"There won't *be* another time."

"We'll ask for you, Ren," I said. Between asking about Ba, Ye Ye, and Ren's curse, it looked like I'd be interrogating the deities for a while. "We'll drag the Dragon King back with us if we have to. You'll get your cure."

Moli leapt back onto the chariot, Ren following close behind.

"Come find us when you're done," Moli said. She lowered her voice and added, "And Faryn? Good luck. Jià!"

The horses whinnied and parted a path between the crowd of disgruntled deities. I watched the tips of Ren's white hair disappear, suddenly wishing I could've been in that chariot with them.

CHAPTER

22

We'd reached the front of the line. The guard standing before us had the yellow body of a tiger and nine—I counted—*nine* red heads with humanlike faces. Talk about an identity crisis.

"Evening," Nezha told the creature. "Looks like you've been busy kicking deities out."

"Me always busy," the creature grunted. It took our golden envelopes into its paws, sniffed them, and then ripped them to shreds. It waved its arms to open the gates.

"Five hundred years, and that thing still hasn't learned how to properly bathe," Yulong muttered as we walked through.

When I looked back, the beast's five million pairs of eyes were staring right at us. They were empty and soulless. I shuddered.

"Oh man," Alex murmured.

The inside of the palace was every bit as elaborate as the exterior suggested. Beyond the golden doors was a long, carpeted hall. Several tall, circular pillars held up a golden ceiling that seemed to stretch onward into the heavens.

Eight empty golden thrones, four on each side, faced each other. A ninth throne—the most elaborate one—sat at the back of the hall.

A large woman sat in the ninth throne, swathed in elaborate silk robes. Even at a distance, I could see the deep frown wrinkles that lined her stern face. Two beautiful young women with long, black hair stood on either side of the woman, holding giant fans made of green leaves.

I recognized the woman on the throne as Xi Wangmu, the Jade Emperor's wife, the Queen Mother of the West. I could barely believe I was seeing her in real life. She looked like a blown-up version of her statue back in the Jade Society. Wangmu niáng niang wore a silver crown on her head, with beads of glittering jewels dangling down to her shoulders. Her red-and-gold robes hung down to her feet and past her arms with big, billowing sleeves. In her right hand she gripped a black staff that curved at the top.

Alex and I fell to our knees. Yulong and Nezha bowed their heads to pay respects to the goddess.

"Five minutes before the banquet begins. You cut it very close, warriors. Nezha. Yulong."

Xi Wangmu's slightly husky voice sounded as old as the Earth itself, and struck me as strangely familiar.

"Apologies, Wangmu niáng niang," Nezha said. He was the perfect obedient subject, except for the fact that his lips thinned and he gripped his spear so tightly his knuckles turned white.

The goddess pointed a finger at a servant. "Show them to their seats. My husband will be arriving any moment now."

The servant led us out of the throne room and into a huge courtyard filled with the sounds of laughter and fireworks that whistled up into the sky, exploding into color high above.

"Faryn," Alex gasped, pointing up. Hundreds of lanterns floated above our heads like bright balloons, filling the night sky with their light. I'd never seen so many in one place before. The gods had pulled out all the stops for the Lantern Festival.

Beneath a towering peach tree, the deities sat around a long table covered in red-and-gold cloth. I recognized a few familiar faces, among them Erlang Shen and Guanyin. They gave us a curt nod before returning to their conversation. Most of the other gods were unfamiliar.

"That's one of the eight immortals, Zhang Guolao," my brother said, pointing out a scholarly looking old dude carrying a tube-shaped bamboo drum with two iron rods. "That's another one, He Xiangu—we met her earlier. And then there's the sea goddess . . ."

Female servants bustled about carrying plates of food above their heads. They wore long, billowy gowns, with red-and-gold layers on top of white inner dresses. Still other girls performed for us in a clearing, dancing and twirling their dresses in a colorful swish while a row of servants played the flute behind them. A couple of servants wore horse heads and were putting on a performance in honor of this year's zodiac animal.

Most of the seats were full already. There were four more empty chairs, two at the end of the table and two near the head.

Suddenly, Nezha doubled over and leaned against the table for support. "I don't feel so well."

"Pull yourself together, Nezha," Yulong hissed. "This is the Lantern Festival banquet. You can't miss it."

"Flying back and forth all day must've given me cramps."

"I have Tiger Balm," Yulong offered, pulling a small jar of the nasty-smelling brown ointment out of his robes. "Stole it before I left San Francisco." When Nezha gave him a look of disbelief, Yulong added defensively, "Hey, Tiger Balm can cure anything."

"Not a stomachache." The boy god shook his head with a grimace. "I'm gonna head out. Tell the Jade Emperor not to wait up for me."

Nezha turned and, so fast I almost missed it, winked at me. He took off, flying up into the sky.

Still trying to process what the boy god had meant by that wink, I looked over at Yulong, only to find that his attention had been diverted by a large man with the head of a dragon and longer, more magnificent whiskers than his son. He wore white robes that shimmered under the light from the lanterns. I guessed him to be the Dragon King of the West Sea, Ao Ji. Beside him sat three other dragon-men who wore robes of blue-green, black, and red.

The Dragon Kings turned toward me and inclined their heads in unison.

"Master of the dragons," they murmured respectfully. After a moment of shock, I quickly returned the gesture.

Since they were dragons, too, would I be able to communicate with them telepathically? I squeezed my eyes shut and concentrated as hard as I could.

"Can you stop making that face and be a normal person for once? You look like you're constipated," Alex hissed.

I opened my eyes. The Dragon Kings were staring at me with strange expressions. Since they were gods and I was a mortal, I guess I didn't have any power over them.

"Fù wáng," Yulong respectfully addressed his father, Ao Ji, getting onto one knee and holding his fisted hands in front of him. Though he bowed his head, it wasn't hard to imagine that he was scowling at the ground before Ao Ji. "My sentence ended after I served the Heaven Breaker in her hour of need, as you said it would."

The Dragon King raised a hand. "You may rise."

Yulong obeyed.

"That was an awfully long time you spent as a horse. You've repented, yes?"

"Yes," said Yulong. "You could have told me it would take five hundred years for the Heaven Breaker to arrive, though."

The Dragon King stared at his son, who ducked his head.

Then Ao Ji threw his head back into a laugh. "My boy! How I've missed you and your jokes."

"That wasn't a joke. Five hundred years of punishment just for destroying your stupid pearl is a little excess—*Hrmph!*"

Ao Ji squeezed his son into a tight hug. "It's good to have you back, ér zi."

Some of the deities wiped tears out of their eyes and sighed in approval, and Yulong blushed as his father released him from the hug. "Wh-why are you being so nice?"

"It's the Lunar New Year. How can any family fight during this special time?"

Yulong just looked at Ao Ji, obviously dissatisfied with his answer.

The older dragon sighed. He raised his hands. "Okay, and maybe it has something to do with the fact that all eight of your brothers skipped the banquet for some silly concert."

"Knew it'd be something like that," Yulong muttered.

"But that means it's the perfect night for father-son bonding." Ao Ji smiled at his son and cuffed him on the ear. Yulong gave in and smiled. The other three Dragon Kings clapped.

"When should we bring up Ren's curse to Ao Guang?" I asked Alex. I had a feeling it would burst these guys' bubbles.

The dragon wearing blue-green robes sneezed. Water spurted out of his nostrils, forcing Erlang Shen and Guanyin to duck under the table. The force of the water slammed an unsuspecting servant into the trunk of a massive peach tree.

Alex swallowed. "Maybe later."

My brother and I settled into our seats at the end of the table. We were like those awkward kids who'd wandered into a friend of a friend's birthday party and didn't know anybody.

The double doors at the entrance banged open, and a pair of men blasting trumpets marched into the hall.

"The Jade Emperor has arrived," a guard announced in a squeaky voice.

The Jade Emperor liked to travel in style. I was sure the guy could've disembarked from his green-and-gold palanquin and *walked* into the banquet hall, but instead he rolled into the courtyard with eight different men to announce his presence: four trumpeters surrounding him in the front and back, and four other men to carry the palanquin forward.

I guessed when you were the supreme ruler of Heaven, Earth, and Diyu, you were allowed to be as extra as you wanted to be.

Once he deigned to step out of his palanquin, I finally got a close look at the Jade Emperor. It was like looking into the sun. Or the face of a man who thought he was the sun.

The Jade Emperor had long, black hair and an equally

long, black beard. He dressed in elaborate gold-and-green robes that matched his palanquin. How could he even stand up with those heavy robes weighing down his frame?

On his head he wore the mother of all hats, a rectangular golden crown. To carry that thing, the Jade Emperor must've had serious neck muscles.

Behind him, Xi Wangmu stepped out of the palanquin.

"Did Wangmu niáng niang get on a palanquin just to move to the backyard?" Alex whispered to me. "So much respect right now."

Everyone bowed their heads as the Jade Emperor and his wife slowly made their way toward the thrones at the head of the table. Once they'd taken their seats, the Jade Emperor smiled.

"My family," he said. He sounded like a normal guy. He wouldn't even make a good radio talk show host. "It's been too long since we've gathered for such a grand feast, although I notice we're missing some . . . attendees."

The Jade Emperor looked at Nezha's empty seat. An uncomfortable silence followed.

"Nevertheless, I wish you all a happy Year of the Horse. May you give yourselves good fortune." The gods laughed good-naturedly. "I have important news—and a fancy new *toy*—to share. Eventually. First, let's eat!"

We waited for the Jade Emperor and Xi Wangmu, who moved like five-thousand-year-old turtles, to get the first pick of the feast. Then I dove into the food, my first real banquet of the Lunar New Year.

There were so many dishes I didn't know what to eat first. Plates of steamed fish, dumplings, long noodles, oranges, and peaches rotated down the table as though by an invisible assembly line.

"Try these," Guanyin whispered, winking as she passed Alex and me two bowls. They were filled with clear soup and contained tāng yuán, balls of glutinous rice flour filled with red bean paste. "You have to eat them during the Lantern Festival. It's tradition."

The tāng yuán melted in my mouth. The food of the heavens tasted—well, heavenly. Each piece of fruit was flawlessly ripe, each bāo zi steamed to mouthwatering perfection. There were no words in any human language that could describe the explosion of flavors that entered my mouth with each bite.

The best part was the bottomless rice bowls and stone glasses. They wouldn't empty, no matter how much people ate or drank from them.

From now on, demons could slay themselves. I was never leaving this island.

After the plates had been cleared, the Jade Emperor held up his hand for attention. "It seems like it was just yesterday that we last gathered here for the annual Lantern Festival banquet. Before I make a special announcement, I'd like us all to clap for two warriors who have joined us tonight, on the last day of the Lunar New Year."

Alex and I shrank back into our seats as the deities broke out in polite applause.

After exchanging a look with his wife, who nodded, the Emperor continued. "As you all know, I called the Heaven Breaker here as part of a test of courage, strength, and loyalty to the gods. She had to pass several trials in order to prove her worth as my future general. Not surprisingly, she has made it."

"She?" spluttered Ao Ji.

I swallowed, feeling my face redden as the deities murmured among themselves. No doubt they'd all thought Alex was the Heaven Breaker. My brother stiffened and remained silent.

"Yes," the Jade Emperor continued. "The Heaven Breaker's successful arrival should come as no surprise, given the strong, mixed blood that runs in her veins."

The gods scrutinized Alex and me. My skin crawled, and heat crept into my cheeks. I waited for the Jade Emperor to claim that our invitations had been a mistake. That we weren't worthy of being here.

"It is fitting that we welcome both warriors to our immortal family on the last night of the Lunar New Year," said the Jade Emperor.

"Both?" Alex echoed in a shaky voice.

"Indeed," said the Jade Emperor with a small smile that didn't reach his eyes. "The Heaven Breaker will become my Heavenly General, but you, brave boy, will join the ranks of my immortal soldiers."

Applause followed the Jade Emperor's pronouncement. Alex pumped his fist into the air with a loud whoop that startled some of the deities. I blinked with shock.

"If only Mao could see us now," my brother said.

Even the idea of the mistress seeing our luxurious glory couldn't bring me to smile. I didn't get it. Any warrior would've given his right hand to be sitting where I sat, in the position to lead the Jade Emperor's army in Heaven. But I only felt empty.

Maybe the gods were rewarding my whole family by granting me this honor. After all, by following the demons' presence to America to better protect the people of Earth, my family had given up everything so I could carry on their glory. Alex and me serving the Jade Emperor would exceed all their wildest dreams.

Ba, Ye Ye, wherever you two are, are you proud?

Why don't I feel proud?

"Now, on to the big announcement." The Jade Emperor stood. Every figure, immortal or human, royalty or servant was enraptured by his words. "The Great War is coming. A war against the demon uprising, far greater than World War I, World War II, or any wars that have ever shaken the Earth. My fellow deities—my family—we relocated to the West hoping that our warriors would mix bloodlines and grow stronger. We hoped the humans would spread word of our greatness to the Western world, so we'd have more followers, and become even more powerful. Yet somehow, their journey to the West has made them forget our greatness, take it for granted."

I shuddered at the power-crazed glint in the Jade Emperor's eyes. Deities nodded up and down the table, though I noticed Guanyin and Erlang Shen didn't look as happy.

"In past wars, we gods have held back our full power for fear of destroying humanity," said the Jade Emperor. "But the humans have proven that we deities can be powerful even without their loyalty. This time, only the most loyal humans will be spared our wrath. And when we defeat the demons once and for all, Earth shall return to a golden age of the gods once more."

CHAPTER

23

Most of the deities shouted in celebration and raised their stone glasses. "Gān bēi!" They clinked and downed their drinks. Xi Wangmu gave her husband a satisfied smile, and the servants resumed their dancing and singing.

Guanyin half-heartedly raised her glass in toast. But instead of digging into her food, she began murmuring with Erlang Shen.

I turned to Alex and was glad to see that he, too, looked stunned by the Jade Emperor's declaration.

"Is the Jade Emperor saying he's gonna commit genocide on . . . the human race?" I spluttered.

"He's saying he wants us—I mean, *you*—to lead it," said Alex.

The realization made want to empty the contents of my full stomach.

"No way." I shook my head so hard I almost gave myself whiplash. "Nope. Not gonna happen. This is—this is *madness*. How can the gods not see it?"

Alex coughed and squinted at his untouched plate of food. "W-well, I kind of see where the Jade Emperor is coming from . . ."

"You *what*?"

He was kidding. He had to be kidding.

"Like, people like Mao and Mr. Yang. They're clearly abusing their power," Alex said, the words coming out of him all in a rush as though he'd been holding them back for a long time. "They made our lives miserable, Faryn—making us do all those chores, calling us names, disrespecting Ye Ye. It wouldn't be the *worst* thing if people like them, you know . . ."

Dread filled the pit of my stomach. I almost couldn't speak. I couldn't believe these words were coming out of my own brother's mouth.

At least Alex had the decency to squirm and look uncomfortable. "Plus, the Jade Emperor did say he's going to spare the loyal humans."

"So it's okay to kill the humans who *don't* pray to the gods?" I demanded.

"I didn't say—"

"You did."

Alex bit his lip and kept his gaze trained on the table.

Fireworks still shot up into the sky, forming patterns I

hadn't noticed before. Pictures of horses. Outlines of deities. The words *xīn nián kuài lè*, or "Happy New Year." They glittered in the air for their one shining moment of life before dissolving and falling to the Earth.

But now, the lights looked threatening rather than pretty.

Ye Ye had always told me to turn to prayer whenever I was in trouble. But it wasn't exactly like I could pray to the gods to help me get out of the gods' clutches.

Still, I squeezed my eyes shut and prayed to the only person who might be able to help. After all, he'd come to me in a dream and helped me escape from the Red Prince.

Ye Ye, I need to get out of here. Take me to Ren and Moli. Cindy You's concert. Anywhere but here. I can't be the Jade Emperor's general. I'm sorry.

Nothing happened. I peeled my eyes open and was shocked to see that a familiar male deity looked right at me.

Wenshu, the god of wisdom and Ye Ye's master.

Something shot up through a tube behind him. He snatched it out of the air.

It was a small white note. A prayer note.

My prayer note?

Wenshu didn't even look at the note before crushing it in his free hand, scattering the white dust in the air. It swirled high above, glittering in the light from the lanterns. The deity stared at me coldly for a few seconds that seemed to span an eternity.

Then he turned to speak to the Dragon King of the North.

Wenshu had just intercepted and destroyed my prayer note.

"A-Alex?"

Before I could tell him what Wenshu had just done, a plate appeared between us, held up by a servant's pale, dainty hand. Two ripe, pink-and-white peaches sat in the middle of it.

"Special delivery," said the girl. "Two peaches of immortality. Eating one peach will extend your life by three thousand years."

"We never ordered these," I said.

"Of course we did," said Alex. "Don't listen to my sister—she's an idiot."

Alex grabbed the two peaches, tossing one to me. He held the other in his shaking palm, a hungry look in his eye.

He raised his peach to me with a grin. "To immortality?"

My peach felt cold in my palm, even though the air up here was lukewarm. The deities had all begun digging into the peaches the servants passed around the table. But even though the fruit looked delicious, I no longer had an appetite.

I placed my peach on the table. "I'll never accept immortality. Not like this. And don't you dare eat that peach, Alex Liu."

The peach trembled in his hand, where it was inches from his mouth. "Just because you're the Heaven Breaker doesn't mean you get to tell me what to do."

"I'm not telling you as the Heaven Breaker. I'm telling you as your sister. Just me. Just Faryn Liu."

"Oh, give me a break," Alex spat. "You're clearly ordering me around as the *Heaven Breaker*. You've been looking down on me the entire time we've been on this quest. Don't deny it. And you *aren't* better than me, by the way. In case you've forgotten, we were both raised as outcasts."

"Alex—"

"Being immortal means we'll finally be better than Mao, Luhao, Mr. Yang, and all those idiots who hate us," my brother said, his eyes turning watery. He blinked furiously, as though to hold back tears.

"Alex . . ."

"If you get to be the Heaven Breaker, I at least deserve to be immortal, too. Otherwise it's just not fair."

"Alex!"

I knocked the peach out of Alex's hand. He yelled. The deities around us gasped. By refusing the peaches, I'd defied the Jade Emperor, the ruler of all the heavens.

I guessed Alex and I wouldn't be staying for dessert.

"Y-you—insolent little—!" Xi Wangmu cried.

"Time to go out in style," I said, grabbing Alex's hand and refusing to let go even when he tried to wriggle away. Turning my pin into a spear, which knocked over half the stone glasses before me, I channeled the power of my weapon and shouted, "Dragons, get us out of here!"

Something red flashed past me. More gasps and yells from the deities.

We have come to rescue you, Heaven Breaker.

A huge, familiar red dragon swooped down on the table, scattering cups and bits of food everywhere.

"Catch that menace!" Ao Ji shrieked. He'd stood up and spilled wine all over the tablecloth.

The four Dragon Kings began squabbling.

"That dunderheaded dragon came from *your* sea, *you* handle it."

"What are you talking about? Obviously an ugly beast like that had to have come from *your* filthy waters!"

Hands clamored to grab the dragon, but it was too quick. My eyes widened when the dragon shot straight at me. Behind it, I could see other dragons swooping in—the ones we'd rescued from Chuangmu's hotel, and more.

"Protect the Jade Emperor," yelled He Xiangu, one of the eight immortals. "And grab the Heaven Breaker!"

Ao Ji lunged for me. Alex reached for me, too, his eyes full of shock. With a gust of wind, the dragon swooped in. Its claws gripped the back of my shirt as well as Alex's. It yanked us out of our seats and flew us up and away.

The dragon navigated an impossible maze in the sky, weaving in between lanterns and fireworks. My brother's voice came from behind me. "I think Nezha's going Third Lotus Wushu on all of Heaven!"

I looked down to see that the eight immortals' banquet had dissolved into chaos. Dragons descended on the ruined table and sent the servants screaming, while the deities struggled to fight the airborne creatures left and right. Nezha rode a white dragon and led the charge on the banquet. Had this been part of his plan all along?

The harsh wind forced me to shut my eyes. My stomach swooped, and I screamed as the dragon brought us spiraling downward. The dragon plowed past something hard and solid.

"Hey! No unauthorized persons allowed back here," a gruff voice yelled.

The dragon's claws released me, and I tumbled about three feet before falling onto solid ground. A second *thud* and groan told me Alex had landed, too.

Get your friends to safety, Heaven Breaker. The dragons will join you soon.

Wings flapped above us. I opened my eyes in time to see the red dragon fly out the door.

I took in my surroundings: a soundboard, black benches, lots of microphones and wires. A broken keyboard in the corner. Scattered sheet music on the ground.

And distant chants of "Cindy! Cindy! Cindy!" muffled by a thick red curtain.

"Where are we?" Alex groaned, sitting up and wincing.

"I think . . . we're backstage at the chūn jié wǎn huì," I said.

"Great. We traded immortality for a stupid concert. Everything always has to go *your* way, doesn't it?" Alex spat. "Are you happy now?"

"Alex, I'm sorry, but this isn't the time."

He must've realized, like I had, that there had to be a reason the red dragon had dropped us here and told us to get our friends to safety. A reason Nezha had launched an attack on the Lantern Festival banquet.

Something big was happening tonight. Much bigger than us, and dangerous. We had to find Ren and Moli.

There was nobody around, but footsteps thundered somewhere nearby.

"This way!" someone yelled.

Guards. Alex and I scrambled to our feet, searching for an escape route. I knew we were thinking the same thing: if the guards caught up to us, they'd throw us out of the venue with pleasure.

Worse, they might take us back to the Jade Emperor, and I couldn't deal with that war-crazed tyrant now. Or ever.

Grabbing Alex's hand, I yelled, "Run!"

We turned—and almost ran straight into a woman who stepped out from stage left, to tumultuous applause and encore requests from the audience. She wore a sparkly red gown that fanned out past her ankles. Her face was caked with makeup, her short hair so glossy it practically glowed. Her lips formed into a round O when she saw us.

Cindy You opened her mouth to scream.

"Wait!" a familiar voice yelled from behind me—Ren's. "I have to talk to you."

Ren and Moli arrived, their clothes torn and faces covered in scratches. They'd fought tooth and nail to get back here.

"Hey, loser." Moli flicked Alex on the forehead. Alex seemed unsure whether to scowl or smile. He settled for elbowing her in the side, and then smiling.

I frowned in annoyance. So Alex would play nice with Moli, but not with me? I was starting to see a pattern. And not a pretty one.

"Ā yí," Ren said to Cindy You politely, pulling something out of his back pocket, "I loved your performance. It was amazing. Spectacular."

"Thank you," the singer said stiffly, "but you didn't need to come all the way back here to—"

"I think you should see this." Ren handed her something small—a photograph. *The* photograph.

Understanding flooded me at once as I considered the similarities in their features.

Cindy's eyes flickered over the old, yellowed picture. She turned it over, and then turned it back again. "Why are you giving me a picture of myself?"

"M-my father gave it to me." Ren was shaking. I reached out and grabbed his hand, and he squeezed it gratefully. "Jianfei. It's a picture of . . . his wife. My mother."

Cindy You's mouth fell open.

"Jianfei, my father," Ren repeated, sounding desperate.

"You—you remember him, right? That woman in the picture is you, right?"

"I . . . why, yes, it—"

Before Cindy could finish her sentence, several guards emerged from a door behind us.

"Preparations are finished," one announced. "And you should see what's going on at the immortals' banquet, my lord. Nezha started a food fight or something—"

The chatter abruptly stopped as the guards' gazes swept over us. Cindy's attention shifted away from Ren to someone behind me. I turned around to see a bunch of men wearing sunglasses and business suits. They growled, narrowing their eyes at us.

"No trespassers allowed back here," one said. "Do you fans have no shame?"

"W-we were just leaving," Alex said.

"No, stay." Cindy stuffed the photograph back into Ren's hand. "You four spectacular fans came all this way to see me, and I'm so flattered." Her lips curved into a smile. "It'd be a shame if you didn't get to see the real show."

As if on cue, a familiar, silky woman's voice boomed out on the other side of the curtains. "Do I hear more song requests for Cindy? Wonderful!"

Cindy cursed and turned toward the stage.

"You're doing *another* encore?" Moli gawked at the singer. "Girl, you've been singing for two hours."

The curtains parted, revealing a female emcee in an

elegant black gown with a rose on one shoulder. She scowled and waved at the singer. "Get up here, you—"

The emcee stopped and blinked at the four of us.

Chuangmu, the goddess of love. She'd escaped the destruction of her hotel. She was here. Hosting Cindy You's concert.

"What're you doing here?" I asked, dumbfounded.

Before I could sort out what was happening, Cindy whipped her gown around, and it burst into flame. "I'll show those idiots an encore!"

I was too stunned to scream. Alex grabbed Moli. Ren pulled me back, tugging me along as he ran for the exit.

Cindy's feminine laugh turned into a boyish one. The laughter was followed by a loud crashing noise that shook the whole stage.

Cindy was no longer . . . well, Cindy. In the singer's place stood a familiar demon lord, one we thought we'd beaten back in D.C.—the Red Prince.

"I missed you brats at my banquet last night," the demon lord snarled, "but I'm glad we get to enjoy this one together!"

I fell back, speechless. The Red Prince was joined by the beast that was supposed to be long dead, that I'd helped Erlang Shen kill on Lunar New Year's Eve. This time, the creature was fully formed, the size of a small building, its scales a glistening blood red.

The nián.

CHAPTER

24

"Y-you," Ren stammered at the Red Prince. "You're alive?"

"Didn't you say you killed the nián?" Alex whispered to me. The creature shook out its mane, digging its claws into the floor. "That thing looks pretty alive to me."

The Red Prince threw his head back and laughed. "Better get used to demons not staying dead. King Yama's power over Diyu is weakening. Many more demons are coming. And no matter how you try to kill us, we'll be back before you know it."

The nián let out a low rumble of agreement, its eyes glowing like yellow orbs as it pawed at the ground.

"No, you idiot boy," Chuangmu shouted up at the Red Prince, stomping her heel against the stage. She ignored the roar of the nián as it turned toward her. "When I saved you in D.C., this is *not* what we agreed to."

"She followed us. I *knew* I smelled knockoff Chanel," Moli sniffed.

My mind leapt to the sense I'd had of being trailed back in D.C.'s Chinatown. Now it all made sense. "But how?"

"She must've snuck in by disguising herself as part of Cindy's team," Alex murmured.

"Weren't you on Xi Wangmu's side?" I cried at Chuangmu. "You should be helping us!"

"Xi Wangmu turned against me when she decided to help you humans escape my hotel," the goddess spat, her eyes glowing with rage. "It seems I choose all my allies poorly."

Chuangmu thrust her microphone at the Red Prince and turned her back to us, which I guess meant we'd just been dismissed. "The deal was that we take Cindy You out of commission, disguise you to put on this concert, and *then* wreak havoc on the Queen Mother of the West. Now, get back out there and finish your finale."

The demon lord sucked in a huge gust of air and blew it back out—as fire. Samadhi fire. The flames shot into the curtain, searing through the fabric and tearing it down in one blow.

"Now *that's* what I call a grand finale," the Red Prince bellowed.

"Why are you demons so—so—*demonic*?" asked Chuangmu.

A cloud formed under her feet, and she shot up into the

air, the flames chasing her as she soared over the panicking crowd and out of sight.

Although my brain screamed at me to run and never look back, I pulled out Fenghuang and faced the demon lord with my spear in front of me. He now sat on top of the nián, and I craned my neck to meet him at eye level.

I'd beaten both these demons once. I could do it again.

But before I could lunge toward the demon lord, his guards rushed between us, meeting my spear with their swords.

"Our demon lord is busy, can't you see?" one of them growled, jerking his head toward the fiery mess that had once been the curtains. The fabric fell to the stage, which burst into flame.

The screams of hundreds of deities filled the concert venue. They clamored over each other to be the first to fly away from the outdoor auditorium on their clouds. Several stagehands and minor deities threw water onto the fire, but the Red Prince's demon flames only grew.

"We need the help of the dragon kings to put out those flames," Ren shouted, panting and wiping sweat off his brow. I could tell he was having a hard time breathing "I'll . . . I'll try to turn into a dragon. One of them might listen to me then, and—"

"Too risky," I said.

You don't trust me, the look on his face said.

But I knew how much it cost Ren's humanity to let the

dragon take over—and I couldn't let him do it. Couldn't lose more of Ren.

Smoke clogged my lungs. But I had to keep fighting. If we didn't stop the demon lord, he could wipe out hundreds with his samadhi fire. Even the deities didn't stand a chance against the evil flames.

Something warm and hard thudded against me.

"I've got your back," Ren yelled. He notched an arrow and shot it at the nearest demon.

As one unit, Ren and I fought off the demons. The pressure of his solid, warm back pressed against mine reassured me that he was still standing. Still fighting. Though they couldn't stand against Fenghuang, the Red Prince's bodyguards were relentless in their attack against me. They slashed down everything in their path: music stands, microphones, each other. I slashed them into oblivion with my spear, but more kept coming.

Alex and Moli met the demons head-on, slicing their swords and parrying the attacks without fear. I slashed Fenghuang's tip down a row of charging men. They vanished, their souls turning into wisps that floated away.

A demon ran at me, his sword pointed at my heart. I parried his blade, sending him bowling into two other men. They tumbled to the ground in a tangled heap of ugliness and confusion. One of them tried to stand up, but Moli shrieked and beaned him in the head with a box of wires. He went down again with a groan. She sliced him in half with her sword, and a ghostly white wisp floated from the ground, all that remained of the demon. Moli wiped her brow and shot me a thumbs-up.

Another demon snuck up on my brother, raising a sword high in the air, but I was on him in an instant. Fenghuang pulsed beneath my hands.

"Get away from my brother, freak!" I slashed my spear down with speed and power that I'd never known I had in me, the crystallized point slicing through the guard as though he were made of nothing more than water.

"Th . . . thanks," Alex panted, wiping ash off his face.

"Shut up . . ." It was so hard to breathe now. ". . . Idiot."

Though I'd meant the words to come out hard, my voice, clogged with smoke, betrayed the fear I'd felt the moment I thought Alex had fallen victim to the demon.

While his henchmen held us off, the Red Prince tossed ball after ball of flame into the audience. His men ripped down the remains of the curtain and wadded up the flaming fabric, throwing it into the crowd. Young deities screamed as the flames consumed them. They burned up right before my eyes.

The walls caught fire, the flames climbing and licking the ceiling.

Eyes and lungs burning, I ran at the Red Prince—and prayed. Praying to the gods I'd just turned my back on left a sour taste in my mouth, but I didn't see another choice.

Deities, give me the power to kill this demon lord.

That same low female voice responded. *I have the perfect weapon for you, Heaven Breaker.*

Something fell into my sweaty hand. I opened my palm. A white lotus flower.

The deity's voice entered my head again. *Guanyin's lotus bed trapped the Red Prince once, hundreds of years ago. This is my refined version of the weapon, which will stop him—and his samadhi fire—again.*

I chucked the flower as hard as I could at the demon lord. When it landed on the ground in front of the Red Prince, it grew to the size of a small couch. The flames leapt off the ground and walls, sucked into the bed of the lotus flower.

The Red Prince's eyes widened when he realized the air was clearing, that his flames had been conquered.

"Wh-who—? What? Impossible—" The demon lord kicked the nián with his heels, but the beast didn't react quickly enough.

Two thick green vines shot out of the lotus, yanking the Red Prince off the nián and into the depths of the flower. He screamed, "Not again!" and thrashed. The flower's petals and leaves grew, sucking him inside.

"Where's the real Cindy You?" I shouted. "What did you do to Ren's mother?"

"Why do you care what happens to a silly mortal woman?" the Red Prince spat. His eyes widened with fear as the vines crawled over his face. Trapped and defenseless, he looked, for the first time, quite pitiful. "Help me!"

"Not unless you tell me what you did to Cindy."

"This isn't the end, stupid girl," the Red Prince shouted as the vines thickened over his eyes. "I'm only the first of the demon lords breaking out of Diyu. Just wait till you face my masters—the demon kings. You and all of Earth will—"

The rest of the Red Prince's threat was lost. He vanished. The flower shrank into the ground and disappeared.

"The nián," Ren shouted. The huge beast had lunged out into the crowd of scattering deities. As I looked, it reached out a scaly paw to swipe up a young male deity who was wearing Cindy You gear from head to foot—and swallowed him whole. Then the nián ate another deity. Then another.

I watched with horror as the beast swelled in size with each deity it consumed, its deafening roars drowning out the screams of the fleeing gods and goddesses. Within seconds, it had doubled in height, standing at least thirty feet tall. The nián stormed over the deities, each step as loud and heavy as an earthquake. The young gods and goddesses flooded through the doors, until only a handful of the braver ones remained behind, wielding everything from swords to hairbrushes as weapons.

If I had to guess, these deities were disciples under the major gods and goddesses. They were basically food for the nián.

"How are these deities so powerless?" Moli yelled as she

took down one of the Red Prince's last guards with a slash of her sword. "Can't they just fly away or something?"

"They can't," Alex realized. He dove in front of Moli, who hadn't noticed a second guard creeping up on her. "These deities are so minor, nobody prays to them. They've got no power."

Ren gave me an imploring look. "C'mon. We've gotta help them."

With a jolt, I recognized the warning signs of his transformation: shifting eye color; pale, sweaty face.

"Ren—"

He leapt over the stage and sprinted toward the nián. Each of his arrows met its mark in the nián's body, but the demon merely swatted at them like they were splinters.

"Ren!" I screamed. His figure was tiny compared to the hulking beast.

Please, master. The rumbling voice of Ren's dragon entered my head. *Let me transform and defeat this demon.*

I bit my lip. It was true that unless he turned into a dragon—sacrificing part of his humanity—Ren didn't stand a chance. No warrior did. This powerful version of the nián wasn't one that the warriors were equipped to handle.

But the fear of loss wouldn't leave me. My mother, father, grandfather—I'd already lost so many loved ones. I couldn't lose more of Ren, too.

"What're you standing around for?" Moli demanded,

wiping at a cut on her cheek. Her ruined sleeve came away wet and red with blood, but she was too busy glaring at me to notice. "You're the Heaven Breaker, aren't you? I *know* you can stop them."

She grabbed my hand and yanked me in the direction where Ren had disappeared into the crowd, and Alex was pushing past deities to try to reach our friend.

Shoving through the crowd and raising Fenghuang into the air, I channeled my thoughts into the spear that had slain so many beasts already.

Please take on your dragon form to help us, Ren.

Ren drew closer to the beast. The spear shook uncontrollably in my hand, searing white-hot.

Ren was only feet away from the nián, which had turned its great gold-and-red head toward him, its mouth parted to reveal razor-sharp teeth. Ren's form bubbled. His limbs shot upward.

Alex stumbled out of the crowd, and the nián's yellow eyes snapped onto him. With a shriek, Moli let go of my arm and rushed over to aid my brother.

I brought the spear in front of me and prepared to lunge forward. But an unseen force slammed into me. I stumbled back into a bunch of deities.

No, Heaven Breaker. The familiar voice of the female deity again. *You are to wait.*

"What?" I spluttered, so stunned that my spear nearly

slipped out of my hand. The screaming deities pushed me away, farther from Ren. He was now a fully fledged green dragon, facing down the still-bigger nián with Moli and my brother by his side. My heart pounded wildly. "*Wait?* The Red Prince might be gone, but there's another demon destroying Heaven!"

I've changed my mind. I command you to wait. Let the nián teach these pitiful deities a lesson. How dare they throw a concert, accidentally let in demons, and make a mockery of the Lantern Festival banquet.

A realization hit me like a blow to my gut. Every time I'd prayed to the gods using Fenghuang's power, that low voice had entered my head. And at last, I could pinpoint why it sounded so familiar.

I pictured the regal woman who sat next to Jade Emperor. Xi Wangmu, Queen Mother of the West.

She had been controlling me all along.

CHAPTER

25

The goddess's power seeped into me, turning my blood into liquid fire. My vision sharpened. Details popped out at me. I could see the fissures form in the wall as it cracked, leaving the entire side of the raised auditorium exposed. The wall fell and crashed into the Atlantic Ocean, hundreds of feet below.

Ren, Moli, and Alex beat back the nián, dodging each swipe of its massive claws. But I was useless. Rooted to the spot by an invisible power.

Wait, Heaven Breaker. Let those who mocked our great tradition suffer awhile for their sins.

I tried reaching out to Ren with my thoughts, but his head was filled with incoherent fragments of rage. A small part of my brain screamed at me to *move move move*, but the compulsion to obey Xi Wangmu won out.

Do as I say, and you will be rewarded with the highest of

honors. Your heritage will make you unstoppable. The greatest general there ever was.

Fenghuang grew unbearably hot beneath my palms. My blood sang. My vision zoomed in on a crate of Cindy You fire-crackers pushed off to the side. On the colorful scales of the nián. On the sweat that beaded down my brother's forehead and the droplets of blood that oozed out of the scratches on Moli's cheek.

If I obeyed Xi Wangmu—stood here and did nothing, let-ting the nián attack the minor deities—would that make me brave? A strong warrior, worthy of my father's memory, wor-thy of the gods?

Or would it make me a coward?

Use Fenghuang, but do not let it control you, my grandfa-ther had insisted in my dream.

The spear had helped me slay many demons. I couldn't bear to part with its power. I couldn't let it control me.

Rage, warrior. Xi Wangmu again. *You will break this world for me. You will break the Earth—and bring on a golden age of the gods.*

The nián swiped its paw and sent Ren skidding across the floor. Moli and Alex lunged forward and dodged as the beast's fangs missed them by a hair. Deities continued streaming out of the ruined auditorium, leaving only the bravest ten or so behind.

Mao's sneer swam in my mind. The daughter of a traitor, she'd always called me. Strange.

Xi Wangmu had praised me. Strong. Powerful.

But I didn't feel like any of those things, either. I was just . . . me. Faryn Liu. A girl who wanted to be the warrior her father once was.

Why couldn't anyone else understand that?

My grandfather's younger face swam in my vision. Now, more than ever, I needed his help. I needed to pray. I didn't know if he'd hear, I didn't know if he'd be able to escape or help, but I had to try. I took a deep breath, closing my eyes and clasping my hands in front of me. *Please come to Peng Lai Island, Ye Ye. We need you.*

When I opened my eyes again, I threw Fenghuang with all my might, through the hole in the ruined wall, into the seas far below. Xi Wangmu's voice disappeared, as though I'd turned a volume dial. Gone, too, was the heat of the power that had crackled through my nerves only moments before.

The gods' will had abandoned me. I'd never become the Jade Emperor's general now. Yet I'd never felt more powerful, self-assured. In control.

A loud whooping noise sounded from above me, followed by a bird's screech. I looked up—and dove out of the way before a huge, brilliantly red phoenix nearly took my head off.

"You called, sūn nǚ er?" A blast of wind blew against the back of my head as the phoenix landed. I turned around and found myself facing—

"Ba!" Alex cried from somewhere behind me.

My brother shoved me out of the way and knelt in front of the figure before us: a broad-shouldered, handsome twenty-something man with black hair pulled back into a short ponytail. He wore a long-sleeved white shirt that was tucked into brown pants. His intelligent black eyes were so familiar.

"That's not our father," I whispered. "That's . . . Ye Ye."

"Huh?" Alex's jaw dropped. "No way. This guy is, like . . . young. And cool."

Ye Ye shouted and pointed behind us.

The nián beat back a row of deities with its claws and picked up speed, charging toward Ren and Moli. Even in his dragon form, Ren looked small next to the monstrous creature.

"Ah Li. Falun." Hearing those familiar names, the ones only my grandfather called us, made tears prickle in the corner of my eyes. Ye Ye's eyes were solemn—and, I was surprised to see, watery and red. My grandfather *never* shed tears. It went against his Wise Mentor image.

"Ye Ye," I cried, "everything is a mess. San Francisco is in trouble, along with a bunch of other Chinatowns, and now this—"

"San Francisco is holding up well. Don't worry," Ye Ye reassured me. "Wang and the other warriors have been taking their duties seriously, protecting the people of San Francisco. But I don't have much time. Wenshu will know I've escaped from his study soon. Before then, we must kill this beast lest it destroys the minor deities."

"Ye Ye—" Alex said in a choked voice.

"How are you here?" I spluttered.

"Wenshu's security was lax today, since he came to attend the banquet. I might have, ah, given the guards a slip." A mischievous light glinted in Ye Ye's eye. "Falun, Ah Li, don't look so pathetic. You're warriors. Now, tell me—what does the nián fear most?"

Though I was feeling dizzy with the adrenaline of the fight and revelation of Ye Ye standing right *here*, I could still recall the answer with perfect clarity. If there was anything the Jade Society warriors knew about the beast that emerged in the Lunar New Year, it was this: the nián feared one thing, and one thing only.

I knew what I had to do.

I dashed over to the crate of firecrackers with Cindy You's face on them, Ye Ye and Alex on my heels. Lighting a red firecracker, I flung it at the nián. It exploded on the demon, showering it with sparks. It roared and swiped away the debris. My brother pitched a second firecracker at the nián.

"Throw the firecrackers!" I yelled at the motionless deities. I overturned the crate and dumped the red-and-gold objects onto the ground. Ye Ye lit up firecrackers as easily as if his hands were made of fire themselves, sending the crackling objects soaring into the nián's face.

Even if they were useless with swords, the deities seemed to be good at setting off firecrackers. They snatched up the fallen red-and-gold objects and chucked them at the nián.

Moli rushed toward me as though prepared to grab fire-crackers, too, but I held out my hand to stop her.

"I'll take care of the firecrackers. You finish the job," I told her. And then, with a grin, I added, "Warrior."

A silent understanding passed between us. Then, she returned my smile with a wild, animalistic scream. Turning around, Moli leapt forward at the moment the nián covered its eyes with its paws. She arced her sword blade through the air, slicing off part of the demon's writhing tail. There was no fear or hesitation in Moli's movements. Only the determination of a warrior.

Pride swelled in me.

"Like I'm gonna let you have all the fun yourself!" Alex called, racing across the floor and joining Moli and Ren in their attack.

Weaponless, I hung back, tossing firecracker after fire-cracker at the beast. The nián hissed and roared, batting away firecrackers and covering its eyes. The flying objects kept coming. Ye Ye's phoenix soared through the air, screeching and clawing at the beast's face, adding fury to the fire.

"I was worried about you when you couldn't come right after I used the prayer note," I shouted at my grandfather. Side by side, we scooped up the remaining firecrackers and chucked them at the nián. By now, the demon was a writhing mass of burning gold and red scales. "What happened? Are you safe?"

"Wenshu passed a new rule. His disciples are no longer

allowed to communicate with mortals—or leave the study."
Ye Ye grimaced, wiping sweat and ash off his brow. "But I had
to warn you, sūn nǚ er."

I had a whole list of questions I needed to ask my grandfather, but there wasn't time. We'd run out of firecrackers,
and the nián looked very much un-slain. My eyes searched
the floor for a weapon, anything I could use to fight.

"Use this," said Ye Ye.

I found myself holding a short, double-edged silver
sword, smaller than both Alex's and Moli's. A far cry from
Fenghuang.

Ye Ye laid a hand on my shoulder. "A true warrior needs
no special weapon, Falun. It is the warrior that makes the
weapon, and not the other way around. Your strongest weapons lie here"—he pressed a hand to my forehead—"and here."
He patted my chest, right above my heart.

My fingers clenched around the sword hilt. Ye Ye was
right. I didn't need a powerful weapon like Fenghuang to fight
well, especially not if it came with the bossy voice of the Queen
Mother of the West.

The skills Ye Ye had taught me made me a true warrior.

The lines on my grandfather's face tightened. He brought
two fingers to his lips and whistled. The red phoenix flew
away from the demon and toward Ye Ye. "And now, sūn nǚ er,
mount your dragon. We end the nián once and for all!" He
climbed onto the red phoenix.

"Ren," I shouted.

Master. I had no idea how I heard him—I'd thrown away Fenghuang, the weapon that was supposed to give me the power to command the dragons. Yet it was his voice, his scaly green head, his black eyes that glued onto mine. The dragon flew away from the nián and toward me, and I leapt onto his back.

Side by side, Ye Ye and I soared high above the chaos, the nián's yellow eyes tracking our every movement.

"I'll distract it," Ye Ye shouted. "You take it out."

Before I could respond, the phoenix plunged downward, taking my grandfather with it. The nián snarled and swatted at the phoenix, but the huge bird was too quick. It zigzagged to avoid the claws and got in a good peck at the nián's neck with its beak.

Leaning closer to Ren's ear, I urged, "Now!"

Ren dove.

The wind whistled past my face. I grasped the sword tightly and prepared for my only chance to deal a fatal blow. This time, I knew I wouldn't feel the protective might of the gods.

Yet power surged into me nonetheless, accompanied by the voices and images of the warriors shouting around me.

My attack was fueled by the warmth of Ye Ye's guidance. The strength of Ba's knowledge. The courage of Moli's defiance. The steeliness of Ren's self-acceptance. The weight of

Wang's and Luhao's dreams. The unwavering belief of my brother, who screamed, in that split second before I attacked— "End it, jiě jie!"

As the demons grow more powerful, so do the gods—and warriors.

At last, surrounded by the red-and-gold debris of the fire-crackers and waves of golden energy that emanated from the warriors and into me, I knew what Ye Ye had meant. The gods didn't give me ultimate strength.

My friends and family did.

The combined force of my comrades' will allowed me to slash downward with pinpoint accuracy. The momentum of Ren's descent, combined with the sharpness of the blade, severed the nián's head from its body in one slice.

Ren soared over to the phoenix. I couldn't keep a grin off my face. Ye Ye nodded and gave me a look full of pride.

The remaining deities shrieked and scattered as the giant, fanged head bounced on the floor. The demon's body collapsed with a *thud* that shook the ruined auditorium. Then it disappeared into a wisp of smoke.

"Piece of cake," Alex panted. He looked down on the rubble of burned firecrackers and seared cloth, the only signs that the powerful beast had rampaged only moments ago.

Moli swatted him on the head. Then she kissed him on the cheek. Alex's face turned fire-engine red.

Cue barf alert. I turned my eyes away as Ren lowered me

to the ground. Shakily, I climbed off his back. My heart was pounding and I felt light-headed, but a realization filled me with elation.

On the last day of the Lunar New Year, I'd killed the nián at the height of its power. Without the help of the gods. With only my friends—and family.

Ren shifted back into his human form. I turned to him, ready to throw my arms around him and give him the most enthusiastic hug of his life.

A voice boomed above the ruined concert hall, the low tenor of it causing the walls and floor to tremble and startling Alex and Moli away from each other.

"Liu Jian," the unseen man rumbled. "I know you're here on the island somewhere. You dare disobey me and leave the study, disciple?"

My grandfather froze, still hovering in the air on his phoenix. It was strange, seeing the fear that washed over his face, turning his eyes wide and alert. In my memory, Ye Ye had never been afraid of anything.

But this wasn't the Ye Ye I'd known, I told myself. Not exactly. Ye Ye was a deity now, a disciple of Wenshu.

Turning his sad eyes to us, my grandfather urged his phoenix up higher.

"Ye Ye?" Alex called with desperation.

I couldn't be losing my grandfather. Not again—not when I'd finally gotten the chance to see him.

There was something caught in my throat. Something burning in my eyes. "No, please—"

"Ye Ye, I'm your grandson . . . right?" asked Alex.

"Alex!" I spluttered.

Ye Ye jerked, slowly turning around to face Alex. "What kind of silly question is that? Of course you are."

"Your blood-born grandson. Am I your blood-born grandson?"

I waited for Ye Ye to confirm Alex's question again. To erase the doubt, the fear in Alex's expression. What I didn't expect was for tears to build up in my grandfather's eyes. The young confidence seeped out of him. His shoulders slackened. He looked like a tired old man again.

"I have watched over you since you were a one-year-old infant. In my heart, you are my own flesh and blood, sūn zi."

The breath deserted my lungs.

"In your . . . heart?" Alex swallowed. "So it's true. We aren't related."

"It's a long story to explain, Ah Li. I'm afraid we don't have time." My grandfather fixed Alex with a pained look. "All you need to know for now is that you are my grandson, and I'm proud of you—both of you. I will sneak you a prayer note when I can. Now, I must return!"

Ye Ye's phoenix soared upward through the hole in the ruined roof.

I looked back at Alex. His heartbroken expression reflected ten times the sensation of crushing loss that I felt. "Alex—"

My brother shook his head, stumbling away from me. "No. No. It can't be."

"Alex—"

"I was right," Alex muttered, distraught. "I knew it."

I moved forward to comfort him, but he pushed my hand away. "Alex, listen, it doesn't matter if we're not related by blood."

"Of course it does!" said Alex. "You don't understand."

Moli stepped between us. "Faryn's right, you know. You're family, and family sticks together. You wouldn't have survived without each other! Don't you get how special your sibling bond is? I would've done anything to have someone like—"

Something cracked above my head.

"Faryn, look out!"

A force slammed into me, causing me to sprawl across the floor. I heard a sickening *crash* behind me. Gasps from the deities.

My brother's inhuman-sounding scream of pure anguish. "No, Moli!"

Through a haze of pain and confusion, I peeled my body off the ground and turned my head.

I struggled to process what was going on. Ren had run after Alex, who was pawing through a mess of broken glass and shattered wood that lay where I'd stood moments ago.

The deities spoke in hushed voices, backing away from my brother. His hands closed around a body.

Moli. Bloody and battered. Unmoving. Surrounded by shards of glass, the remains of a huge lighting rig that had slammed into the ground.

My vision swam. I didn't understand. I wanted to retch.

The sounds of horses whinnying diverted everyone's attention. The golden chariot, pulled by our trusty four horses, soared overhead, and landed next to Moli. The horses must have felt their mistress's distress.

One nudged her with his muzzle. Moli didn't move.

My chest tightened. A nearby deity shook my shoulder. "We owe you warriors a great debt," he told me, inclining his head. "But first, you need to leave. The Jade Emperor is on his way. And he isn't happy."

As if confirming the deity's words, thunder boomed above us.

"Leigong," a young female deity near me said as fearful whispers rustled through the crowd. "The god of thunder is furious. It's beginning."

I wobbled to my feet. My chest and head felt hollow. Ren tugged at my hand, pulling me into the chariot. He and Alex picked up Moli's body and heaved it onto the bench in front of me with what must have been inhuman strength.

"Moli," my brother kept repeating. "Moli. Moli."

The horses flew upward. Yet even the cool night air

whipping against my face couldn't shake the emptiness from my insides.

I was certain that Zhao Moli had just saved my life—by sacrificing her own.

CHAPTER

26

The horses soared above the lanterns and remnants of the concert hall. The minor deities scattered into the streets. The pí xiū that had been carrying the prayer notes stormed around the city, thrashing and plowing down everything in sight. Cindy You's billboard had toppled over onto the ground, taking with it many red paper lanterns and decorations that had hung on buildings.

A short way away, the eight immortals' palace was in an uproar, the banquet table upturned. Flashes of light from magic and shiny weaponry showed me that the dragons and deities were still fighting. I couldn't tell if the gods were battling the dragons or each other.

"Demons at the Lantern Festival," Ren said, his body quivering. "That's gotta be a first."

Alex clung on to Moli's nearly motionless body. Tears streamed clear tracks down his soot-covered face.

"Wake up," he pleaded, over and over again.

My brain wouldn't process the image. On top of Ye Ye revealing the truth to Alex and then being forced to leave, Moli couldn't be dying. It wasn't fair.

The horses had only enough energy to drop us beyond the wall, on the beach. I disembarked and keeled over into the sand.

Alex lay Moli's body on the ground, fingers fumbling for her wrist.

Moli's breaths were ragged. Thick streams of red liquid ran down her lips. I scrambled closer. Just moments before, she'd been helping us take down the nián. The picture of a true, fearless warrior.

How could Moli, one of the most strong-willed girls, whom I'd known for my entire life, look so weak and helpless now?

"Moli, y-you have to fight this," I said. "I promised to teach you how to fight well, and you still kind of suck at it. You can't leave us yet."

Moli let out a laugh, though it quickly dissolved into choking noises. "Sorry I . . . wasn't a better . . . student. But thank you . . . for being such a . . . good teacher."

There were so many words I wanted to say to my former best friend—words that had hung unsaid between us for years—that in my panic, I couldn't figure out where to begin. *I hate you. I'm sorry. Thank you for saving me.*

Those last words finally bubbled out of my mouth, as the tears escaped my eyes. "Thank you," I whispered, and Moli nodded.

"No no no," Alex kept muttering, tears splashing down onto Moli's rapidly heaving chest. He cradled her head and clutched her hand to his cheek. "You can fight this. I know you can."

A light tap on my shoulder and the scent of pine told me Ren was by my side. His eyes filled, and he squeezed my hand.

When Moli spoke, her voice was so weak we had to strain to hear her. "I . . . can't . . . die yet. Not on . . . the Lunar New Year . . ."

The last of the fireworks exploded above. The light flickered and faded, and then the only sounds I could hear were muffled shouts behind the wall.

"I'm so sorry, Bà ba. I left on . . . the Lunar New Year, and . . . I can't go back." Moli gasped, a tear streaking down her cheek and landing in the long, black hair that fanned out beneath her. "I couldn't . . . protect you."

"Your father is safe, Moli," I said softly. "The warriors are protecting San Francisco well."

Even though I knew she'd heard me, Moli's expression didn't change. She didn't seem to be speaking to us but rather to the kindhearted father she'd left behind. "I'm sorry I . . . I never . . . honored our family."

"You did honor them," Alex said fiercely. "You're the most kick-butt charioteer who ever lived. There's no *w-way* your father wouldn't—wouldn't be proud. Tell her, Faryn."

I managed to get the words out beneath the force that was cleaving my chest in two.

Moli coughed. "The Society . . . doesn't deserve you . . . either . . . warriors." She reached out a trembling hand and clung to my robe, telling me what she had to say was life-or-death important. "Faryn . . . Alex . . . all those horrible things . . . when I was younger . . . I'm . . . sorry . . ."

I squeezed her hand, letting her know I accepted the apology.

"Forget all that. It's in the past," Alex said. "Just live. *Live.*"

Moli's bloody lips pulled together into a small, ironic smile. She cupped my brother's tearstained cheek. "*You live, brave warrior . . . both of you . . . prove them all . . . wrong . . .*"

Her voice drifted off, and her body stilled. Her hand fell limply to her side.

"Moli?" Alex's fingers scrabbled at the back of her hand. "No. No, no, no. Not like this."

Moli's blurry body swam before my vision, until I saw only the young girl who'd ridden horses with me in the courtyard.

Beside me, Ren hung his head. His face was covered in ash, as was his hair, which now looked gray. His hand squeezed mine.

"She—Moli will be fine," I blurted out. "She sacrificed herself to save me. The gods will look favorably upon that, and they might deify her, like they did Ye Ye. M-Moli might even be able to visit you in your dreams."

Confusion flickered in his dull eyes. "Dreams?"

"Yeah. Like how Ye Ye visited mine."

My brother's breath hitched. "Huh? What are you talking about? This is the first time we've heard from Ye Ye since . . ."

A realization slammed into me. In all the chaos since D.C., I'd forgotten to tell my brother about my dream. "When I used my prayer note, Ye Ye visited me in a dream. He told me how to defeat the Red Prince back in D.C., and . . . Alex?"

"You were getting messages from Ye Ye," he said quietly, "and you didn't tell me?"

"I'm sorry. I only got one, and I didn't mean to hide it from you. It—slipped my mind—"

"Oh, right. Slipped your mind. Like telling me about you slaying the nián back in San Francisco slipped your mind? I thought there were no secrets between us, but ever since you became a fancy warrior, you've changed."

I opened my mouth to protest, but Ren interrupted me. "That's not what your sister's saying. You're twisting her words. You're not thinking straight." He sighed, dropping his eyes to Moli's still body and looking away, his chin trembling. "None of us are thinking straight."

"You've always been the cool one," Alex accused. "Mastering martial arts. Slaying demons. You're everything Ba and Ye Ye—and even the Jade Society—always wanted, a warrior for the gods. I'm just the geeky loser who reads a lot."

"That's not true," I insisted. Alex had looked out for me this whole time—we'd looked out for each other. It was his voice, in that moment of clarity I had before defeating the nián, that had guided me to victory. "Alex—"

"Yes, it's true. That's why the gods gave you Fenghuang, and not me. That's why Ye Ye visited your dreams, and not mine. What a joke. Now I understand why you're so much more skilled in combat than I am. It's because we aren't even related."

"That doesn't have anything to do with—"

"We don't look like the other warriors, but we don't look like each other, either." His eyes lit up with wild accusation. "That's why the people at the Jade Society always picked on me more than they picked on you. You must've known this whole time we weren't related. You've been laughing at me. Haven't you?"

"What are you saying? Of course I didn't know, and I was never laughing at you."

He let out a short, bitter laugh. "Tell me the truth, Faryn. *In your heart*, was I ever your family?"

My brother might as well have twisted a knife into my heart and yanked the whole thing out. "Alex, y-you've always been my family." The tears tumbled out of my eyes, thick and heavy and fast—the opposite of my words, which came out slow and choked. "You're my brother. M-my dì di. We've been through everything together. Bullying. Ye Ye's training. Ba's disappearance. You aren't just part of my family. You're my *only* family. Just because we aren't related by blood doesn't change anything."

"You're right. It doesn't change anything. It changes everything."

With shaking hands, Alex pulled something out of his pocket. Ba's notebook. He turned around and chucked it into the waves of the ocean, which lapped it up hungrily. The black leather-bound notebook filled with my father's research, the clues to his whereabouts, was . . . gone.

My heart nearly stopped. "Wh-what have you done, Alex? How are we going to find Ba?"

Alex's eyes still streamed tears. But they were cold. Dead. "None of that stuff matters to me anymore. Don't you get it? I have no relationship with Liu Bo. I don't care about finding him. No wonder he abandoned me. I'm not his son."

He spat out the words with vehemence. So strongly that I almost believed him.

I picked myself up and sprinted unsteadily toward the waves. Ren got up with me, as though reading my mind. Ba's notebook couldn't have sunk too far. I could save it. I had to.

Something flew down from above and landed between Alex and me, kicking up sand and forcing me to back away. It was the red dragon—with Guanyin on its back. The white dragon touched down right behind the red one, and Nezha slid off its scaly back. Erlang Shen arrived on a black dragon, with his red dog, Xiao Tian Quan, right behind him.

I thought of Nezha's "stomachache" at the Lantern Festival banquet. Had he planned to duck out all along, rescue Alex and me from the banquet, and start a fight among the gods?

"Some rescue you planned, Nezha," Erlang Shen grumbled.

"It'll be easy," he said, putting on a high-pitched voice that sounded nothing like Nezha's. "'We'll grab the mortals and split. We definitely won't set anything on fire.' Weren't those your exact words? And now look." The warrior god thrust his spear in the direction of the city beyond the walls, where smoke rose high into the clouds. "We should've skipped this whole banquet to begin with."

"The point of attending the banquet was to make sure these kids ate the peaches of immortality," Nezha said defensively. "How was I supposed to know that demons were going to sneak onto the island?"

Peaches of immortality? Uh-oh.

"We didn't eat those peaches," I blurted out.

"Clearly," Nezha grumbled.

"That Chuangmu," Guanyin added darkly. "Bargaining with demons now after falling out with Xi Wangmu. Some of the minor deities will stop at nothing for power, especially as the humans slowly forget them."

The way she was speaking, it sounded like these deities were aiming to rebel against the Jade Emperor. But before I could ask what exactly their plan was, Nezha let out a gasp. "Oh."

His eyes had landed on Moli. Guanyin's hands pressed to her lips.

Erlang Shen pointed his spear at Moli. "What's happened?"

He must have found the answer in our eyes, because he didn't press further. At his feet, Xiao Tian Quan whimpered, and his ears drooped.

Nezha lowered his hand to Moli's wrist. Guanyin knelt down too, head bowed in respect, and waved her green staff over Moli.

"Wh-what're you doing?" my brother demanded, clasping her limp hand more tightly.

Guanyin murmured something, and Moli's body disappeared. Just like Ye Ye's had.

Alex's eyes widened. "No."

"That girl's soul will do just fine in Diyu," Guanyin reassured Alex, but my brother remained stone-faced.

We stared at the spot where Moli had lain only moments ago.

After a few minutes had passed, Erlang Shen coughed and broke the tense silence. "My uncle's reign is coming to an end. I can feel it in my bones."

"I think that's the others coming after us," Guanyin pointed out. The sand beneath our feet shook. "They must've broken past the other dragons."

"Get on your chariot, warriors," Nezha snapped. "The Jade Emperor is going to send out a search party for you four—" He caught himself, with a sad look at the empty space where Moli had been. "Three, I mean. You need to leave."

"The Jade Emperor is going to call a search party for a couple of mortals?" Ren asked in disbelief.

Nezha shook his head. "Not mortals. He's looking for his powerful weapon. The . . . Heaven Breaker."

"Powerful weapon?"

"The Jade Emperor's looking for this, right?"

My brother crouched over in the water, the waves lapping at his ankles. His hands closed around something shiny that had washed up on the shore.

Alex turned his eyes toward me. They looked empty, but his lips curled up into a smile.

My heart lurched. "But . . . I threw it away."

Only the Heaven Breaker was supposed to be able to pick up Fenghuang. But my brother lifted it as though it were featherlight and twirled it in the air. He caught it easily, as though the weapon had been made for him.

Alex was the Heaven Breaker now, not me. But how?

"Hand that over, boy," Erlang Shen said, his hand outstretched, a greedy gleam in his eye. But Nezha flung his arm in front of the warrior god's chest and shook his head firmly.

"Put that down, Alex," I pleaded. "We've got to leave. Now."

"What a shame," Alex said. "This spear deserves a better owner—one that appreciates it. Don't you, Fenghuang?" He twirled it in another circle, his eyes following its movements with wolfish pride.

I swallowed hard with a realization. Xi Wangmu's voice. Of course. The evil goddess controlled the weapon, and she'd chosen my brother to be its next master. The next Heaven Breaker and leader of the Jade Emperor's army.

"Fight it, Alex," I urged. "You're stronger than that voice. You know becoming the Jade Emperor's general is wrong. Remember Moli. She wouldn't have wanted . . ."

"We don't know what she would have wanted. Moli is dead." Pain, raw and unfiltered, flashed across Alex's face. "Moli didn't deserve to die," he whispered.

"No. And neither do any of the other people the Jade Emperor will ask you to kill for him."

Alex's grip around the spear relaxed. I was so close—*so close*—to convincing him; I could tell by the anguish that pulled his eyebrows together.

Please, deities, let my brother return to me.

But I had no powerful spear—not anymore. No prayer notes, incense sticks, or offerings. The voices of the gods had deserted me.

Alex's rage shifted into pain. "Don't you dare speak Moli's name. You're the reason she's dead."

The words slammed into me. "I'm just . . ." I swallowed hard. "I'm trying to protect you."

"I don't need a stranger's protection." He spat out the word *stranger* as though it had left a foul taste in his mouth. "I'm the new Heaven Breaker, chosen by the gods to lead Heaven's army into glory with Fenghuang."

As he spoke, his outline glowed, causing all of us to shield our eyes. When I peeked out from under my arms again, the dragons had frozen. Their huge, now-blank eyes fixed on Alex.

"H-hey, good dragons. Eyes over here," Nezha said, snapping his fingers.

Instead, the three dragons flew over to my brother and settled around him. Even with his glow, Alex appeared tiny sandwiched between the great beasts.

"What's wrong with the dragons?" Erlang Shen asked. Xiao Tian Quan barked.

I knew, with a sinking heart, what had happened. The dragons had only obeyed me, their former master, because the position of Heaven Breaker had been vacant until I picked up Fenghuang. But not anymore. Now, Alex was the Heaven Breaker, and master of the dragons.

Beside me, Ren jolted. A flash of pain passed over his face, and his body began quaking. His eyes flashed blue once more.

"No, Ren. Fight it. You're human enough to stay with me. Look at me," I insisted. If Alex took command of the dragon inside Ren and wrenched him from my side, I'd be completely, utterly alone. No Alex. No Moli. No Ren.

Ren's body stopped shuddering. He shook his white hair. His eyes cleared, reverting to their green and black colors. Had my plea worked?

Alex's golden eyes met mine across the sand. I couldn't be sure, but I thought they looked sad. He gave a small nod. And then I understood. He'd *let* Ren stay by my side.

Why? Why, after siding against me, against *humanity*, would my brother still be looking out for me?

Shouts came from behind the wall, followed by a *bang*. The guards burst through the doors of the circular entrance. Behind them came a palanquin that could only belong to the Jade Emperor. The swarm of guards pointed their spears at us and yelled.

"We need to leave—now," said Nezha.

He dove over the side of the chariot and took the reins. Took Moli's place, I realized with a jolt. The horses calmed in seconds under his control.

"Fleeing feels like cowardice," Erlang Shen grumbled, but he leapt into the chariot, along with Guanyin.

"Come, Faryn." Guanyin's kind eyes crinkled as she smiled at me. She spoke in a soothing, motherly voice that made it nearly impossible for me not to do as she asked. "You'll be safe with us."

Alex stood there, surrounded by the dragons. I extended my hand to him. The chariot lifted a few inches off the ground. The wind whipped my hair around my face until I could barely see. Alex remained where he stood, glowering, his curly hair, now golden, rising around his head, shining in the night.

"Alex, you've got to come," I shouted.

The horses climbed higher into the air at Nezha's urging. My brother shook his head. He might have been crying. I was now too far away to see, and tears blurred my vision.

"Alex!" I screamed, the wind whipping away my words. He turned his back to us and walked toward the Jade Emperor.

Golden footsteps trailed behind him in the sand. The Emperor welcomed him with a strong clap on the shoulder. Xi Wangmu waved at the guards who'd begun flying after our chariot, as if calling off their pursuit.

I tried jumping out of the chariot—but hands pulled me back. Ren's.

I slapped them away. "Don't touch m—"

"Let him go, Faryn," Ren said.

"But he's my b-brother," I choked. "I don't care if we aren't related by blood. We've done everything together. Everything. And now—now he hates me." My voice came out so small I barely heard it myself.

Ren tucked a loose strand of hair behind my ear. His eyes, when they held mine, shone with conviction. "Alex isn't saying he hates you, Faryn. He's saying he needs to find his own path."

Numb with disbelief, I sat back in the chariot as the Jade Emperor slammed the door shut, blocking Alex from view. The palanquin departed, and with it, the boy I'd called brother for eleven years. I watched until the palanquin became a speck in the night.

Then nothing.

CHAPTER

27

We rode on in silence, leaving Peng Lai Island far behind. The horses charged forward at Nezha's coaxing. Erlang Shen and Guanyin pulled up on either side of us on their clouds, with Xiao Tian Quan right on the heels of his owner.

I'd saved the minor deities, but I'd failed everything else. I'd lost Ye Ye—twice. I hadn't found Ba. I'd even lost the one person who'd always stuck by me—my brother. Numbness settled in my chest.

"You're sure the warriors have prepared suitable quarters for us, right?" Erlang Shen asked Nezha. "We better not be squatting in a pathetic hole with a bunch of sniveling humans."

"All I know is that they're expecting us," Nezha said. "They've been praying for our help for ages, anyway."

It sounded like we were on our way back to San Francisco. If there was even a San Francisco to go back *to*.

Erlang Shen sighed into his hands. His dog barked and chased its own tail in excitement among the clouds.

Ren kept staring at his picture of his mother, which was now frayed and burned around the edges. I winced in sympathy. Right after he'd found her for the first time in his life, Ren's mother—or at least, who we thought had been his mother—had turned into a demon lord and tried to burn down Peng Lai Island.

"Hey." I nudged Ren. "We'll keep looking for Cindy. The real Cindy. She's gotta be out there somewhere. Your real mom, I mean."

His lips twitched upward in the first smile of the day. "Yeah. We'll find her. She's a celebrity, after all. I just . . . I hope the Red Prince didn't do anything to her. I hope she's okay." Ren's eyes fell upon me. "Did you get to talk to Ao Guang, or . . . ?"

My heart thudded. I shook my head, staring down at my toes.

"It's okay," he reassured me. "I'm sure we'll see him again. Besides . . . I'm beginning to think that having this dragon with me isn't such a bad thing, after all."

"Really?"

"Yeah. I used to be scared of transforming, but now I'm not. Not as much as I was at first, I mean. I've begun to trust this dragon a lot more—ever since I met you."

I couldn't stop the grin from spreading across my lips, or

my heart from giving a strange little leap. "That's great to hear. But no more breaking stores, okay?"

Ren returned the smile with one of his own. "No more breaking stores."

"No more what?" Guanyin popped up before Ren and me. She took the seat in front of us—the one Alex had vacated—and pressed a warm hand over mine. "Worried about your brother, Heaven Breaker?"

I knew Xi Wangmu had been influencing my brother. Twisting his mind with her vile words. But how much control did the goddess have over him, really? How many of Alex's parting words were his own?

"I'm not the Heaven Breaker anymore," I mumbled.

"What makes you say that?"

"You saw what happened just now," I said dully. "Alex took Fenghuang. Alex took the dragons. And here I am, weaponless and dragonless. It's pretty clear who the Heaven Breaker is now."

Guanyin nodded slowly. "I won't lie. Xi Wangmu controls Fenghuang, which means she effectively chooses and controls who the Heaven Breaker is. Now she has decided your brother will take that role."

"I knew it," I groaned.

The goddess held up her hand. "It *would* seem as though you've lost your power. But you'll do well to remember this, warrior—power isn't measured only by the size of a weapon. You have at least three deities on your side, and we deities don't bother with mortals who lack potential for greatness."

Guanyin winked. She flew out of the chariot and joined Erlang Shen and Nezha in the front.

The silence stretched between Ren and me as we rode on, over oceans, cities, and greenery. Then the scenery below shifted as we approached a city located on an island populated with impossibly tall buildings and surrounded by towering bridges. I recognized a few striking landmarks from afar, like a statue holding a torch high into the air. The Statue of Liberty. I'd never been to New York, but I knew enough from the news and some American history textbooks to recognize the landmark.

As we edged closer to the ground, Nezha slowed the horses. We'd come to another ruined Chinatown. Red paper lanterns had been strung, though halfheartedly, on the few buildings that hadn't been seriously damaged. The streets were filled with rubble, and cars were upturned and parked haphazardly in the middle of the road. Smoke and an air of gloom hung over the city.

The gods were silent as they took in the scene. I couldn't speak, either.

"Is this Manhattan's Chinatown?" I asked.

"It was," Nezha said grimly.

More like Manhattan's ghost town. There was almost nobody out on the streets.

"What is this, Nezha?" Erlang Shen narrowed his eyes at the boy god, betrayal written across his face. "You promised me the mortals would be falling over themselves to welcome

327

us. And instead you take me to this—this—this barren wasteland?"

"I promised you a place where mortals would send you all the prayers you could ever want, you power-hungry fool," Nezha snapped. "This is it. If you don't like it, you can go back to being your uncle's puppet. The Jade Emperor's plan will guarantee the destruction of humans—and of us. But go on."

Erlang Shen must've hated that idea, because the warrior god fell silent. His stiff shoulders told me he wanted nothing better than to pummel Nezha, though.

Guanyin shook her head. "You'd better straighten out your attitudes before we meet the New Order warriors."

"New Order warriors? Have you heard of them?" Ren whispered to me.

I shook my head. Moli's death and Alex's betrayal weighed on my shoulders like a mountain. "Why are we here? Why did you save us back there at the Lantern Festival banquet?"

Erlang Shen rolled his three eyes. "Haven't you mortals caught on already? We saved you two because we—the little boy, the goddess of mercy, and I—are raising a rebellion against my senile uncle the Jade Emperor, before he plunges us into a war unparalleled by any before."

Ren let out a breath, the air whistling past his teeth. "Let me guess. You want us to join your cause."

Erlang Shen's grin stretched across his face as the chariot dipped. "That's right. As much as I hate to admit it, mortals, if we deities are to save the world from the Jade Emperor's stupidity, we're going to have to team up with your kind, along with the forgotten deities. And we're going to need the help of the Heaven Breaker."

I sighed. "I already told Guanyin. I'm not the Heaven Breaker anymore."

Before the warrior god could respond, we landed on the rocky ground with a jolt. "Ow! Are you sure you have your charioteer's license, Nezha?" Erlang Shen growled.

"I've had mine longer than you've had yours!"

As the deities bickered, Erlang Shen's words ran through my head.

An uprising. A rebellion. A war on Heaven. It sounded dangerous, like something Ye Ye would never approve of, that Liu Bo would run toward. It sounded like certain death. But it also sounded like stopping the Jade Emperor and Xi Wangmu from destroying humanity. And it sounded like a chance to prove to Alex that he was truly my brother and belonged at my side.

"I'm in," I said.

"You are?" Ren echoed.

"Yeah. And you are, too."

"I am?"

"Let's kick some Jade Emperor butt."

Erlang Shen's grin widened. He rubbed his hands together. But a voice interrupted him before he could speak.

"It's the deities!"

We all turned around to see a shabby-looking man come

out of a nearby rundown temple. He wore a tattered long-sleeved white shirt and long, black pants. Other men and women peeked out nervously from behind him, streaming out of the temple.

I was stunned. They were warriors, but not the homogeneous Chinese warriors I was so accustomed to seeing. This was a diverse group of people who hailed from all walks of life. Men and women with complexions ranging from pale white to dark brown. Girls carrying swords and other weapons alongside the boys.

Xiao Tian Quan barked. He leapt from Erlang Shen's side and landed on the ground, his tail wagging. The people in the crowd began whispering. But for the moment, I had eyes only for the man who stood in front of the New Order warriors.

He looked different from the last time I'd seen him. Different from the only picture I had, too. His hair was longer and whiter, tied back into a short ponytail. His beard had grown out, and there were far more wrinkles and cuts on his face than there had been in his portrait.

On the first day of the Lunar New Year, the gods took my grandfather from me. On the last day, they took my grandfather a second time—along with my brother.

But in doing so, they'd returned someone else.

"Ba," I whispered.

DEMONS AND DEITIES THROUGH THE DYNASTIES

A Glossary

Hello! Author here. I want to preface this glossary by saying that I drew the below definitions and interpretations of Chinese mythology from my own research and experience, including the stories I learned growing up. Primarily, I drew from the classical Chinese text *Journey to the West* by Wu Cheng'en and the guidebook *Chinese Mythology A to Z* by Jeremy Roberts. There are other versions of Chinese folklore out there, so this is not by any means a comprehensive guide. But I do hope it will teach you a little bit about the mythology that appears in *The Dragon Warrior*—and make you want to learn more!

DEITIES

Chuangmu: Chuangmu is the goddess of love, sleep, and those who love sleeping. Many pray to her for a good night's rest. And she's sure to grant plenty of rest to those who ask—as long as you don't annoy her.

Dragon Kings: The Chinese believe in five Dragon Kings, four who rule over the seas and one who commands them all: the Dragon King of the North Sea, the Dragon King of the South Sea, the Dragon King of the East Sea, the Dragon King of the West Sea, and the Dragon King of the Center. Hmm . . . I'm seeing a pattern in their names. These beings live in crystal palaces beneath the water. The Dragon Kings don't just own pearls and jewels, they *eat* them. Sounds like an expensive grocery list. They're powerful enough that they watch over the seas, move mountains, and create massive tidal waves. Plus, every year the Jade Emperor relies on them for reports about the seas.

Erlang Shen: Erlang Shen's official title is "True Lord, the Great Illustrious Sage," which is pretty apt since he's an epic warrior. He's the god of war and waterways. He's also the nephew of the Jade Emperor. Erlang Shen has a third, truth-seeing eye in the middle of his forehead that can sense if a man is honest or not. The eye also gives him X-ray vision, not to mention a surefire way to mess with humans and demons alike. In many stories, his loyal dog, Xiao Tian Quan, never leaves his side. Don't mistake Erlang Shen for a dog-loving softie, though. Those two combined have and will really mess things up in Heaven. Xiao Tian Quan may be small, but he's fierce and powerful, and he helps Erlang Shen subdue evil spirits.

Guanyin: Guanyin is commonly worshipped as the goddess of mercy. In some traditions, she's considered male, but in others, she's considered female to better represent the qualities of mercy, compassion, and purity; traits customarily thought of as feminine. Many pray to this goddess in the hopes that she will relieve suffering or provide help to others.

Jade Emperor: If you thought the Jade Emperor seemed intense at the Lunar New Year banquet, wait until you hear more about him. His full official title is "Peace Absolving, Central August Spirit Exalted, Ancient Buddha, Most Pious and Honorable, His Highness the Jade Emperor, Xuanling High Sovereign." The fancy title isn't just for show. He rules all of Heaven, Diyu, and Earth.

Becoming the Jade Emperor was no easy task, though. Once just an ordinary immortal, he hid in a mountain as he passed more than three thousand trials, each lasting three million years. There he cultivated his Tao—the Way, or the process of things coming together while transforming. Wild, right?

The Jade Emperor finally emerged strong enough to defeat the mega-powerful demon that had been wreaking havoc on Earth. Everyone was in awe of the Jade Emperor, mostly because his beard had grown super long while he was busy passing all those trials. Anyway, after he got rid of the demon, the deities named him their supreme ruler.

Nezha: Some of Nezha's many titles include "Third Lotus Prince," "Third Prince Lord," "Marshal of the Central Altar," and "Marshal Zhong Tan."

Basically, the story of Nezha goes like this: Nezha's mother was pregnant with him for three and a half years, which was understandably concerning. One day, she finally gave birth—not to an adorable Chinese baby, but to a lotus (or in some versions of the tale, a ball). So Nezha's father, Li Jing, like any good, gentle parent, whipped out a sword and sliced the lotus wide open to reveal a boy wearing a flaming bracelet on his right wrist. Totally normal birthing process in ancient China. A priest stopped by the family's house and told the parents to name the boy Nezha.

When he grew up, Nezha used two weapons: his spear and cosmic rings. They were so gobsmackingly powerful that when he swam in the sea with them, they shook the Dragon Palace of the East Sea. The Dragon King of the East Sea didn't like that, so he sent a messenger to wrestle the weapons away from Nezha. Well, Nezha didn't like *that*. He retaliated with one blow of his rings and defeated the messenger. The Dragon King liked that even less, and he sent his third son, Ao Bing, to teach Nezha a lesson. Once again, Nezha struck with his cosmic rings, and Ao Bing shrunk from a vicious dragon into a puny human. They had a giant battle, and eventually Ao Bing lost, because Nezha's just that epic. From then, Nezha was revered/feared as one of the strongest warriors in the land. So I guess the moral of the story is, really long pregnancies can give babies dragon-defeating powers.

Wenshu: Wenshu is known as the god of wisdom, and he speaks with a boom-y, echo-y, holier-than-thou voice. Don't think he's all brains and no brawn, though. Wenshu rides a big, fierce green lion and carries a double-edged flaming sword in his right hand that symbolizes wisdom's sharpness. In his other hand he holds a blue lotus flower that contains the Perfection of Wisdom Sutra, which he can also use to defeat enemies by reading from it and boring them to death.

Xi Wangmu/Queen Mother of the West: Xi Wangmu is the wife of the Jade Emperor. She is associated with the phoenix, the complement to the Jade Emperor's symbol of the dragon. Many stories depict Xi Wangmu as the guardian of the immortal peaches, which is no easy task, because everyone and their grandmother always tries to steal them. Sick of chasing thieves away for eons, Xi Wangmu was bound to grow cranky and kind of evil. Who can blame her?

Yulong: Yulong is the third son of the Dragon King of the West. After he accidentally destroyed his father's great pearl, Yulong was sentenced to death. However, Guanyin, goddess of mercy, took pity on Yulong and saved him from execution—but under one condition. Yulong had to become a horse and accompany a monk on a dangerous journey west to obtain some Buddhist holy scriptures. After helping him complete the mission, Yulong was deified.

DEMONS AND CREATURES

Dragon: Since ancient times in China, many Chinese have believed that they are "龙的传人" (lóng de chuán rén), which translates to "Descendants of the Dragon." According to this belief, the Chinese evolved from dragons. Pretty cool origin story, right? A dragon is thought to be a symbol of luck and wealth and is often associated with jade. They are also portrayed as powerful and mighty, which explains why thunder and lightning accompany them when they fly. Dragons can do pretty much anything: swim, fly, guard the gods and their treasure, make it rain (literally and figuratively), become a convenient form of transportation . . . you name it, they've got you covered.

Fenghuang/phoenix: Originally, the term "Fenghuang" referred to two divine birds who often appeared in Chinese mythology. "Feng" refers to the male, and "huang" refers to the female. In translations, "Feng" and "huang" became combined and known to some as a phoenix. But while Fenghuang looks like a Western phoenix, it's actually a divine bird that symbolizes peace, prosperity, virtue, fortune, the harmony of male and female, and yin and yang. It's often paired with a dragon in Chinese mythology and imagery, with Fenghuang as the female and the dragon as the male. Fenghuang is also, of course, the name of the coolest weapon around: the Heaven Breaker's spear.

Hú lì jīng: The hú lì jīng, or nine-tailed fox, is a demonic and cunning fox spirit that must consume ten human hearts every century to grow a new tail. Once the hú lì jīng grows the ninth tail, it reaches the ultimate level: gaining the ability to be . . . a human. Seems like a letdown to me. If I put that much work into growing nine tails, I'd better transform into a dragon, the Jade Emperor, or something equally spectacular!

Nián: Nián means "year." It also happens to refer to a big, fearsome demon.

The nián plays a big role in Lunar New Year celebrations. The story goes that a long, long time ago, a bunch of scary monsters dominated Earth. Those creatures included the nián. Every Lunar New Year eve, the nián would do annoying things like mess up the festivities and eat humans, which made it kind of hard for people to enjoy themselves. One Lunar New Year, when the nián was doing its mass-destruction thing in a particular village, an old man came along. He saw the panic, and he asked why everybody was running around screaming. After the villagers explained, the old man showed the nián his red underclothes. For some reason this scared the monster more than anything the humans had threatened it with, like weapons, animal patrols, and mass pollution. (I'm kidding. It was actually the color red that had scared the beast.) The villagers took the old man's lead and flashed the nián with *their* underclothes, too. The nián stopped its rampage and ran away.

Red became the lucky color of the Lunar New Year. People put red paper on their doors every Lunar New year since, and they beat red drums and set off red firecrackers to make a racket and scare off the nián. And in case you're wondering, yeah, the mysterious old man was probably a god in disguise.

Pí xiū: A pí xiū is an epic winged creature that's a mash-up of the coolest animals you can think of: it has the body of a lion and the head of a dragon. Females have two antlers, and males have one. I'm pretty sure these creatures could take over the world easily if they wanted to, but they're way more interested in eating money (yes, I said *eating*) and protecting the wealth of their masters.

Red Prince/Red Boy: Known as the "Red Boy" in *Journey to the West*, the demonic Red Prince has also been called the Boy Sage King and is the son of the Bull Demon King and Princess Fan. He cultivated his fire-controlling powers for more than three hundred years, and he reigns over the Fiery Mountains. Like most demons, he's not exactly the biggest admirer of humans.

Yāo guài: The term "yāo guài" refers to demons in general. They're usually evil animal spirits or vengeful celestial beings that practice Taoism, a philosophy developed from Laozi's teachings centered around humility and religious piety, to hone their magical powers. With this power, they do fun stuff like plot total world domination. Often, their greatest goal in demon-life is to achieve immortality and become deified into gods.

FAMILY TERMS/HONORIFICS

Ba (or bà ba): Ba means father. Related: "dad," "paternal figure."

Dì di: dì di is a respectful term for younger brothers that older sisters should use, unless those brothers are behaving badly.

Ér zi: ér zi is a term of endearment for a son. It is also a term for less-than-endearing sons.

Jiě jie: Jiě jie is a respectful term for older sisters that all little brothers should use, with no exception.

Niáng niang: Niáng niang is a term of respect for mother figures, usually those who hold high status, like empresses and goddesses (yes, even the ones with evil tendencies).

Sūn nǚ er: Sūn nǚ er means "granddaughter."

Sūn zi: Sūn zi means "grandson."

Ye Ye: Ye Ye means paternal grandfather.

OTHER TERMS

Ǎn ma ne bā mī hōng: A complicated mantra that can't really be translated into a simple saying. Many Buddhists believe that speaking these words or writing them down will grant attention, blessings, and compassion from the gods.

Diyu: The Chinese version of the underworld or afterlife, Diyu is ruled by a deity named King Yama. It's where both average Joes and bad guys go in the afterlife. So rather than being just a place of punishment, this realm is also a purgatory where souls await reincarnation into the next life. Imagine being in a waiting room for a really, really, really long time, listening to endless moaning and wailing, and eventually being greeted with scary demons wielding sharp, painful tools. Basically, it's like the dentist's office.

Firecracker: Traditionally, firecrackers are set off during the Lunar New Year. Here's the tale behind this zany little invention. Long ago, a bunch of monsters dominated a mountain. They were pretty hideous and awful, and everyone was better off with them out of sight.

One day, a wandering merchant came by, and the Mountain Monsters attacked him. The merchant fought back and managed to escape, even capturing one monster along the way. He wanted to take the creature back home and show him off as a souvenir to his family and friends. (There weren't exactly souvenir shops around in those days, so bringing back a monster was the equivalent of buying a T-shirt.)

Another passing traveler saw the merchant with his captured monster and was pretty alarmed. The traveler told the merchant that ensnaring a Mountain Monster was bad luck. Sure enough, the merchant began to feel sick. The two built a fire out of bamboo sticks so the merchant could rest. This whole time, the other Mountain Monsters had been preparing to get their friend back by ambushing these two travelers. But then the bamboo pieces crackled and made exploding noises as they caught fire. This scared the living daylights out of the Mountain Monsters, and they ran away as fast as they could. The men learned that unless they wanted to end up in more origin stories maybe they needed to stop traveling around mountains . . . Oh, and burning bamboo scares off demons and monsters. So from then on, people used firecrackers to chase away demons during the Lunar New Year.

Hóng bāo: Hóng bāo are red packets filled with money that family elders give to younger family members during the Lunar New Year. The envelopes are usually bestowed in even numbers, because even numbers are more auspicious.

Lunar New Year: The Lunar New Year, or Chinese New Year, is just about the most important (not to mention longest) celebration in Chinese and other Asian cultures. It starts on the first day of the first lunar month and continues for fifteen days. During that time, everyone wears red and eats lots of traditional food, like dumplings, Chinese cabbage, and fish. It's also important to say nice things to relatives, friends, the weird barefoot uncle who's always sleeping through family gatherings, and everyone else who will stand still long enough to listen.

Nián gāo: Nián gāo literally translates to New Year Cake, but I think of it as "the yummiest dessert of Heaven, Diyu, and Earth." Many eat this sticky cake during the Lunar New Year. People will bake nián gāo with sweet red bean paste filling, jujube paste filling, or no filling at all. You can also eat this cake for breakfast, lunch, and dinner—just don't let anyone catch you.

ACKNOWLEDGMENTS

Writing a book is a scary quest, and doing so as an #ownvoices diaspora author is both an extra privilege and an extra responsibility. Just like the dragon warrior, Faryn Liu, I couldn't have completed this quest without a group of amazing people in my corner.

First, to my incredible editor Hali Baumstein. Hali, where do I begin? You saw the heart of this story so clearly from day one, and worked endlessly to challenge me to shape it into a better book than I could've even imagined it to be. Thank you for your kindness, your wisdom, your support, and your enthusiasm for my writing. I couldn't imagine crafting my stories with anyone else!

To my superhero of an agent, Penny Moore. My life changed when you offered me representation in early February of 2018. You are not only a dream agent, but a dream maker, a sharp and wise mentor, and a true champion for your authors. Thank you for always seeing the heart of my stories so well, and for being a fierce advocate for diverse representation in kid lit. You've changed so many lives, including mine, and will change many more. I truly could not have asked for a better agent!

To the publishing team at Bloomsbury, whose overwhelming support and enthusiasm for my book has been more than I could have ever asked for: Diane Aronson, Erica Barmash, Liz Byer, Danielle Ceccolini, Phoebe Dyer, Beth Eller, Courtney Griffin, Melissa Kavonic, Erica Loberg, Cindy Loh, Donna Mark, Elizabeth Mason, Brittany Mitchell, Annette Pollert-Morgan, Sarah Shumway, Lily Yengle, and Sarah Yung. And thank you to Vivienne To for the beautiful cover art. Thank you all so, so much for believing in a story about a Chinese American girl who saves the world. It means everything to me.

To my very first Twitter writer-friend, Amélie Wen Zhao: when we met, I knew you were special, but I had no idea how special, nor how much our lives would change just shortly after we met. We've joked that we're cousins, but I truly look up to you as the older sister I never had, whose footsteps I've followed in the publishing world. Thank you for offering me so much: from your whip-smart editorial insights, to your knowledge of balancing corporate and author life—to your very own apartment! I'm inspired by your empowering and beautiful writing each and every day, and I'll fangirl over your books—and you—until the end of time. To Becca Mix, one of the kindest, funniest, and most generous people I know: thank you for making Michigan more bearable, and for being a constant light in my life. I still laugh over how on-brand it is that we became friends by fangirling over Amélie's book *Blood Heir*. Thank you for always being able to cheer me up with your jokes, for always speaking up for what is right, and for being my role model. Your compassion and empathy are truly limitless, and I admire you endlessly as an author and friend. And, you have the BEST cats! To Grace Li: I still can't get over how lyrical and exquisite your writing is, how powerful and hauntingly tragic. I'm blown away by your intelligence, your talent, your kindness, and your endless support. Who else but you could have the brains to be both a kid lit author *and* a doctor? I can't believe you've kept up with reading my super-extra amount of books, and have understood the heart of my diaspora stories so well. I don't deserve your friendship, but I'm so grateful for it every day, and I can't wait to keep reading your amazing stories, #ownvoices or otherwise, until the end of time! To the gracious and humble Molly Night: you are one of the most compassionate people I know, and it shows in your incredible work. Thank you for writing the Chinese stories I so desperately wanted to read as a child. We've both faced and fought against gatekeeping in the industry to get our #ownvoices stories out there, and encouraged each other along the way. I'm so proud of all that you've accomplished, and to call you my friend. And I don't care what anyone else says, you will always have the BEST chocolate!

To my friends, cheerleaders, and CPs, who read through countless drafts of this book and cheered me on. Aly Eatherly, your friendship, sharp editorial vision, and publishing wisdom have been invaluable to me. Francesca Grandillo, your kindness and powerful writing amaze me every day. Lyla Lee, we've had many ups and downs together—so grateful to have your friendship on this journey! Britney Shae, I can't thank you enough for your friendship and your continuous enthusiasm for my stories. Cassandra Farrin, I'm so grateful for your support, and beautiful and emotional stories, which break my heart and mend it over and over. Jamar Perry, I couldn't have made it without your friendship and without us cheering each other on through this wild publishing journey; thank you for sharing your important #ownvoices stories with me, and for always being there as a friend. June Hur, thank you for being one of my very first writer-friends—your words are pure magic, and your hair is gorgeous! Priyanka Taslim, thank you for cheering me on and letting me read your incredible, magical #ownvoices stories in turn. Elinam Agbo, your friendship and endless enthusiasm has meant so much to me—thank you for being one of my first Michigan writer-friends! Ana Franco, you're always so bright and kind—I love your writing and I couldn't have done this without you. Aneeqah Naeem, you are one of the most generous writers I know, and I'm lucky to be on this journey with you. Roselle Lim, you are one of my favorite authors, and I'm so honored to be able to call such a kind, talented, and generous author my friend. Shealea I, thank you and so many other online book bloggers for supporting Asian authors—it truly means more than we could ever say. Adam Gaylord, George Jreije, and Jessica Jade Ng, thank you for all your guidance and feedback on this book, which would not have seen shelves without your help.

To my mother and father: thank you for bringing us to this country, for forcing me to go to Chinese school against my protests, and for ensuring that I grew up with rich stories from our culture, including the classic tale *Journey to the West*, which inspired much of this story. (We had our own journey to the West, and it's been pretty successful, if I may say so myself.) I'm proud of who we are and where we come from, and I'm proud to be your daughter. To my little sisters, Jessie and Ember: if you're reading this, you owe me dumplings.

Finally, to you, the reader: Faryn Liu would like to say thank you for giving this book about a Chinese diaspora heroine a chance. And, if you're reading this during the Lunar New Year, you'd better run. The nián is coming!

FARYN'S STORY CONTINUES IN . . .

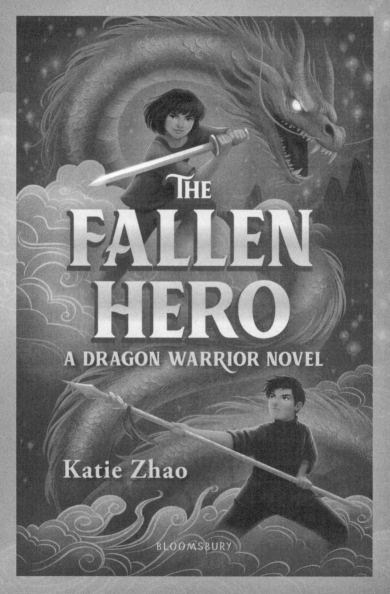

Read on for a sneak peek!

Ba," I whispered.

The man I could've sworn was my father blinked and squinted. Confusion darkened his features. "Who are you?"

My stomach dropped. "Faryn Liu. I'm . . . I'm . . . I'm your daughter?" *The daughter you left behind at the Jade Society in San Francisco's Chinatown eight years ago. Remember?*

I hadn't imagined reuniting with Ba this way. We stood among rubble and ruins, the remains of Manhattan's Chinatown. Torn red paper lanterns scattered across the streets and hung limply from buildings. Nearby, produce stands had toppled over, spilling fruits and vegetables onto the road. And instead of welcoming me into his warm embrace, apologizing for abandoning me and promising we'd stay together forever, my long-lost father stared at me with no recognition in his eyes.

Something awful had happened to Ba along his journey, costing him his memories. That was the only explanation. He couldn't have *really* forgotten his daughter. Right?

"I'm sorry, girl," Ba said, shrugging helplessly. "I'm not your father. I-I'm afraid I don't have any children. Would you like me to help you find him?"

"I . . . N-no. That's okay." Embarrassment burning my cheeks, I turned away. My heart sank into my stomach with dread. A nightmare. This had to be a nightmare.

"I'm sorry, Faryn," came a quiet voice.

I turned toward my friend Ren. The wind ruffled his white hair. His eyes, one green and one black, flickered from me to Ba and widened with sympathy.

Great. Why did Ren have to witness this shameful scene—my own father not remembering me? I shook my head to indicate that this conversation was over. This wasn't the time or place to explain to Ren all my family-related troubles anyway. Around us, the battle had died down, but the threat of danger still hung in the smoky air. I turned my gaze to the crowd of warriors behind Ren. Dirt-smeared men, women, and children stood before me amid rubble that layered the street. Some of the warriors held swords and shields in their hands, and others held bows and arrows. One confused kid had a Nerf gun. The warriors stared at Ren and me in near-silent awe.

No, not at just Ren and me. At *us*. The deities of legends

surrounded me—Nezha, the boy god; Guanyin, goddess of mercy; Erlang Shen, warrior god.

We'd just landed in Manhattan's Chinatown after fleeing the gods' banquet on Peng Lai Island, where we'd learned about the Jade Emperor's plans to destroy disloyal humans. It looked like we'd come a little late. The demons had already destroyed much of Chinatown.

"Warriors of the New Order," Guanyin said with a grim smile, "you've fought bravely today to protect the people of Chinatown."

"It's the gods," gasped a silver-bearded old man. He dropped his sword and shield and knelt. Weapons clattered to the ground as everyone behind him did the same. "Help is here. We're saved."

"You may rise," said Guanyin. In a scattered, clumsy motion, the crowd obeyed. "I'm afraid we come bearing bad news, brave New Order warriors. The Jade Emperor will not be sending reinforcements."

"*What?* Why not?" demanded a tall, beefy-looking man.

"Mr. Wan! Show respect for the gods," hissed the short man beside him. Slowly and reluctantly, Mr. Wan inclined his head toward the three gods in a display of respect.

An old man stepped out from the crowd, carrying himself with the confidence and poise of a god. His long white beard flowed down to his belly. He wore a gray robe, and a sword dangled from its belt on his waist as he bowed. "My name is

Xiong," he said in a deep, soothing voice. "I am the master of the New Order. What brings you to our society, gods?"

I thought the reason was obvious, but maybe Xiong wanted to be polite. Like, "I'm pretty sure you've come to help us win the war but maybe you're just dropping by to say hi" polite.

Guanyin, Nezha, and Erlang Shen exchanged glances.

Erlang Shen spoke next. "We three—I, Erlang Shen, along with Guanyin and Nezha—will help you vanquish these demons. Our combined forces are enough to stop the demons from rampaging. We need not involve the Jade Emperor himself."

Ren twitched and turned toward me, his eyes full of confusion. I knew why: the gods were withholding important information—the Jade Emperor wasn't only *not* sending reinforcements, but he was also actively *using* the demons to get rid of all the pesky, "disloyal" humans. I guess the gods figured sharing this information with the warriors right now wouldn't exactly boost morale.

Erlang said his piece with such conviction that even I almost believed it. Plus, the god's threatening sneer told us that if we *didn't* believe him, the demons would quickly become the least of our worries.

"Warriors." Nezha pointed toward the crowd with his flaming spear. "The battle isn't over. You must do your ancient, sworn duty and protect the people of this Chinatown." He raised his weapon high.

In a clumsy wave, the warriors pointed their weapons

skyward, too. I didn't stop watching Ba. My heart clenched when his sword came up last, as though he wasn't quite sure what was going on.

A roar ripped through the street. Gasps and screams rose from the crowd. A huge, black, bearlike demon flew out of a collapsed building and leapt straight for the chariot—straight for *me*.

I reached into my hair to pull out the hairpin that could morph into my trusty spear, Fenghuang. My fingers met thin air.

Then I remembered. The powerful weapon was gone. My brother, Alex, had taken it, leaving me defenseless in the face of the demon. Worse—there was no *way* Alex could pull off that hairpin look.

"*No!*" My father's voice rang out loudly and clearly, like he'd shouted in my ear. A second later, hands shoved me out of the way.

"Oof!" I careened into the other end of the chariot, and pain shot through my rib cage. I opened my eyes. Ba lay on the ground, unmoving. Before I could scramble over to him, several other demons charged out from behind the first, scattering the warriors. Nezha and Erlang Shen were on them in a flash. They batted demons out of the way left and right, as easily as if they were made out of paper. Guanyin floated high above, clearly intending to take care of the largest demon that had tackled Ba.

A demon with red skin burst out of nowhere, headed straight for—Ba. Instinctively, I leapt forward to defend him.

"AUGHHHHHHHHHH!" From the fore of the crowd, a tall boy dove in front of us. It looked like he was going to take on the demon by himself.

"Jinyu!" someone screamed. *"No!"*

I watched, paralyzed, as the demon swatted away the tall boy like he was nothing. Jinyu flew into a building and then crumbled to the ground, motionless.

The demon turned its eyes back toward Ba and me. The gods and warriors were busy with their own battles. We were on our own.

Panic numbed my senses. But strangely, my thoughts were clearer than ever. My father was defenseless. A boy might have just *died* in front of me. And if I didn't want there to be any more deaths, I had to bring down the demon myself.

My mind and body entered overdrive. I grabbed Ba's sword from the ground, drew it back, and let out a battle cry. The demon charged straight at me. It swiped a great paw so close to my face that I felt the sting of claws just barely missing my skin. The demon roared and drew back its paw for another attack. I didn't think. Didn't pause. I lunged forward and drove the tip of my sword's blade upward, through the neck of the beast.

The demon let out an ear-piercing scream of pain, a ghastly, inhuman sound that nearly tore my eardrums.

I collapsed onto the pavement. Stabbing sensations shot up my palms and knees. Ba's sword skittered away at the foot of a food cart, at least three feet out of reach. I tried to stand to retrieve it, but a horrible pain tore up my right foot. The pain escalated until all I could do was bite my lip and hope the tears stinging my eyes didn't spill over.

"Finish the demon off!" a warrior shouted nearby. "It's almost done for!"

The warriors roared and surged forward in a wave toward the downed demon. Then the world grew blurry around me and disappeared.

Someone touched my arm and shook me. Ren's concerned face peered down. Dimly, I registered Ba's motionless form still lying inches away.

Before I could reassure Ren I was fine—or, at least, still alive—the world faded to black.

Six Months Later

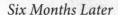 was having those strange dreams again, the same ones I'd had ever since arriving at the New Order. I found myself up in Heaven among the gods without a clue as to how I'd gotten there. I couldn't speak or move, and nobody was ever able to see me. But I could see *them*.

I dreamed of my brother wearing his new black battle armor. Sometimes, Alex was alone. Sometimes, other Heavenly soldiers accompanied him. Once, I'd even seen Alex using the power of my old weapon Fenghuang, a mighty white-tipped golden spear that gave the wielder the power to lead all dragons. He commanded a whole crowd of dragons in a vast garden.

This vision was the clearest yet. I stood in an enormous

hall. Alex paced the red carpet right in front of a golden throne, holding his battle helmet under one arm. I wanted more than anything to run up and hug my brother, even if he'd hate that. Too bad I still couldn't speak or move.

From the throne came a woman's dark, silky voice. "Heaven Breaker, you seem disturbed today."

My heart slammed in my chest. Even though I couldn't see the speaker from the shadows, I'd recognize that voice anywhere: Xi Wangmu. She was the Queen Mother of the West and wife to the Jade Emperor, the ruler of the Heavens. She also happened to want all demons destroyed and didn't care if that meant wiping out humanity in the process. Really charming, that one.

"Those pesky Jade Society warriors are stirring up trouble," Alex reported.

The Jade Society in San Francisco—where I used to live with Alex and our grandfather Ye Ye. Last I'd heard, they were still in recovery mode from the near destruction of the society during the Lunar New Year. Hope bloomed in my chest. Were the warriors growing stronger?

"I put a stop to their antics, though." Alex stopped pacing and stood up straight, puffing out his chest. "I went down to Earth and threw their ringleader—Zhao Boyang—into Diyu, where he'll await punishment by King Yama."

Oh no. Back when Alex and I had lived in the Jade Society, Mr. Zhao had been one of the only adults who'd treated us with unconditional kindness instead of questioning our half-warrior parentage. I pictured the man's crinkled eyes and gentle smile and shook my head.

Alex had thrown Mr. Zhao into the Underworld so easily. When had my brother become so cruel?

"Your old society, soldier," Xi Wangmu said softly. "Your old ally Zhao Boyang. Don't you feel terrible for punishing him so?"

"No." Alex's reply was swift. Cold. "Those who interfere with our plans must be punished. No exceptions."

"Excellent. Truly excellent, my Heaven Breaker." Xi Wangmu said *my Heaven Breaker* like she was tasting the term on her tongue. It made me want to puke. "Speaking of plans, for the upcoming Hungry Ghost Festival, we will—"

"Faryn!"

A familiar voice awoke me from the dream with a jolt.

"Alex?" I sat up straight, knocking the side of my head against something solid—the wall. "Ow!" Rubbing my head, I looked up. A towering pile of books was stacked on the table in front of me, bookshelves lining the walls. My gaze landed on a confused-looking boy, around eight or nine years old. He was slightly chubby. He had short, stubby black hair, and there was chocolate smeared on his mouth—from the Choco Pie he held in his right hand, probably.

"Ah Qiao. What're you doing here?"

"Looking for you. I knew I'd find you in the library. You're in here a lot these days!" Ah Qiao chomped down on his Choco Pie. Crumbs spilled onto the table.

"I'm researching something." Since realizing Ba had lost his memories, I'd done my best to try to find a cure. I'd gone through every memory-related book in the library at least three times but still hadn't found a satisfactory answer. The weathered book I'd fallen asleep reading—*Restorative Potions*—seemed the most promising. Only problem was, the chapter titled "Memory-Restoring Elixirs" was mysteriously blank.

"Researching? But you're always sleeping here. Don't you have your own bed?"

"I am not always sleeping here," I said defensively.

Ah Qiao pulled his phone out of his pocket. "I have pictures. Wanna see?"

"No! Hey, don't you have homework, or training, or someone else to bug—?"

"Faryn!"

I jolted, sure that this time I'd heard Alex's voice. But no. The person who'd arrived at the door was Ren. Not my brother, who'd betrayed us and was plotting gods-knew-what with Xi Wangmu. Ren, my friend, who could sometimes turn into a fifteen-foot-tall dragon. You know, just normal puberty stuff for an average thirteen-year-old kid.

The hope of seeing Alex had briefly bloomed, but now it disappeared. I swallowed my disappointment.

Get a grip. Alex is gone. He chose to leave you. Just like Ba. Just like how everyone else in your life has left you.

Every day, I thought about Alex and how he was a top contender for the Worst Little Brother Ever award. Six months ago, during the Lunar New Year, when little brothers were supposed to give their older sisters compliments and nice presents, *my* little brother had decided to give me the gift of utter betrayal. While I saved the world from the wrath of the fearsome nián demon, Alex decided to become an evil turd. Guess who *didn't* get a hóng bāo, a red packet of money, for good behavior.

"I heard you in the hallway," Ren said. "You were yelling pretty loudly. Something about a demon-Alex. I thought maybe the library was under attack or something." He raised his hand so I could see he'd drawn his sword.

"Of course the library wasn't under attack." I frowned. "The demons have been gone for six months now, remember?"

The combined forces of warriors and deities had helped to beat back the demons in Manhattan's Chinatown—for now, at least. We'd heard hardly a peep of any demon activity since the end of the Lunar New Year. The warriors had different theories. Some believed the demons were gone for a good while. Some believed the demons were regrouping for an even bigger attack in the future.

"You're lucky you *weren't* under attack," Ren said. "I would've been the only one around to help you."

"Why? Where'd everyone else go?" It was rare for the New Order apartments to be empty. The warriors took up all the rooms in a six-story apartment complex right outside China-town. As the Elders had explained when we'd first arrived, the building was guarded with ancient magic that made it look like a doctor's office to any outsiders. This meant the warriors were very safe, because *nobody* ever wanted to go inside a doctor's office.

The New Order was the Jade Society 2.0. Clearly, the New Order warriors had gotten a much bigger chunk of the budget the gods had allotted warriors for building their societies. The apartment complex was way bigger on the inside than it appeared from the outside. It had everything a warrior could possibly need: a training ground in the basement, apartments on the first and second floors, a dining hall on the third floor, a library on the fourth floor, a game room on the fifth floor, and even a spa on the sixth floor.

"Everyone's gone to the temple, of course," Ah Qiao said loudly. "Don't tell me you forgot what day it is."

In the aftermath of my dream about Alex, it had slipped my mind. "July 31st. It's the day before the Hungry Ghost Festival."

One of the biggest celebrations of the year, the Hungry Ghost Festival was a time for the living to reunite with their dead ancestors and friends. It was more of a formality now, since the warriors were no longer powerful enough to *actually* summon the dead. Still, the holiday always reminded me of the family I'd never known—Mama, my mother; Nai Nai, my grandmother; Gu Gu, my aunt; Jiu Jiu, my uncle. They had all passed away before I was born. This year, my grandfather was also on my mind. Ye Ye had passed away during the last Lunar New Year and now lived as a deity in Heaven. The thought brought a pang to my chest.

Every warrior needed to be alert for demon activity during the Hungry Ghost Festival, just like on every holiday, when the demons grew stronger—and especially this year, the wake of the demons' attack during the Lunar New Year. And I'd almost slept through the prefestival ceremony. The worst part was, Xiong, the master of the New Order, was just about the strictest guy on the planet. He once made me run ten laps around Chinatown because I forgot it was my turn to sweep the dining hall floors. I guess a guy named Xiong, which literally means "fierce," is bound to be one tough cookie.

"Xiong's speech starts soon. Ah Qiao, you should get going. I need to speak with Faryn."

"No! I don't wanna go to the dumb—"

One hard, penetrating stare from Ren was enough to silence Ah Qiao. The little boy gave me a sullen look, as though asking for backup. I just looked at him.

"Fine," Ah Qiao grumbled. He tossed his crumpled-up Choco Pie wrapper into a nearby trash can and ran out the door.

"We should head over to the temple, too." I stood up.

"Wait. First I have . . . something important to . . . to think about," Ren mumbled, shifting his bag.

"More important than the New Order's preparations for the Hungry Ghost Festival? Do you *want* to run laps for Xiong? 'Cause I'm telling you right now, it's not fun."

"I-I've been summoned," Ren confessed. "To the palace of the Dragon King of the Center Sea. For training. The Dragon Kings sent me a vision in my dream. I saw the palace. This dark, ugly cloud surrounded it, and—and the Dragon Kings told me if I went to the palace, they'd train me for battle."

My heart sank at the thought of Ren leaving me on my own. We hadn't spent a day apart for the past six months. "Oh. What . . . what are they training you for?"

"Apparently, word of my—uh—special situation has spread pretty far. The Dragon Kings are worried that without their training, I'll be a danger to those around me."

"Th-that's ridiculous," I spluttered. "You haven't hurt a single soul since arriving at the New Order!"

Ren still appeared hesitant. "Not *yet*. I'm sure it's because the gods have been strangely quiet, so all the dragons—mine included—have been quiet, too. So have the demons. I don't like it. I don't like it at all . . ."

"Yeah, I prefer war," I said sarcastically.

"I didn't mean it that way. All I'm saying is, things have felt *too* peaceful lately. Feels like . . . something big is about to happen."

Katie Zhao is the author of *The Dragon Warrior* and *The Fallen Hero*. She grew up in Michigan, where there was little for her to do besides bury her nose in a good book or a writing journal. She graduated from the University of Michigan with a BA in English and a minor in political science; she also completed her master's in accounting there. She wrote *The Dragon Warrior* during her last year of school, in between classes. In her spare time, Katie enjoys reading, singing, dancing (badly), and checking out new restaurants. She now lives in Brooklyn, New York.

www.katiezhao.com

@ktzhaoauthor